The Monster Man of Horror House

DANNY KING

Jone '20

To

Ben

Happy Birthday!.

Love

Bu

ISBN-13: 978-1500609450
ISBN-10: 1500609455

FOR JOHN & HELEN
For being such smashing grandparents to
mine and Jeannie's little monsters

ACKNOWLEDGEMENTS

My thanks to Clive & Jo Andrews, Jeannie King, Robin King, Michael King, Andrew Crockett and the late Ronald Chetwynd-Hayes for each helping me with this book. Also to the amazing Heike Schrapper for helping to T-Cut the typos from this book. Thank you one and all.

Contents

CHAPTER 1:
SECOND TO LAST HOUSE ON THE LEFT

In any neighbourhood, in any town, there'll be a scary old house. It'll be overgrown, run down, uncared for and forgotten. And more often than not it'll be occupied by a scary old man who will more or less fit this same description. Time addled, weathered, blistered and peeling, this old man will shuffle around the district keeping himself to himself, harvesting his neighbours' skips and thinning out Post Office queues whenever he wafts in to collect his pension.

He'll also be blissfully ignorant of the fact that he's the local oddball.

He'll think of himself as quiet, unassuming, frugal and sage, a maverick to be sure, but a wily one at that. And he'll make the classic mistake of thinking that if he minds his own business, everyone else will mind theirs. If only.

It took me a few months before I realised I was the scary old oddball in my street. I'd always thought of myself simply as John: hard working, conservative, thrifty and solitary, if occasionally ripe on hot days, but what did that matter when I lived on my own? It was my house; I could smell how I liked in it. Besides, I remembered reading somewhere that soap clogged up your pheromone holes and it was them that got women hot under the petticoats, not Daz and Old Spice and all that load of old poof's water. Not that I went in for any of that sort of nonsense any more either. My libido was like my old army sidearm, in a box somewhere under a load of old crap and it hadn't fired a shot in anger since Aden. No, I was happy to potter about in my shadow, keep the world at arm's length and save a few pennies towards my dotage.

I'd moved into this house in 1972. Back then it had been a smart two-bedroom end-terrace bungalow with a side garage and front and rear gardens. It had cost me the princely sum of three thousand pounds at the time, and despite the fact that I hadn't cut the lawn, cleaned out the guttering or wiped the windows since, I reckoned it had probably kept its value.

Of course, I didn't plan to end up this way, a lonely old buzzard whose sole purpose in life seemed to be ridding the world of Oxtail soup, one tin at a time. I mean who does? But life had simply got the better of me. When I was young, and I mean waist high to a cricket, I'd dreamed of being a sailor, of seeing the world and of exploring new lands, which is about as far away from how I'd ended up as it's possible to get. I guess I'd just been shipwrecked against a different fate, that's all. Most people are if you think about it.

But as I say, because mine had been a gradual decent, rather than a spectacular plummet, I was oblivious of the fact that my reputation was somewhat on a par with the scrap metal merchant's dog. That was until the neighbourhood kids started taking an interest in me – a telltale sign of one's standing in the community if ever there was one. Of course, I didn't understand why they'd singled me out for their intrigues at first, but single me out they had. Spectres knocked on my front door all hours, whispers emanated from the knotted jungle that was my back garden and my milk was no longer left to be collected from my front door step, but rather poured through my letter box in the small wee hours of the morning. What wags they were.

After four weeks of this nonsense I decided to take a long hard look in the mirror and realised to my dismay that I was Thetford's kooky old oddball.

Like I say, all neighbourhoods have at least one. In my

day he was called Harold and he lived in a cottage at the end of my road. He'd got on the wrong side of a German shell in Ypres and looked a fearsome monster, with hooks for hands and a face screwed on all wrong. Me and my pals were terrified of him and made up stories of what fate befell any child who tumbled into his clutches. This inevitably led to us venturing into his garden after dark to test our mettle and trample his tomatoes. He used to roar at us as we scarpered away, over the wall and into the night, and we took his roars to be the homicidal rages of frustration at missing out on catching us to fill his pies with, when really he probably just wanted us to bugger off and stop pissing in his watering can. Poor old Harold; he'd gone through hell and back on the battlefield only to find it had followed him home and into old age.

It's funny, I hadn't thought of him in some fifty odd years. Not until the pranks began in earnest on my own doorstep. And that was when I realised I was his reincarnation.

Of course, none of their parents would do anything about the little bleeders when I tried complaining to them.

"My Tommy ain'done nothink I'm telling ya and you can't proov nothink otherwise, you fackin' stirrin' old *caant*. Go on, fack off away from my *haas*, you faackin' old scarecrow, you stink!"

Not like in my day. In my day had one of my neighbours come to the door with a complaint about me, I would've felt the lick of my dad's belt across my back without so much as a right to reply. Oh yes, children learned to respect their elders in my day and no mistake – except poor old Harold now that I come to think of it. He'd complained to everyone but no one had taken the blindest bit of notice of him. I guess at the end of the day no one likes an oddball, young or old, because oddballs are always complaining about something, whether it be kids in their vegetable patch or Catholics in the town planning office, so why pander to 'em? Short shrift and the bristly end of a broom is all they understand.

I can appreciate this. I honestly can. In the cold light of day, after a period of cold and careful reflection, I can genuinely see how I might not have listened if I'd lived next door to myself either, but this didn't make my neighbours' indifference any easier to bear, especially when my bins started doing handstands on the garden path the night before they were due to be collected. Little bastards!

Things got so bad that I even daydreamed about going to the law, but I quickly got over that. Me and the authorities don't make for good bed fellows (I don't like those nosy parkers knowing my business), so I took the one course of action left open to me and decided to do something about my pest problem myself.

One of the many benefits of living the way I do is you always have the materials for any job, be it knocking together a chicken coop in the garden, repairing an old vacuum cleaner from parts or building a guillotine in your basement, whatever you like really, so I set about knocking nails into walls, rigging wires on pulleys and fixing bolts to doors until I'd engineered a solution to my woes.

I'd built a trap.

"That'll do," I concluded to myself, admiring my handiwork as I freshened up with a post-toil handkerchief bath. "Now all I need is a drop of bait."

I left a fiver in plain sight on the sitting room table for three nights running but no one broke in to swipe it, so I figured a more obvious approach was called for and dug out my dad's old bowler hat.

My dad had worn a billycock all his life and it was one of the few things I had to remember him by. I'd never worn one myself, because the fashion had come and gone by the time it had reached my head, so I'd simply stuck it in the back bedroom and left it to gather dust for the last four decades. But finally, some forty years to the day after it had last seen action, I reached it down from atop the wardrobe, gave the brim a wipe with the back of my cuff and set it upon my crown at a jaunty angle. And you know what, as I admired myself in the hallway mirror, I have to say I looked a right pillock. Well they didn't go out of fashion for nothing, you know.

I grabbed my coat, dug out my shopping basket and headed for Tesco's.

I had a fair idea of the hoodlums who were responsible for my torments and knew whereabouts they liked to congregate too, so I sounded general quarters and set course to put myself in their sights.

One of the fringe benefits of being the town oddball is that you can get away with dressing like one, so no one paid me or my fetching new headgear any heed – not until I passed the little scummers bumming smokes in the alleyway by the side of the supermarket. The stifled sniggers and hoots of derision that tumbled from their direction told me they approved, so I doffed my peak at a couple of confused Tescolites and headed inside to see what treasures awaited me on the dented tins shelf.

I was out and about a lot over the next few days, always in my bowler and always in sight of my persecutors. They followed me around, giggled hysterically and took to shaping McDonald bags on their heads to match my hat. They were very excited by this latest development indeed, so I kept it up until they were champing at the bit to knock it off my head and take it for a spin.

Satisfied the groundwork had been laid, I set the hat on the front windowsill of my bungalow, in plain view of the street (once you got past the overhanging hazel branches of course) and settled in for a busy night.

CHAPTER 2:
NOCTURNAL VISITORS

"You get it yet?"

"Nah, *fackin'* knocked it on the floor. Hang on, hold the window open, I'm going in."

"Tommy don't!"

"*Fack* off bottler."

"Shut your *maaf*, I ain't no bottler!"

"*Fackin'* make me."

"*Fackin'* all a' yous lot, shut it or you'll wake the old scarecrow up for *fack's* sake."

"Ain't me, it's Farny."

"*Fackin'* grasser."

"*Fack* off!"

The leader of the pack climbed through the window and dropped into the gloom of my front room. Barely able to contain his squeals of delight he grabbed my dad's old hat and stuffed it back through the open window to his mates outside.

"Got it! Here, grab it will ya!" he told them excitedly, clambering back up onto the windowsill to make his escape. The boys outside giggled triumphantly and started passing it from head to head when they noticed their leader had yet to join them.

"Tommy, you coming or what?"

"Hang on. Look at this!" he said, spotting what else I'd left for them amongst the clutter.

A few yards from the window, I'd pushed back a couple of my taller scrap heaps to air a stretch of carpet. My poor old Axminster hadn't seen the light of day since 1982 and it didn't get much of a respite now because I heaved my bait up from the basement and set it down

12

amongst the shadows. It would've been difficult to make out what it was from the overgrown weeds of my front garden, but once a person was inside, my front room's newest feature stood out like a horrifyingly sore thumb.

"It's a coffin!" Tommy told his mates .

"What?" came back their reply.

"It's a coffin. Scarecrow's got a *fackin'* coffin in his living room!"

"Where?"

"I can't see."

"You're lying."

Tommy steeled himself and edged towards it, watching his footing amongst the clutter and bracing himself to run at the first creak.

"What's inside it?"

"Tommy don't, let's go."

"Shut it bottler!"

But Tommy ignored his mates' and continued towards the coffin until he was within touching distance of its scratched cedar lid.

"Ho-ho-hoo," he chuckled to himself with ghoulish delight as he felt along the lip for a finger-hold.

"Tommy, what are you doing?" a needy anxious voice called from outside, but Tommy was feeling reckless and he heaved at the heavy lid, cracking it open an inch until the bolts I'd screwed into the hinges stopped it from opening further.

Inside the coffin a sudden movement had him dropping the lid and soiling his socks as he tumbled back in fright. "Jesus!" he squawked, scrambling back across my front room and up onto the windowsill before recovering his courage. His friends outside had done considerably better than he and had practically made it back home and into their pyjamas in the same space of time, but curiosity and a lack of a reaction from the bungalow's resident

"Scarecrow" soon had them back and sniffing around my casket once more.

Only now there were two of them inside my house.

"You lift it, I'll look inside," they concocted as Tommy dropped to his knees and pushed his peepers against the crack.

"*Fackin'* Jesus!" he yelped once again when something spun within, tumbling back onto his buns and scrambling over his chum who was already halfway through the window.

This time, it took them a full hour before they returned, but return they did. Three of them climbed in through the window this time – Tommy, the one they called Farny and a Ginger lad – leaving the littlest outside to sniffle and blubber to himself in protest.

"What is it?" asked Farny holding the lid.

"I don't know, but it's horrible," Tommy replied, and Ginger who was on his knees beside him echoed these sentiments.

"D'you fink it's the scarecrow like, and he sleeps in the box or somefink?" he asked, prompting the Farny, who was holding the lid, to pull his fingers out, much to the dismay of his pals' noses.

"*Fackin'* conehead twat!" Tommy groaned, holding the wet squidgy mess that used to be his face before realising his fingers were full of tears and not blood. "Stupid *twat.*"

"It's a girl," Ginger said, pushing the lid up long enough to take another peek.

"Tommy, please let's go home," snivelled the fourth musketeer through the open window.

"Barry, get in here," he was told for his troubles.

"No, I don't like it," he replied.

"*Fackin'* bottler!" was Farny's assessment and Ginger agreed.

14

"Pissin' his pants he is."

"I ain't, I just want to go home," he pleaded, but Tommy wasn't having any of it.

"Barry, you get in here right now or you ain't hanging out with us no more."

"I'll tell mum," Barry threatened, prompting a chorus of chicken clucks until Barry silenced his tormenters the only way he could – by climbing through the window. He was supremely reluctant I can tell you that. I've seen panicking bluebottles who've found their way through open windows faster than Barry, but he eventually joined his peers, only to continue his protestations at close quarters, though he was now so fear-pitched that only dogs and Superman could hear him.

"Look inside the coffin, Barry," Tommy told him, cranking open the lid and inviting as much fear as he could muster into his little brother's life.

The gang went through another round of "bottler" "no I ain't" "shut it" "jus' *fackin'* do it" before Barry finally took a gander, and when he did his gasp all but silenced the others.

"Who is she?" he quivered, but the others didn't get a chance to answer for at that perfect moment I yanked the first of my strings and slammed their point of entry closed behind them.

Eight pairs of socks were left on the carpet behind as they fled to escape, but the window was now sealed and the glass reinforced with clear plastic in case they tried to smash their way out.

"WHO'S IN THERE!" a tape recording boomed from the darkest shadows of the room, buffeting them towards the open door and they broke en masse, clambering over each other in heart-wrenching panic as they tumbled out into the hallway. Naturally, a whole heap of boxes barred both exits, front and back, but a third door invited them to step inside, offering them a hiding place from the increasingly heated recordings that were blaring out from the half dozen different speakers dotted around the house.

"WHERE'S MY AXE?"

"This way!" Tommy ordered and the rest all followed without a second's independent thought.

They got two steps into my basement when they realised it offered no way out, but by the time they knew this it was too late, the door slammed shut and the steps fell away, plunging them down a long slide and into the darkness below.

"Gotcha," I chuckled to myself, locking home the heavy steel bolt as I listened to their howls of terror.

CHAPTER 3:
BASEMENT FEARS

I left them to stew in the darkness for thirty minutes before returning to the door. Imagination is a powerful weapon and I wanted their little minds primed for the night's entertainment.

I cracked back the bolt and shone a torch into the blackness. Huddled on the floor and sobbing their eyes out were Farny and Ginger; they'd waved the white flag and were resigned to meeting their makers with as little dignity as possible (well fair enough, they were only twelve), while Tommy was clutching a hand trowel he'd found and shielding his baby brother behind him. The torchlight temporarily blinded them all and Farny and Ginger cranked up the volume while Tommy tried to kill the air before him with scything swings.

"Let us out you *facker*! Let us out or we'll call the cops!" he warned.

"Why haven't you already?" I asked, knowing full well why not. I'd stacked most of my lead on the floor in the room above, meaning they had as much chance of getting a signal on their mobiles as I had of getting a column in *Ideal Homes*. "Phones not working boys?" I cackled.

"I want to go home," Barry blubbed, unable to hold it in any longer.

"I expect you do," I scowled, "but we so rarely get what we want."

Before me, the basement steps had dropped away to a forty-five degree angle, turning the stairs into a highly polished slide. Now I brought my old automatic into the glare of the torchlight so that they could see it and warned them away from the bottom step.

"Against the far wall. Move it. Do as I say and you might even get out of here alive," I enticed.

The lads moved to the far wall and after a little more shepherding, occupied the battered and tattered sofa I'd forgotten I owned until I'd shifted all that bleeding lead upstairs. I yanked a lever on the wall at the top of the stairs and the steps in front of me now clanked back into a usable flight. I descended carefully, keeping the barrel of my Browning on them at all times.

I reached the basement and felt for a switch I'd concealed behind a shelf, flicking it on to illuminate a forty watt bulb screwed into a lamp in the corner. Around that forty watt bulb was an old sheep's skull. And as the beams of light broke from its cracked eye sockets and cruel leer the boys gasped as one, as if their worst fears had just been realised, so I told them to be quiet otherwise I'd turn them into fixtures and fittings for the rest of the house.

"Now then," I said, pulling up an old oil drum to sit down on in front of them (as my bleeding back was killing me). "Strap."

Judging from their faces they must've misheard me and thought I'd said "strip', so I pointed to the left of the sofa to where Tommy found a long leather strap affixed to the frame. After a little more encouragement he passed the other end along his mates and Ginger at the far end fixed it to a hook I'd screwed in just below the armrest. It wasn't exactly Hannibal Lecter's car seat, but it was enough to keep them from rushing me if I needed to scratch myself unexpectedly.

"Okay boys, let's start with your names shall we?" I said.

Tommy told me he weren't saying nothing, which was admirably defiant if a little redundant seeing as he was wearing a cap with Tommy written across it. Barry however coughed his guts up, as did Farny and Ginger, who turned out to be called Ralph Farnsworth (or Farny to his friends) and Colin Dunlop (or Ginger to friend and foe alike).

"My name is John Coal," I told them, lowering my gun and feeling around in my jacket for my pipe. "And this is my home you're trespassing in."

"You let us go right now or I'll tell my dad on you!" Tommy threatened once more.

"Then tell him," I said, filling my pipe. "Go ahead and tell him."

Tommy sat mute for a moment while the impediments of this threat bounced around inside his hat.

"Can't tell your dad if I don't let you go, can you?" I put to him.

Tommy didn't answer, but the seriousness of the situation was fully understood by his little brother Barry, who appealed to my better side for mercy. It's so often the way with children; up until the age of ten you can wave hedge trimmers and garden shears at them and they'll genuinely believe you'll cut off their legs if you catch them. But all that goes for a toss once they hit their horrible teens and overnight develop a working knowledge of English law. At Tommy's age he probably knew – or at least thought he knew – that I couldn't really hurt them, not *really*, not without risking prison and retribution and life and liberty. But a little knowledge is a dangerous thing because every once in a while a cocky young buck runs into a dangerous old coot who's not entirely full of piss and vinegar. And when that happens all the *habeas corpus* in the world ain't going to help them blow out another birthday cake.

Now it was up to me to convince them I was this self-same dangerous old coot.

"Sorry boys, this ain't nothing personal but I can't have you little sneaks creeping about my property. I have too many secrets buried here and if you don't want to join them you'll do well to stay clear, if you know what's good for you."

"What secrets?" Farny blurted, as if I was just going to tell him after that whole flannel.

"The blackest kind of secrets: murder and death, blood and demons," I hissed, metaphorically holding a torch under my chin. "That's why I came to this shitty little town; to escape the horrors. And it's why I keep myself to myself; not for my own sake, but to protect those around me, for if these secrets ever saw the light of day it would mean death and destruction to this whole worthless backwater," I said, laying it on a bit thick while at the same time putting the boot into their neighbourhood.

"You're full of shit," Tommy said. "My dad says you ain't nothing but an old tramp who's got a house and that if I don't want to end up like you, I should forget about school and come roofing with him."

As gratifying as it was to be a part in Tommy's careers advice, I saw that my rhetoric would be taken as empty unless I could back it up with a few specifics, so I mulled over my options and lit my pipe, taking a long hard draw on its nib before flavouring the stale basement air with a blue grey plume.

"Is that right?" I speculated. "I guess fathers tell their children all kinds of things, don't they? My own father was no different, a very persuasive man. Of course he's dead now; he died a great many years ago but when he was alive I would've done anything for him. Anything. Well… almost anything."

PART 1:

LIKE FATHER LIKE SON

i

My father, Reginald Coal, was an extraordinary man, made all the more extraordinary by the fact that he'd had the thorniest of beginnings. Born to an unwed mother, abandoned to luck and wrapped in the blood-soaked blankets he'd been delivered in, it was by the slenderest of miracles that he'd been found before the early winter frosts had got the better of him.

The Lloyd's housekeeper, about to turn in for the night, thought she'd heard a cat screaming in pain in the alleyway outside and went out to shoo it away lest it disturb the mistress of the house, only to get the fright of her life. I guess the intention of my grandmother, other than to rid herself of the shame of having a child of love in such judgmental times, had been to place my father with a well-to-do family. The Lloyds were certainly that, boasting a proud lineage, a box at Ascot and a pile in stocks and shares that would keep them in clover until the crash of '29. But families like the Lloyds didn't keep their proud lineages by taking in every waif and stray to pitch up in their coal shed.

"Take it with you," was Mr Lloyd's assessment when the doctor told him that young Reginald was out of danger.

"Certainly," the doctor toadied.

So rather than seeing a life of comfort and privilege, Reginald spent his first ten years in the local orphanage, starved of love and Vitamin D. It could've turned out so differently for my father but then in the spring of 1932 the Reverend Charles Eckett took pity on the gangliest waif in St Mary's of the Blessed Salvation (and Norwich) and offered him the thing orphans the world over spend their

23

days and nights dreaming of – a home and a family to call his own.

The good Reverend and his wife weren't able to have children of their own you see so they'd done the Christian thing and plucked a child off life's scrap heap. And as far as they were concerned, the more wretched and pitiful that child was, the brighter the gesture shone.

Reginald Coal knew clean sheets and warm embraces for the first time in his short life and he took to them immediately. He lost the rickets that had blighted his early years, filled out his shirts and year-by-year became a man. In fact, had Chancellor Hitler not gone and sidetracked my dad's progress by invading Poland, he might've even gone to Oxford or Cambridge. Instead he went to North Africa.

Like so many men who saw action in the war, my father rarely spoke of his experiences, but he must've been in the thick of it because he started out a humble private in Tobruk and ended up a Captain by the time he got to Rome and he had a chest full of medals to show for the journey.

Amongst those medals was the Victory Cross.

Oh how Granny Coal and the Lloyds would've loved to have been seen with Reginald now.

Yet he never made a big deal of his decorations. They were simply symbols that he'd done his duty, nothing more. He'd lost too many friends along the way to exploit his ribbons for his own gain, so when he returned from the war he put them in a biscuit tin, swapped his peak cap for a billycock and turned his thoughts to furthering his education.

And so after two years and a thousand candles worth of revision Reginald Coal finally made it to Oxford.

"Why was he still called Coal?"

"What?"

"Why was he still called Coal? Why didn't he change

his name to Eckett like his new dad, the Reverend?" Tommy asked.

"He'd had the name Coal for the first ten years of his life. It was given to him because of where he'd been found," I explained. "The Reverend thought it important that my father not forget his origins. Anyway, stop interrupting," I chided, tapping my pipe against the oil drum and reaching into my pouch to replenish my smoke.

Now this was quite a feat for a boy born to an unwedded mother and left to die on a filthy slag heap. And it was even more of an astonishing fete when you consider that while he'd been studying for his exams, he'd been working a full-time job to support mother and me. I'd been born in 1945 almost nine months to the day the RAF had flown the celebrated Captain Coal back from Italy for a week of richly deserved leave, so we were here and waiting for him in a country cottage just outside King's Lynn when he returned for good in 1946. My mother, Rhea Eckett, was the Reverend's niece, and my father had presumably married her out of duty to his adopted father or because he'd figured patience was no longer a virtue once the air started to crack with machine-gun fire. I don't know, maybe I'm being a little hard on my parents. Maybe my father genuinely loved my mother and connected with her in ways that only the heart could understand. It's possible, but knowing her for the miserable, nagging old shrew she'd been, despite her being my own beloved mother, I'm sure Captain Coal VC could've done better.

After five more years of cramming, revising, studying and working, my father was eventually called to the bar in 1953 and he went on to become one of the finest criminal barristers of his generation.

He represented them all over the next fifteen years he did, from Donald Copper, the bodies in the deep freeze killer (hanged) to sir Henry Davenport-Fielding, the maid-

murdering adulterer with friends in high places (also
hanged – his friends were obviously out the day he needed
them). Of course my father had his successes too, like
Penny Wilson, the Wimborne widow who escaped the
rope only to see out her days knitting scarves from her
Holloway cell – the same scarves that each of her lovers
had come a cropper against when they'd tried to break up
with poor Penny. And then there was Ryan Douglas, the
Colchester kidnapper, not only acquitted of any
involvement in the disappearance of Beryl Ashby, but
celebrated on the underground poetry circuit after his
anthology, *Through the Eyes of a Ghost* was published to great
acclaim following his trial. It charted his and Beryl's
turbulent relationship and his [suspected] hand in her
abduction and murder, and turned the young Ryan into a
cause célèbre. In fact, he might've gone on to even greater
literary heights had Beryl's father, Gordon Ashby, asked
him for his autograph when he'd come off stage at The
Black Cat instead of stabbing him in the neck. Still,
Gordon Ashby made for a very sympathetic defendant in
his own right and it bolstered my father's reputation no
end when he represented him in the subsequent trial and
stood by his side throughout – right up until the trapdoor
fell away beneath him.

But then that was the fifties for you. Forget about
your pop stars and matinee idols, the kidnappers and
killers that filled the papers in those days were just as big a
names as any wobbly legged singers that flashed the pan –
especially when one of them 'took the drop'. So through
his tireless support of sensationalist murderers and his
impeccable war record my father became a household
name.

Now I have to say right off the bat that I'd always
been in awe of him, perhaps even a little afraid if I'm
honest. Not because he was a harsh man – quite the

opposite in fact – but because he was such a good and admirable man. Throughout my early years, I couldn't help but feel that I never quite measured up to my father's own impossible standards. Of course he'd never said anything unkind to me, nor was he ever judgmental or cruel, but his praise always fell short of wholehearted and his gratitude for chores performed was perfunctory rather than sincere.

But like I say, please don't think poorly of my father because he wasn't a bad man. I was just a disappointing child if truth were told.

Mother left us for that great dress shop in the sky in the autumn of '62, which was very hard on me at the time, being that I was an only child and all, but I tried not to linger on it because I didn't want to appear milk soft in front of my father. Instead, we simply tightened our routine to take in the slack, learned how to use the mangle and did enough housework between us to ensure we were never out of vests, socks or clean handkerchiefs for the week.

I'd left school by this time and was doing my apprenticeship with a local electrics firm. I wasn't the academic type, which was another regret of my father's, but I made up for this by repairing the television set when it blew a valve shortly before the Queen's Speech on Christmas Day of the same year.

"That should do it," I said, turning the knob on the front of the box and almost choking on my nerves as the television hummed and crackled for a full thirty seconds before eventually a dot of light unfolded on the glass and a picture appeared to fill the screen. I turned up the sound and *Good King Wenceslas* filled the living room to serenade us on our day of enforced confinement.

My father studied the picture for a second or two then looked at me and nodded.

"Good show, John. A fine job," he said, before

settling back in his armchair to hear Her Majesty's thoughts on this past year.

And there you have it, the nicest thing my father ever said to me. It made me feel ten feet tall and so proud I could've sung, though that would not have done at all. Instead I just sat there with my father listening to the Queen's speech without hearing a word of it.

It was the best Christmas I ever had.

ii

Six weeks later, in the depths of the blackest February I had ever known, my father came to me in the night. He woke me from my slumber, from my very bed, shaking me with a terror in his eyes and a sweat on his brow. I'd never seen him like this before. I'm not sure anyone had, not even the Germans, but a fear had gripped him as if the very hounds of hell were after him, so I grabbed the scotch off the sideboard and did what I could to calm him down.

"I didn't mean it. It wasn't my fault!" he sobbed over and over again as he wolfed down his whisky and cradled his knees.

"What father? What didn't you do?" I asked, but he could barely bring himself to look at me, let alone answer. "Father, please tell me," I implored and father eventually took an almighty belt of scotch and muttered something under his breath that barely qualified as a croak. "What?" I had to ask several times before I finally made it out.

"I killed someone," he snivelled. "I killed a girl."

To say I was stunned doesn't really do my reaction justice. I was knocked flat by a wrecker's ball, brushed off, straightened out, put back into my pyjamas and stood on my feet again, all within the blink of an eye.

My father had killed someone!

My father had obviously killed lots of people – they didn't give VCs to mildly curious bystanders – but they'd all been German or Italian and they'd been out to kill my dad first.

But a girl?

My dad had killed a girl?

"Who was she?" I asked, now trembling in the darkness almost as much as my father.

"I don't know," he sobbed. "A girl of the street. A girl of easy virtue."

"Easy virtue?"

"Oh God, don't look at me like that John, I didn't know she was a madam, I swear I didn't," he said when he saw me baulk.

"I believe you father," I quickly assured him. "But what happened?"

My father didn't say anything for a few seconds; he just held out his glass for more scotch and looked to me in pity. I half-filled his tumbler then reached for a glass myself. I normally wouldn't have dreamed of taking a drink in front of my father, but I surely needed one and reasoned my father would cut me some slack now that he'd taken to killing prostitutes.

"It's cold out there," he started. "It's bitter to the bones with a fog so thick you'd need an axe to get through it in parts. So when I saw her standing by the side of the road shivering, I just thought she needed a lift home. I swear John, I swear on my father's good name I had no idea she was a harlot."

This was my father all over. He was such a good man that he sometimes bordered on the naïve. Ridiculous really when you think about it, especially for a criminal barrister, but more often than not my father's blind spot was the evil in other people.

"Of course she readily accepted," he almost laughed,

shaking his head at his own stupidity. "But then once we got out into the Lanes I realised my mistake when she… well, let's just say she drew my attention to the true nature of her occupation."

I blinked a few times in the darkness, none the wiser as to how she might have done this, but shocked all the same, as was the reaction that was called for.

"Go on," I urged, despite my mind's eye lingering on the passenger seat of my father's car as he examined the young lady's credentials.

"Well I er… I thanked her for her kind offer, but regretfully declined, then fostered her with a few shillings to compensate her for her inconvenience and offered to drop her back at her place of business."

"Where was it father?"

"It doesn't matter. But I never want you going there, you hear me?" I immediately promised him that I wouldn't, although it occurred to me later that I couldn't very well avoid the place if I didn't know where it was.

"Anyway, the young lady accepted my shillings but then said she recognised me from the papers and said it would cause a right stir if it were known this big shot barrister was out at night picking up tradeswomen in the night – if I knew what she meant."

"What did she mean?"

"Blackmail John. She meant to cry wolf or worse if I didn't feather her nest. Oh John, there's no fool like an old fool," he lamented.

"You could've gone to the police, dobbed her in for a tart," I argued.

"It would've been my word against hers."

"Then it would've been no contest," I said.

"Perhaps to you, John, and to some of my friends, but I am a criminal's barrister. I am on the side of the enemy as far as the police are concerned and how they would love the chance to bring me down," he explained, before staring into the shadows at the carcass of his tattered career and wondering how a lifetime of unblemished service could've brought him to this.

"So is that why you killed her?" I finally asked.

"What? Good God John, no!" he reeled. "I wouldn't kill a fly to protect my reputation, let alone a beautiful young girl. How could you even think such a thing?"

"I'm sorry father, I didn't think."

"No you didn't," he chided. "It was an accident, plain and simple. When I told her to do her worst, she started to scream and attacked me. I only meant to defend myself but I'm afraid I must've under-estimated my own strength."

"Of course, father."

"John, the last person I'd fought was a burly German Quartermaster and I'd only just come through that encounter by the skin of my teeth. I think maybe I'd had a flashback and brought the same force to bear on this poor unfortunate as I'd done on the Jerry," he mourned.

This was even more tragic; not only was my father an innocent caught in the machinations of a conniving tramp but his own traumatic war experiences had emerged to play a part in his undoing.

"What will you do?" I asked.

My father just shrugged and shook his head.

"Hang," was his assessment.

"What! But you can't," I spluttered, knocking my glass clear across the room.

"I'm afraid it's inevitable. As night must follow day, I shall take the ride to Tyburn."

My dad's theatrical euphemism aside I could scarcely understand what he was saying. He was a war hero, one of the bravest of the brave and decorated by the King himself. In recent years he'd established a reputation as a much-respected public defender of lost causes. If anyone was the victim of this sordid affair, it was he. Could they really hang him for this?

"She was a sex worker. When a girl of that profession dies in such circumstances the motives are almost always assumed to be likewise, sexual. And that is a stonewall Capital crime. No mitigating circumstances. No clemency. Just three clear Sundays and an early morning appointment with the rope."

"Oh father," I finally broke down. "This is so unjust, so unfair. Surely there's something we can do?"

"No son, when I go to the police in the morning, I must tell them everything and put myself in God's hands."

The surprises were coming thick and fast tonight and this latest revelation almost knocked me across the room to join my shattered glass.

"You mean the police don't yet know?"

"No," he replied.

"But I thought…"

"What?"

"I thought they knew. From the way you were talking, I thought they already knew."

"No," my father blinked in all innocence. "Why should they?"

"But where…?" I shook the questions from my head and took a moment to order my mind. It's funny, but my father's profession and mine weren't as different as he thought. As an electrician, my job was all about tracing connections and finding faults. If something didn't work, I needed to be able to see it in my mind as a three-dimensional circuit diagram in order to locate the problem, and now I applied the same mindset to my father's predicament.

"When did this all happen father? What time?"

"About an hour ago, I think. Maybe two," he told me.

"Did anyone see you pick up the girl?"

"I don't think so, especially not in that fog. John what are you getting at?" he asked, but I brushed his question aside with a few more of my own.

"Where is she now?"

"She's dead!" he snapped, his hackles rising at my impertinence.

"Yes, but where is she?"

My father glared at me in the gloom and I thought for a moment he was going to tell me to go to hell in a handcart, but instead he continued to pull dead rabbits from his hat when he told me she was still in the car.

"In the car?"

"In the garage," he added and we both fell into our thoughts. Time was ticking away, but the next move had to be right, so I used up a few more precious seconds to make sure all the light bulbs lit up in order, then took the scotch from my father's hand.

"Go to bed."

"What?"

"Go to bed," I repeated. "And don't say anything to anyone, especially not the police. I'll sort things out for you, father."

"Sort things out? What do you mean sort things out?" he demanded.

"Father, what's done is done and no one can undo it. But it would be senseless of you to sacrifice yourself for the sake of an accident."

"But what choice do we have?" he gawped.

"My God if I'm ever in trouble do remind me never to hire you," I sighed.

"John…?"

"I'm going to get rid of her. Break the connection."

"Get rid of her? Break the connection. Just like that? Toss her out like a piece of garbage you mean? My God

John, that it should come to this…" my father once again started to sermonise, but for the first time in my life I stood up to him and told him to shut up.

"Your sense of right and wrong is going to put a rope around your neck, which might be fine for you and your twisted sense of morality but what about me? I need a father. I need you in my life. Your clients need you. The world needs you. You're a good and important man. You can't make this stupid gesture just to appease your own conscience. It's selfish. You have to be stronger than that," I told him.

My father didn't know what to say. He simply stared at me in open-mouthed consternation as his boy became a man before his very eyes, then he lowered his gaze and nodded sadly.

"So be it, John. If it means that much to you, we will do it your way," he eventually agreed.

I snatched up his car keys and headed for the garage, but my father called to me before I'd reached the parlour door.

"John?"

I looked back as he stared up at me from out of the darkness. "I… I just want you to know that… I'm very proud of you," he finally said.

I didn't reply. I merely nodded then headed out to dispose of the dead hooker my dad had brought home tonight.

iii

She was just as my father had said, slumped in the front passenger seat of his Morris Oxford and as lifeless as an empty dress. I approached her with caution, afraid of what I might see, but needlessly so for there were no obvious signs of violence about her. Her head was not bashed in, nor her features marked. Her hair was a little ruffled and her blouse torn, but other than that she looked for all intents and purposes as if she were simply slumbering against the window, awaiting a kiss from a handsome Prince to rouse her.

I loaded a pick and shovel in the back of the car and opened the garage door.

The night was still thick with fog and as cold as the grave but it barely registered with me, I was too intent on the task in hand. I pulled the seat belt around my passenger to stop her falling across me as I drove and pulled out into the night.

I took it slow. I had no choice, visibility was reduced to a radiator's width but I made my way across town and towards the Lanes. There were a few secluded spots up there that picnickers used by day and courting couples by night, though I couldn't see how anyone would want to expose so much as an ankle to this frozen night. Still, as the unfortunate girl in the passenger seat could testify, there were still a few hardy all-weather souls out there who needed to be catered for, so I continued with caution.

I circled the Lanes looking for the dirt trail that led to the lake and finally found it on my third pass. The track was muddy, but frozen solid, so I bumped and bounced my way down to the shore and parked up a few yards from the water's edge, just in front of a twisted knot of skeletal trees.

No other couples had made it out here this evening, so I unhooked my passenger and caught her as she fell across my lap.

My God she was lovely: young, beautiful and no longer bedevilled by the cares of this world. I actually felt quite revolted at these thoughts and a choking bile clawed at my throat as the realisation hit home that my father had done this.

My father had snuffed out this light!

She was barely a year older than me and my father had killed her.

Okay, it had been an accident, he'd not meant to do it and if he could've taken it back then he would have, even at the ruination of himself, but still she was dead. She was young, beautiful and fair. But she was dead. And she had no one but herself to blame.

This travesty was enough to stir me to do what I had to do, so I climbed from the car, grabbed my tools and went in search of a suitable resting place.

In amongst the trees, maybe thirty yards from the car, I found a small clearing. The ground was thick with dead leaves, which was perfect as I could use them to cover my works, so I kicked the crackling carpet aside and started swinging the pick.

But the ground was frozen solid after two straight weeks of frosts, turning the dirt to concrete. I'd been digging like a maniac for almost thirty minutes and had barely cleared two inches of topsoil. At this rate I'd still be here in April when the picnickers returned so I threw down my pick, mopped my brow and had a rethink.

I couldn't just leave the girl out for anyone to find. According to my father, time was everything when it came to criminal investigations, so it was important to buy as much of it for ourselves as we could, to muddy the memories and erode any physical evidence my father may have inadvertently left.

I racked my brains and thought some more.

Under the leaves? Could I just cover the girl with leaves and hope no one would stumble across her? No – animals would sniff her out and this place was rife with dog walkers. I had to put her beyond the snout, but where?

That was when I noticed the lake.

Like the ground, the lake was frozen over, but unlike the ground, I didn't need to smash my way through six cubic feet of granite-hard mud to get rid of my problems; a single hole a foot or so wide would do just as nicely.

I recovered my wafer-thin grave with leaves and headed out onto the ice. It easily supported my weight without the slightest creak, so I guessed it must've been a good six inches thick, but ice has a siren-like habit of being at its thinnest in its very deepest, so I braved my weight until I found what I reckoned to be the centre of the lake.

I swung the pick and the crack reverberated around the woods like a gunshot, chipping a tiny dink out of the ice, but otherwise barely troubling its sheen. I brought the pick down again, smashing the ice in the same place and wincing as the boom shook frost from the shoreline branches, but there was no way around it. Five minutes of cracking was preferable to six hours of huffing and puffing, and as the night was still thick with fog any passers-by might be unlikely to locate the source of the commotion, so I pressed on, swinging the pick and smashing my way through to liquid water. I was eventually rewarded after three or four dozen swings with a splash, then worked to widen the hole until I almost slipped in myself.

It was now a little before six in the morning and the roads would soon be busy with milkmen and early risers. I couldn't let myself be seen by potential witnesses so I ran back to the car to fetch the object of tonight's exercise.

I half-expected her not to be there when I finally found the Oxford. My mind had run amuck while I'd worked on her watery tomb, pushing back the boundaries of this nightmare to terrible conclusions and I'd come to convince myself that she hadn't been dead, merely grievously wounded, so that it would be left to me to either finish her off or nurse her back to health as I saw fit.

Alas the Lord had left me with no such dilemmas. She was still as dead as before and awaited my return with glassy eyes.

Let no man say my father didn't know how to kill young women.

I pulled her shoes from her feet and stuffed them into her blouse to save me from losing them en route, then grabbed her under the arms and dragged her from the passenger seat. She was easier to drag once I got her onto the ice, but just when I thought the finishing line was in sight I was all at sea again when I couldn't find the bloody hole.

The lake was almost a quarter of a mile long and it was as close to pitch as the fog would allow, so I spent the best part of the next half an hour dragging her backwards and forwards before collapsing through fear and exhaustion. I could've dragged her past the hole by a matter of inches and not spotted it in this darkness, so I decided to strike out alone and locate the hole unencumbered before returning for the body.

Another ten minutes of sheer unadulterated terror passed before I eventually blundered into my own handiwork. My foot disappeared into the icy portal and I only stopped myself from taking a mariner's nap by flinging out my arms and legs out either side, though the crunch of bones on jagged ice almost crippled me with pain.

I hauled myself out, screamed a silent scream into the night, but ploughed on nevertheless, ripping off my soaking jacket and jersey and laying them out on either side of the hole to mark it for later. I did the same with a couple of twigs and a brickbat I found on the surface, and laid them all out, thirty feet in all directions. I wasn't going to lose this hole again, of that I was sure. But it was only then, at this moment of minor triumph that I realised my problems had matured with interest.

I'd now lost the girl.

I'd been so intent on finding the hole that I'd done the exact same thing all over again and left her somewhere out there on the ice assuming I'd be able to find her again.

Oh fudgecakes!

The time was now a quarter to seven and the fog was starting to thin. This was something of a mixed blessing as it meant I'd be able to find my charge faster, though it also meant the curtain behind which I was operating was lifting.

I skidded across the lake in great sweeping arcs, almost going out of my mind with frustration and now convinced more than ever the girl had simply upped and walked away, when a cold terror knocked me onto my knees. Somewhere out there in the soup a car door slammed shut.

I stilled my breathing and strained my ears, turning this way and that as I tried to hear more and soon a couple of voices drifted across the ice.

"… out there… on the lake… … some sort a… … … really loud banging…"

"Oh God," I shuddered, the shock of my discovery twisting the fear around my neck like a noose.

I all-but threw myself at the fog, skating across the deadly surface with nary a care for my safety as time was suddenly cut short, both for this task and on earth. Oh it could be argued that I hadn't actually done the deed, that I'd merely been trying to cover up after the fact, and I couldn't be hanged for that, but I was shrewd enough to know that even if my father stepped forward and took full credit for his night's work, the notion of a father taking the rap for his wayward son fitted the charge sheet so much more snugly than anything approaching the truth. Especially when that father was the famous Reginald Coal

VC QC and all around good egg.

The next sound to rile me was the sound of a dog. It barked like fury and came hurtling out of the mists to skid right past me. The sight of this black mutt almost sent me into a fit but the beast just gave me a cursory sniff before lolloping on his way.

"Jupiter!" came the renewed cries, now barely a football pitch away from me. "Jupiter boy, where are you? What have you found?"

I realised they'd set the dog off the leash to find whatever was amiss out here on the lake, so I turned and followed the dog myself, drawing closer to its excited barking until I could see it bouncing up and down on the spot over the body of my father's former confidante.

I kicked the dog aside, bundled the girl up by the arms, only to have to kick the dog some more as it joined in the fun, yanking her in the opposite direction by the ankles.

"What have you got? What is it boy?" came the excited voices, now closer than ever. That was when I decided to do as my father might in this situation, pulled the belt from my trouser loops and strangled the dog where it bounded. Within thirty seconds it was dead, or at least no longer in contention for Crufts, so I fixed the belt to my waist again, grabbed a couple of ankles and dragged the girl towards the hole.

My pursuers found their dog before I found my hole and they hollered in anger and despair in equal measures.

"Oh God, no!"

"You bastard! You fucking bastard! We know you're out there somewhere and we're going to kill you!" they pledged, but I'd already found my soaking jacket and the hole was now just a short lug to the left.

I had originally planned to say a few words before committing her to the depths, but my newest companions had soured those noble plans so I simply threw her into the crag headfirst and stuffed her legs in after her.

"What was that?"

"Someone's in the drink. Come on!" came the inevitable responses, but my night's work was now done and evasion was most definitely the order of the morning.

I grabbed my jersey and jacket and struck out for the shore. Obviously I'd now lost my father's bleeding car to the fog as well, but I reasoned if I could lose so many other important things on such a perilous night, I shouldn't have too many problems losing the ex-dog lovers on my trail.

I hit the shoreline after a few seconds and scoured the clearing mists for familiar landmarks. Nothing sprang out at me, so I sprinted along the water's edge, tumbling and gliding as I went until I fell arse-over-tit over a protruding tree root that the ice hadn't managed to swallow.

"He's over there the bastard!" echoed the voices, but the good Lord finally cut me some slack when I looked up and saw my father's Oxford jutting out from the trees.

I threw myself at it with a renewed purpose, only to have a minor heart attack when it took me a full ten seconds of frisking to locate my keys, but finally I was thumping the pedals and wheel spinning away without a thought to the poor suspension. I bounced over every frozen rut and dip before my front wheels finally found some semblance of evenness, then clutch, gear and accelerated away like a bat out of the broom cupboard. Shapes were running out of the mists and across my rear-view mirror but I dared not look back, I just ground my right foot into the foot-well and shot myself up the track and towards the Lanes as if the world behind me were plunging into the abyss.

And you know what?

It was.

iv

I arrived home shortly after eight, stashing the Oxford in the garage and locking the doors behind me. I hung the tools on the wall and spent the next thirty minutes wiping the car out with white spirits before I was so spent with fear that I crashed out there and then across the front seats.

I awoke a little while later. I wasn't sure of the time or indeed where I was until the events of the night before came crashing back to me like a terrible dream. But the night had been no dream, as my father standing over me with an anxious look on his face testified.

"Well?" he prompted.

"It's done," I confirmed, causing my father to blow out his cheeks and shake his head sadly.

"Lord have pity on us, your wretched servants," he lamented, before offering me his hand. I hesitated at first, because it was such an alien thing for him to do, but I eventually accepted it with solemnity. "It is a terrible thing we've done tonight, John, but you were right, it was a necessary evil. As God is my witness it was so. And therefore I now propose this pact, that we put the events of this hellish night behind us and swear to the grave that we shall never hitherto reveal a detail of what befell that poor unfortunate creature to any persons outside of this handshake."

My father had a lifelong habit of fancying-up the vernacular but I think what he was getting at was "I won't tell if you don't".

"Yes father," I agreed, only to turn white when I remembered my companions from the ice. "But wait, I was seen!"

42

My father jumped two inches to the left. "Up close?"

"No, as I drove away. They'll have the car's regis…" I started to panic, only to stop mid-fret when I rounded the back of the Oxford and found it was already missing its plates.

"It's all right John, I took them off last night," he told me. "Just as a precaution."

I accepted this explanation for what it was; simply relieved that he'd had the forethought to do this when I myself hadn't, but a few days later I did start to wonder when he'd taken off the plates.

And why.

There was nothing in the papers about ladies in lakes or murderers on ice, just a small piece in the local rag about a gamekeeper's dog being killed by an ice fishing poacher. The gamekeeper was distraught, not least of all because the poacher had shown him a clean pair of heels, and there was a phone number at the end of the article together with an appeal for information.

I breathed a sigh of relief and gave thanks that this whole sorry ordeal was behind me but this relief didn't last long, for within days of our inaugural father/son activity night the old man was at it again.

"Oh John, John!" he cried, shaking me from my nightmares for the second time in a week and wearing his now familiar expression of panic. "Wake up, wake up, we're in trouble again!"

The previous adventure had been, hands down, the worst experience of my life, so you can imagine my reaction to this latest development. If you can't, there was an old joke doing the rounds back then that summed it up: The Lone Ranger and Tonto are out on the plains when all of a sudden they are surrounding by a war party of angry Sioux. The Lone Ranger turns to his sidekick and says:

"Looks like we're in trouble, Tonto," to which Tonto replies, "What's all this *we* shit, Pale Face?" My response wasn't quite on a par with Tonto's, although this sentiment did pop into my head.

"We're done for, we're done for," he sobbed, and once again I couldn't jog any sense out of him until I'd first lubricated his chords.

"She saw me! She knows!" he kept saying, dangling tantalizing fragments of our predicament in front of me.

"Who saw you? Who knows?" I pressed, topping up my father's glass and pressing him as much as I dared.

"Her friend," he finally said. "Another harlot. She must've been with the other one the night I picked her up and she says she saw me. Phoned me at the office she did. Phoned me just like that."

"What did she say?" I gulped, the ground disappearing beneath my feet like a Tyburn cellar.

"She says she's going to tell unless I pay her five thousand pounds," he said, screwing up his face in disgust. "It's always money with these whores, isn't it? If she were out for justice, or wanton to avenge her friend then I could at least understand that, but money? Why is it always money with these people?"

"Do we have five thousand pounds?" I asked.

"No, not unless we sell the house, the car, my medals and the shirts off our very backs, and even then we'd probably still come up short," he totted. "But you can forget about bargaining with these villains, even if we had the wherewithal to pay her, she'd simply demand double the next day and tell the police once she'd bled us dry regardless. No John, I'm afraid we're done for this time."

I allowed these thoughts to thoroughly deflate my spirits before risking my father's wrath.

"But, does she know about me too?"

My father looked at me thunderstruck and all but

choked on his fury. "Of course she knows about you, you stupid boy! Who do you think I'm worried about? Myself? Good God boy, you've got a pretty low opinion of me to even dare ask that!" he fumed.

"No no father, I didn't mean… "

But my father was in no mood to write off the insult and continued to wail about how he'd happily lay down his life if it was up to him, and how he regretted ever letting me talk my way into this sorry situation before I was finally able to get a word in.

"Of course father, of course. I didn't think, please I'm truly sorry," I pleaded, and my father said he should think so too. He glared at me with glassy contempt before the indignation finally crumbled to leave me with the sting of a *faux pas* as well as a death sentence hanging in the air.

"No, this has gone far enough already," he concluded. "We must go to the authorities, offer ourselves up and make our peace with this world."

It was amazing, that this same bloke who couldn't pass a noose without sticking his head through it was the same bloke who'd won a Victoria Cross at Monte Cassino.

"Father, surely there's something we can do?" I beseeched.

"I don't see what," he obstinated.

"Let us at least go and see this woman and try to reason with her. We can surely do that, can't we?"

"And have it known that we were trying to wriggle out of our responsibilities even when the game was up? I'd rather hang," he hawed, which was the sort of Victorian attitude that saw many a good Captain go down with the ship when there were rubber rings and lifeboats to spare, but one to which I found hard to relate. So, at the risk of further enraging my father, I pleaded with him to be allowed to go and see this girl for myself. Just to try.

"After all, you did say it was me you were concerned

45

about," I snivelled. "I'm not ready for this, father. Please, not me father, please?"

My father sucked his gums for a moment or two then frowned with supreme disappointment.

"If you must, John. If you must," he finally relented, before turning his back on me.

v

My father suggested I borrowed the Oxford to pick her up and gave me a head-to-toe description of our persecutor to take with me. I left shortly after sundown and cruised the streets past her place of business, parking up just across the road until I saw a girl fitting this same description being dropped off by a light blue Ford Anglia at around 9pm.

I was so anxious about the impossible task at hand that I didn't even take a peek at who'd dropped her off, instead I simply started my engine when he drove on and cruised over to where she was stood, winding down my passenger window as I went.

The girl approached and climbed in without nary a word, so I put my foot down and took us away from the glare of the streetlights and towards the thick shadows of the Lanes.

"It's ten bob for hand, twenty for a blowy and thirty if you want to go all the way," she told me, rattling off the menu as if I'd come to order breakfast from a drive-thru.

I stole a quick glance at her as I played for time; she was a pretty girl for sure, similar to the girl whose acquaintance I had made a few days earlier, with bold features, long eye lashes and scarlet lips, though as pretty as she was, she had a hard look about her that intimidated me without her having to try.

"Nervous?" she asked when I still hadn't answered.

I tried to gulp down my fears and answered as best I could. "A little."

"You're a young 'un, aren't you. First time?"

"What?"

"Is it your first time with a lady, sweetie?"

"No," I replied, not fully taking her meaning. "I've been with lots of ladies before."

My passenger smiled. "Of course you have, Valentino. Of course you have. Well then dearie, what's it to be?"

I figured we needed a quiet place to speak, although I have to admit I still hadn't worked out what I was going to say, so I played for time and told her I just wanted to sit a while. She seemed fine with this, but warned me it would still cost me half a nicker whether we did anything or not, so I agreed and pulled off the road, mounting the verge to take us into the trees.

I killed the engine and plunged us into total blackness, but righted this by switching the headlights back on.

"Romantic," her silhouette commented. "Money?"

"Oh yes," I remembered, searching through my pockets for a note I was convinced I had, only to find coins. "Can I give you change?" I asked. She frowned but held out her hand all the same.

"I'm not a bloody slot machine, you know ," she said, dropping my shillings into her purse. "Right then, I'm all yours," she said, slipping a cigarette between her ruby red lips and flicking a lighter several times before the car filled up with smoke. "Sure you don't want to…" she started, pulling my hand onto her left breast.

Despite my earlier claims, this was the first time I'd touched either of a girl's breasts, left or right, at least while she'd still been alive, but I wasn't here to indulge boyhood fantasies so I pulled my hand away – after twenty seconds or so.

"I'm sorry," I spluttered, "but I simply need to talk."

"I see, one of them are you?" she concluded. "Okay then dearie, let's hear it? See if you can shock me."

I took a deep breath and tried to compose myself, but failed to come anywhere close to collected so I simply came out with it.

"My father didn't mean to kill your friend, it was an accident, honest!" I blathered, catching a fag in the face as it flew clean across the front seats between us.

"… 'ere, you what?" she coughed.

"It was an accident," I repeated, trying to hammer this particular point home before she scarpered, "please don't go to the law, you'll be doing us both a great injustice."

"Go to the law? Killed who? What on earth are you talking about?" she gawped. "… 'ere, you're not one of them weirdos are you mate, because I mean it, if you try anything funny I'll fucking stick you," she warned me in no uncertain terms, reaching into her bag to pull out a little pocket blade after several seconds of rummaging.

"No please, I'm not going to try anything funny, I just want you to listen," I pleaded, but she wasn't in much of a listening mood any more.

"Look darling, I don't know what you're talking about, but when I hear talk of killing and the law I don't want to know, all right? You can just drop me off where you picked us up and we'll forget about the lolly," she said, scattering my coins onto the floor of the car as she held me at bay with her penknife.

This had gone badly. Not as badly as I'd thought it might go admittedly, but badly all the same and I wondered if I'd picked up the right girl from her reaction, although she did fit my father's description to a tee. I decided to salvage what promises I could before calling it a night. "So you won't go to the police then?"

"Believe me dearie, you drop me off and I won't tell

no one about this hullabaloo, you have my word," she promised, so I took that on face value and started the car.

"Okay then," I agreed, but no sooner had I twisted the keys in the ignition than a shape appeared out of nowhere from behind the passenger seat and wrapped a red and white tie around my passenger's neck.

"What the…!" I yelped, jumping out of my skin as her head whipped back into the shadows. In the reflected glare of the headlights I could make out my father's grimacing expression behind her, his jaw clenched into a vicious scowl as he brought all his might to bear on that silky snare.

"Hold her arms. Hold her arms!" he barked at me, ducking this way and that as she tried to stab him over her shoulder.

"What are you doing?" I shrieked, launching myself at the horror but having to fight my way past the girl's frantic heels as she lashed out at the steering wheel. I grabbed my father's wrists and tried to pull the tie from his grip, but he was too strong for the both of us and he held me at bay as he wrung the last few throes from her quaking body.

"Stop it! Stop it!" I screamed, only to crash headfirst into the dashboard when a three-inch blade sunk into my side up to the hilt. I writhed against the seat, trying my damnedest to scream in agony but unable to draw a breath, only to catch the girl's eyes one final time. They burned with hatred and despair, locking onto me as if sheer wrath alone might somehow save them from that ever-lasting blackness, but it wasn't to be; a few final flickers of consciousness extinguished behind her pupils and her eyes turned grey.

My father continued to pull on the tie with a fury that made me feel as if the world was coming to an end, but eventually he relented, flopping back in his seat to gasp with vitriolic release.

"Jesus," he sobbed. "Jesus, Jesus, Jesus, I am your servant."

I didn't know about Jesus but I wasn't entirely convinced myself and pawed at the driver's door until I was able to tumble out onto a blanket of crackling leaves.

I didn't know where I was going, as far away from this nightmare as possible I hoped, but the pain in my side was so great that I could scarcely drag myself across the frozen ground, and all too quickly my father was picking me up and carrying me back to the car.

"You're hurt, my son," he said, dumping me in the passenger seat. The girl was already gone, her body discarded somewhere out there in the night and now my father drove us back home, back to the house we shared...

Back to the place where hellish pacts were brokered...

vi

I must've passed out on the drive home because I came to with a burning fever. I knew I was in my bed, but for some reason I'd been transported out onto the ice. Moving around in the fog were terrifying shapes, hell-bent on ripping me to pieces and throwing me to the wolves for my recent misdeeds, even though I'd had nothing to do with that first killing and no idea my father had been hiding in the car with his own solutions to the second.

I cried with despair, miserable to the core, but knowing I deserved whatever fate befell me for all the suffering I'd been a party to.

The shapes got closer, forming up before my very eyes and emerging from the mist with steely claws when all of a sudden a crack sounded beneath me and the bed plunged on one side.

The ice was cracking!

The ice was giving way!

I finally found my voice and screamed my last scream but it was lost to the night as my bed crashed through the ice and into the black abyss.

I awoke to freezing flannels and icy water bottles. My father was fighting my fever from the outside and making a decent fist of it, though I failed to appreciate this at the time. I simply floundered in my soaking blankets, desperate to escape the pain before succumbing once more to sleep.

It would be another four days before I'd awake again.

"It was touch and go for a while there," my father told me. "I've seen many a good man die from lesser scratches than yours, their veins blackened by poison before they knew to say their prayers. I thought I'd lost you too, John."

"How long have I been asleep for?" I asked; my arms weighted by my side like lead.

"A week."

"A week! But work…?"

"I phoned your boss for you, told him you were laid up with flu. He understood," he reassured me, though to be honest my work was the least of my worries. It had just been the first to pop itself into my head.

"Why did you kill that girl?" I demanded.

"I had no choice John. I had to do it. I hope you can see that."

"No father, I can't. I don't understand," I said.

"John," he started, pulling his pine chair a little closer to my bedside to demonstrate his sincerity, "we would've both hanged if I hadn't silenced her. You were right. You were right all along," he conceded. "You can't bargain with these women. There was simply no way around it."

"But she said she wouldn't go to the police," I reminded him.

"Yes, I know. Just as she would've said anything to get out of that car, John, anything, because she was scared of what you might do," he said. "Just as the young Italian boys we captured in Messina promised us they'd throw away their uniforms and go home if we turned them loose. But we knew they wouldn't. We were on their home soil and we knew they'd rejoin the fight the moment we let them walk, so I shot them all to save my men. It's as simple as that."

"Father…"

"You've not been to war son. You've not had to do these things, and for that I envy you," he said, placing a caring hand on my shoulder. "But you've got to be strong now, just as I had to be for you, for we're not out of the woods quite yet."

This got better and better didn't it? All that death, all that horror and all that murder and we still weren't out of the woods? He had to be bloody kidding!

"This can't be. Nobody saw me pick her up. Nobody saw us in the woods. There's no way she would have told anybody else about her blackmail, so how can we still be in peril?" I gasped.

Father bristled a smidgeon at my less than respectful tone, but he made an allowance for my fever.

"The police have already been here. They have a vague description of the car used in both incidents and they are questioning everyone in King's Lynn who owns such a vehicle. They don't have the exact make or model or indeed the registration number, but I am in the frame by owning that car," he said, before spelling out where this all got particularly sticky. "And I don't have an alibi for either night."

"But surely…"

"But surely nothing. The lack of an alibi is as good as a signed confession in the eyes of most juries. I should know, boy, I've been on the wrong end of more than one such judgement."

"But what can we do?" I asked. "I can say you were with me. I'll give you an alibi."

"That's no good," he dismissed. "A family alibi is no alibi at all. No I need to be seen in public, by independent witnesses whose word cannot be brought into question."

"But, how do we do that?" I fumbled showing my naivety.

My father raised an eyebrow. "There has to be another," he said. "But this time, it has to be done by you."

As you can imagine, I didn't exactly leap out of bed to chase down a bowl of Cornflakes at the suggestion, and the house reverberated with the sounds of terrible rows for three straight days before it eventually fell into silence once more.

"Son, I did these awful things for you, now you must do the same for me. This is on your head as much as it is on mine and I'll not go to the gallows alone," he vowed, completing a spectacular about-turn with hypocrisy to spare.

I could've stuck to my guns and told him to go to hell but he was still my father and I was still in awe and afraid of him in equal measure. But more than that, if he was prepared to kill burly German quartermasters, unarmed Italian boys and defenceless young girls to save himself, what further price was he capable of paying?

So I stopped arguing so vehemently when this thought dawned on me, but I didn't let up entirely. After all, "people will say anything to get out of the car. Anything." I now knew this to be true. And so did my father.

"This has to be the end though father. One more, just one and then we're finished," I insisted. "I need your solemn word." My father regarded me for several seconds as he rolled my condition over in his mind before accepting.

"Very well, this one will be the last, come what may."

He held out his hand and as sickened as I was, I took it and shook it all the same.

"This is a pact John, from father to son. And it cannot be broken by outside forces. Take a girl, deliver her to the Lord in the same manner as the others and set us both free."

There were many things I could've said and probably many things I should've said. But in the event, all I said was:

"Yes father."

vii

Once again the number plates were already on the side when I entered the garage. I looked at them with contempt then climbed into my father's car and headed out into the night.

I didn't know where my father had gone for the evening, but the first thing I did was to make sure he wasn't hiding in the back seat. I'm not sure what I would've done had I found him lurking down there again but I doubt it would've been pretty.

Before he'd left for the evening – all dolled up in his finest tweeds – he'd kitted me out with a pair of black leather gloves, a pair of thick rimmed glasses that sported clear glass lenses and a silken tie with a pre-tied knot halfway up its length similar to the one he'd used a week earlier. That first one was in cinders apparently. Or perhaps my father had lied about that too. I didn't know. One silk tie looked much the same as the next to me.

I headed across town once more, to the place where women availed themselves, and waited until the sexual rush hour passed. This town had one hell of a libido it seemed. As recently as two weeks ago I'd had no idea this sort of thing even went on. And I'd had no idea just how many townsmen participated. I guess I was learning more than I'd bargained for these days and weeks.

A little after two in the morning, the traffic eased and most of the girls retired for the night to count their blessings. One or two of the girls still lingered and I waited until there was just one before I started my engine and rolled over to her corner of the street.

"Looking for business, fella?" she asked, dispensing with her fag with a flick of the finger and metaphorically rolling up her sleeves.

I could scarcely bring myself to answer, so instead I cranked open the passenger side door and invited her in with a nod. The girl slipped in so I put my foot down and headed out to the oh-so familiar Lanes.

"Not seen you about before, love," she commented. "New to this sort of thing are you?"

"You could say that," I replied when I finally found my voice.

The traffic on the roads was pretty sparse, so I was reasonably confident we'd have no one going to the police the next day with tales of plateless Oxfords or similar, though this was the only shred of confidence I possessed.

I pressed on, past the lakes, past the picnicking sites and even out past farmlands until the girl started to shift uncomfortably in her seat and asked me where we were going.

"Away from here," I simply replied. "As far away from here as we can get." I was admittedly a little sketchy on the details, but then this was because I was simply too swamped with raw emotions, although I should've perhaps tried to phrase my intentions a little better as my passenger's alarm bells were now clattering ten to the dozen. I guess getting picked up by some poetic fruit loop is a scenario working girls live with every day and some even prepare for it, because all at once there was a straight razor at my throat and a threat of violence in my ear.

"You stop this car this instant, Jack, or I'll cut you a new grin," she suggested, although she hadn't entirely thought through the strategy.

"If you cut me," I told her, "I'll as likely crash this car and there are deep drainage channels on both sides of the road." The girl took a moment to check and saw the moon flickering off the icy surface of the parallel waterways. Now the weather was still freezing, the ice might've supported the weight of a person, but it wasn't about to support the weight of a careening Morris Oxford. "We won't be found until the next time they're dredged, whenever that may be," I added, which was perfectly true. These channels had claimed dozens of lives over the last forty years or so and some of the dead took years to emerge from the silty black waters.

"Stop this car!" she screamed, the straight blade now trembling in her hands.

"I'm sorry, I can't," I said. "I have to get you away from here. It's for your own good."

"You fucking psycho bastard!" she cried. "I mean it, I'll carve you up!"

I turned to her, my eyes no longer on the road. "I wish you would. You'd be doing me a favour."

Seeing she'd blown herself out, I decided not to elaborate on the evening's itinerary any further and risk provoking a last ditch reaction, instead I gambled on the uncertainty of silence. We drove on like this for several more miles, me holding her life in the balance, her holding mine, until a short way ahead the road turned at a sharp right angle, over a stone bridge and away from the ice-covered conduits. The girl saw this and she saw that I saw it too. She must've taken it for a "now or never" moment because the blade quickly jammed itself back into my gizzard before the road found the channels again, but I didn't yield. Instead I drove on, into the night and towards the place I'd picked out to dump her.

"I'm going to count to three…" she warned me, the edge of her Sweeney comb already drawing droplets I could ill afford to spill. "One…"

"It won't save you," I told her.

"Two…" she continued.

"Do it, and you'll be dead within days," I promised.

"Three!" she declared, but before she could swipe me a new fag hole, I turned off the road and pulled up at our final destination – Fenwold Country Railway Station.

The girl tried to slash me as I stopped but I grabbed her wrist and held on for life, limb and the upholstery.

"I'm not going to hurt you," I finally got around to telling her. "You're safe here with me. Open the glove box and see for yourself." I even demonstrated my sincerity by letting go of her wrists, affording her a free swipe across my kisser if she so desired, but the flicker of hope I was offering was too tantalising to dismiss. "Open it," I urged. She hesitated for a few moments before reaching for the latch and pulling open the glove box. Inside was an envelope full of pounds, shillings and pence and a clean white handkerchief.

"They're for you," I told her, and she fingered the envelope without taking her eyes from mine to find there was close to a hundred pounds inside.

"What is all of this?" she demanded, shoving the blade back into my face. "What do you want from me?"

"I want you to leave town, disappear and never come back," I told her.

"Disappear?"

"Make it look like you've disappeared, like you've come to some harm, you know?" I spelt out. "You'll have to leave all of your things behind but at a guess I'd say I've more than compensated you for your troubles."

"A hundred pounds?"

"Open the hanky," I reminded her.

The girl had neglected the handkerchief in the presence of so much folding money, but now she pulled it out and took a look at what I'd wrapped inside it.

"What is it?" she asked, none-the-wiser.

"It's a medal, a Victoria Cross," I told her. "The highest military medal you can get. It's worth a lot of money, at least a few hundred, maybe even more. You could set yourself up very nicely if you hocked it to the right collector."

"Whose is it? Because I know this much, love, it ain't yours," she somehow guessed.

"It's a relative's," I semi-fudged.

"It's stolen more like," she concluded.

"Yes, but it'll never be reported, I can guarantee you that much, and I've included all the proper documentation so you can get a good price for it with absolutely no comeback, I promise."

"What about my friends?" she said.

"Make some new ones," I suggested. "Make some better ones. Make a new start away from all of this."

"And where exactly am I meant to go?" she asked.

"The first train to Cambridge passes through here in a little over three hours. From there you can get to anywhere you like. Just don't come back here, not for at least ten years anyway. Please, it's for your own good. And the good of your friends."

I could see from her expression that my proposal made no sense whatsoever and it troubled her. Well, we all need our explanations, no matter how thick the envelopes we're given are.

"But why?" she asked.

I figured I had to tell her something, and it had to be an approximation of the truth as there was simply too much to lose risking everything on a bad lie, so I told her as much as I dared. "I need someone to think I've done something bad, something to you, to a girl of the night, if you know what I mean, and this is the only way I can do it without…" I trailed off. "Please, trust me, it's really important."

The girl stared at me hard in the darkness, her mind racing but her razor now ramrod still. It eventually flickered when she came to a startling conclusion.

"Is this about Juney? Are you the bastard who done Juney?"

"No no no," I assured her. "I'm just the poor bastard who's trying to stop it from happening again."

"How? How does this help?"

"I can't say. It's for your own good. Just trust me when I tell you that it will."

"I should report this," she said. "And if you know something about Juney then you should report it too," but deep down she knew I couldn't. She didn't know why, but she knew enough about living on the fringes of society to know there were no blacks and whites out here, only murky greys, and they all overlapped in ways honest decent folks could never comprehend.

"A couple of hundred, you say?" she finally asked, folding away her blade and looking at the VC again.

"Maybe even a thousand," I blarneyed, clinching the deal. There was just one final condition from her.

"I've got some letters from my mum, back at my room. Send them to me and I'll catch your train, they're all I want," she said, handing me a brass latchkey. I agreed and scribbled down my name and number on the back of the envelope, then did my utmost to drum into her the importance of only talking to me when she phoned, not my prostitute-murdering dad, and she seemed to understand without me going into the small print.

"Good-bye then, John Coal," she said, shoving the money and handkerchief into her bra before climbing from the car. "I won't say it's been a pleasure meeting you, but it's been memorable. Stay lucky."

"Yes, you too, er…" I faltered, realising I didn't know her name despite making her a gift of my own.

"Shandy," she told me.

"Shandy?"

"It's what they call me, because I'm half and half," she explained, adding, "I dig girls as well" when the fog refused to lift from my face.

"I see," I pretended, fully five years before I actually did. "Well take care Shandy. Don't come back. And if anyone asks…"

"I know, I know," she replied before I could say the words myself. "If anyone asks, I'm dead."

viii

I snuck into Shandy's bedsit, found her letters right where she'd left them and picked up a few undergarments too. The night was fast turning to dawn, but I had just enough time to get back out to the Lanes to sow the seeds of another disappearance before fleeing the scene.

When I got home the house was quiet. My dad's bed had not been slept in and there were no signs of him lurking behind any fixtures or fittings so I thanked the Lord for small mercies and collapsed into bed, falling into a deep sleep before I'd even finished bouncing.

*

I came to four hours later. The house was still quiet, but there was evidence that my father had been and gone. His tweeds were back in the wardrobe, a cup and saucer sat on the sideboard and the number plates were back on the Oxford.

Despite him being my beloved father, and despite our having slept under the same roof as each other for more or less the last eighteen years, I couldn't help but feel uneasy about being asleep while he'd been creeping about the place this particular morning. Still, I shook these heebies from my jeebies, had a wash and put the kettle on for a richly deserved cup of tea.

That was when I noticed the scrapbook.

I'd not seen it before, but it was a thick leather-clad volume with cuttings bloating out the first thirty pages. Next to it were a pair of scissors and the lunchtime edition of today's *Evening Herald* – minus the front page.

I found the missing page hanging out between the pages of the scrapbook. It was yet to be pasted in but read:

GIRL MISSING: FENS STRANGLER FEARED

The previous page held a similar headline, only this one carried a picture of my father's first victim:

WHERE IS SHE? COUNTRYSIDE SCOURED

And yet another article featured a picture of Juney, my father's second victim:

DEAD! STRANGLER STRIKES

I couldn't believe my eyes, my father was keeping a record of his atrocities, but I flicked back through the book, through headlines and front pages until I realised I was no longer reading about the three girls I knew of. I was reading about at least another dozen.

FENS VICTIM 9: POLICE HUNT MADMAN
RAMPAGE – ANOTHER BODY!
POLICE BAFFLED: STRANGLER STILL AT LARGE
GIRL FOUND IN RIVER

In all, I counted sixteen separate girls who'd either fallen victim, or who were counted as abducted, by someone known as the Fens Strangler and I was just coming to the obvious conclusion that my father was that same Fens Strangler when I realised he couldn't be. Some of the earliest cuttings dated back to 1917, before my father had even been born, and a good proportion of them were from the 1920s, when he would've only been a nipper. He couldn't possibly have been responsible.

I went through the scrapbook again and made a note of all the dates, finding that the murders seemed to come in waves of two or three before petering out: 1917 1925 1929 1939 1944 1946 1955 1962 – the years were there in black and white, there was no escaping the facts.

"The first were done by my father," explained a voice behind me, near separating me from my internal organs. I spun around to find my father setting his billycock on the sideboard while shaking himself from his overcoat.

"I didn't hear you come in," I gasped, hardly able to catch my breath.

"I can be quiet when I want to be," he replied, his eyes studying me carefully while flicking towards the notes I'd been taking. "You haven't pasted the new page in yet?"

"What?" I gawped, before realising what he was talking about. "I didn't know I was supposed to."

My father walked to the kettle. "What do you think I

left it out for?"

I didn't know, and I didn't particularly want to hazard a guess for fear of provoking a mortal rebuke from the strangler. He looked at me as he turned the gas on underneath the kettle.

"Paste it in," he told me.

"Yes father," I agreed, daubing the back of the article with paper paste and slapping it in.

My father glanced at my handiwork over my shoulder. "It's not straight," he scowled, as if this was the most deplorable misdemeanour likely to be found between this album's sleeves. "Pull it out and do it properly before it dries," he ordered, so I peeled the page out again and relayed it, this time with the precision of a veteran draftsman. "Very good," my father grunted.

He refilled the pot with boiling water and brought it over to the table, before pulling up a chair for himself.

"So, you're probably wondering what all this is about," he speculated.

"Umm…" I ummed, unsure just how stupid to play this one. In the event I realised unswerving respect and obedience would serve me better and give me a greater chance of seeing my nineteenth birthday, so I puckered up my reverence and gave my father's accord the kissing of its life. "I was rather, father. I can't seem to make head nor tail of it," I twittered like a right royal nit.

My father nodded. "Well as I say my father was responsible for the first girls."

"The Reverend?"

"Yes, he was a sublime hunter, taught me everything I know. In fact, if it hadn't been for the skills I learnt from him, I might not have come back from the war at all," he said, waiting for me to pip in with "Good old Grandpappa" before continuing when it became clear I wasn't about to.

"Anyway, yes, he introduced me to the sport shortly before the war and showed me how to play it."

"The sport?" I finally said.

"Yes, the sport. I have to say, I didn't take to it particularly well at first, you were much more game than I ever was," he commended, pouring himself a cup of tea from the pot when it was brewed.

"Yes, well... er... I didn't know it was a sport," I felt I had to admit.

"Of course not, and neither did I. Not until I'd smelt a few hares at any rate."

I didn't even go there.

"Your grandfather chose me carefully. He gave me the love and understanding the bitch who'd borne me never had and he educated me to the ways of *womenkind*," he said, almost spitting this last word out before I saw he was actually trying to rid himself of a loose tealeaf.

"The ways of womenkind?"

My father didn't respond immediately. He merely took another sip of his tea, then set the cup down very carefully. "You'll see," he eventually answered. His actions were deliberate and calculated, much like his actions throughout the last couple of weeks. He was grooming me, just as the Reverend had groomed him before.

"But I couldn't do it," he admitted. "I didn't have it in me. At least I didn't think I had until the war came along, then I found strengths I never knew I possessed."

My father flicked a speck of dust from his lapel and straightened his tie. It was his regimental tie, I noticed. I wondered if his alibi from the previous evening had involved some sort of reunion of the chaps, but I didn't have time to dwell on this as my father was rapidly reaching the cake and balloons part of the evening.

"You have these same strengths, John. I saw it in you from that very first evening. And tonight, you've demonstrated beyond all doubt that you are indeed my son." My father cast a glowing eye over me and even allowed a smile to filter through to his thin lips. "I'm very proud of you, John."

If anything, this eclipsed the starchy praise he'd bestowed on me for fixing the telly, but weirdly I didn't feel too happy about it this time around.

"I didn't push you to these actions, John," he said when I didn't answer. "I was very careful. If anything you pushed me. All I did was show you crossroads and you chose your own path. You are a hunter, John. Just as I am and my father was before me. It is in your nature. And it is now up to you to harness these strengths."

"Yes father," was all I could think to say in the absence of any long distance telephone lines between us.

"Good. Well I'm glad we could finally have this little talk," my father nodded cordially. "Needless to say, I expect you to exercise due diligence when it comes to the sport. I've not lasted this long by running about like a crazed maniac, so I think it would be best if we put the Fens Strangler to bed for a few more years, don't you?"

I did indeed. In fact, it was the first thing he'd said in several weeks that I agreed with, so I took what comfort I could from it and decided not to rush into any hasty decisions until I knew whereabouts my head was.

Or moreover, whereabouts it was likely to end up if I made the wrong decision.

ix

My father spoke to me some more over the next few days, educating me as to the ways of 'the sport' and the unGodliness of women in general. They'd gotten us chucked out of Eden, had brought down kings and had

65

even corrupted the poor old Reverend, "curse his folly", costing him a nailed-on bishopry, which is where I suspected all this had really begun.

My father, having been abandoned by his own Earthly mother within hours of his nativity, had been cut from the same cloth as the Reverend, but I myself had no such complaints about the rib-stealers, making me wonder just how fervent my father's beliefs could be that he would assume I'd fall into line right behind him and grandfather. I mean, respectful obedience was one thing but I couldn't help feel he was abusing the privilege.

Naturally, I tried to look as studious as I could for the sake of appearances and my own neck, but every sinew of me wanted to honk into a bucket after "our little talks". My father and grandfather had killed dozens of women between them. Now they expected me to carry on this ignoble family tradition. Of course, people with illicit vices always want everyone else to indulge in the very thing they themselves can't stop from doing just to validate their own compunctions. But this wasn't pouring a mid-morning sherry or sucking off altar boys after evensong, this was murder, the most heinous and dastardly crime of all. It wasn't a sport. It was never a sport. Not in peace. Not in war. Not in even King's Lynn, which I could almost understand. No, I may have been young. I may have helped my father do some terrible things, but I still knew the difference between right and wrong. Didn't I?

Of course I should have gone to the police. I should have but I didn't because I was a coward. I wanted to live and I wanted to carry on doing so for as many years as possible. Was this selfish of me? Perhaps, but I was young, my life had only just begun and there was still so much I had yet to do, like see Great Yarmouth, ride a motorbike, sail in a boat or take a girl out for an evening and bring her back alive again. I couldn't turn myself in, not least of all because my father wasn't letting me out of his sights just in case some hitherto untapped sense of morality got the better of me. No, I had to figure this thing out for myself.

Alas, I didn't get the chance. I thought the Fen's Strangler had been bedded down for a few years but events conspired to rouse him from his slumber early. They'd begun a week earlier, outside Fenwold Country Railway Station and had bounced around the country several times before eventually reaching us via the ringing of our telephone.

"… really don't know what… … of course… yes yes…" came my father's voice, floating up the stairs to draw me to the landing banisters. "Well I'm sure there's been some sort of… yes, of course. No, that won't be a problem. I'll come right away. Thank you. Thank you," he said, setting the phone down, thinking for a moment, and then turning for the stairs. I ducked back into my bedroom and hid as he rushed past, then tip-toed along the landing until I could peek into my father's room. He was tearing through his wardrobe and emptying the drawers of his dresser as he scoured for something in particular, only to turn several shades of scarlet when he came up short.

His eyes lifted to the doorjamb and I fell back to avoid his glare, but he must've seen my shadow recede for he barked at me to make my presence known.

"Sorry father, I was just…"

"Where's my medal?" he demanded, in no mood to dally with my expositions. "Where is it?" he said, rattling his emptier-than-usual biscuit tin.

"I don't know father. Have you checked…" I started to suggest but father cut me short.

"I've checked everywhere! I keep it in here, as you damn well know, so where is it? What have you done with it?" he smouldered.

"Father, honestly…" I got as far as bullshitting before

he barked at me once more.

"Liar! Liar, damn you! Who did you give it to?"

"Father…"

"You gave it to some little scrubber, didn't you? Who was she? Some little tart you were trying to impress? Tell me boy before…" but now it was my father's turn to bypass a full stop when an uncomfortable notion suddenly occurred to him. "You gave it to *her*, didn't you? You gave it to *her*, instead of… oh God. Oh you foolish boy. What have you done? What *have* you done"

"Father please, I can explain," I told him, although I think that was the very thing he was most afraid of.

"Mother said I should never involve you in the sport," he then bemoaned, catching me full in the kisser with the full weight of that one. "She said you weren't up to it."

"Mother knew?" I almost choked.

"Of course she knew. How could she not with all mine and father's comings and goings?" he contended, which was a fair point, if totally fucking insane.

"But…"

"Mother understood the sport for what it was. And she gave me her total and unequivocal loyalty," he vented, rising to his feet and dropping the biscuit tin on the bed. "Now be a man and come clean," he ordered, utterly unmoved by deafening hypocrisy claxons that were suddenly going off all around us. "You gave it to that harlot, didn't you? You gave it to that whore?"

"I didn't know about the sport when I gave it to her. I still thought I was bargaining for our lives, so I paid her off with your medal and made it look like a disappearance. I thought I was doing the right thing at the time," I pleaded wondering if this was a good time to tell him about the mattress cash he no longer had either.

"So you gave her my medal. And how exactly did you explain this benevolence to her?" he asked.

"I… I just made out that I was a Good Samaritan, intent on saving fallen women," I blarneyed, though this blarney barely made it past his eyebrows.

"Did you indeed?" he flickered.

We stood facing each other across the bed for a second or two before I decided to fill the air in-between us with a little more hot air to distract my father from reading between the lines.

"She doesn't know about us, she doesn't have anything on us, we don't have to worry about her," I promised.

"Don't we now?" he replied, chewing on the gristle out of my assurances before asking; "And so what about Sergeant Crow?"

"Sergeant Crow? Who's he?"

"Sergeant Crow is the fellow who's just rang me. He's holding your young strumpet at Lincoln Police Station after she was arrested whilst attempting to pawn my VC. It appears she had all the correct documentation and everything, but the proprietor… well, let's just say he had reservations she'd come about the award on the slopes of Monte Casino."

"The police have her?" I shuddered, the blood immediately pooling in my ankles.

"Yes, and they have a few questions too. So now I'm going to have to travel to Lincoln, avail myself to their sniggering inquiries and attempt to convince them that I gave her the medal myself," he fumed, leaving out the part about *how* he was going to convince them of this – more less *why*. "Stupid useless boy!"

"I'm sorry father, what can I do?" I submitted, already mentally packing my bags as I paid lip service to my father's tune.

"Yes…." my father growled. "What *can* you do?"

I let the question hang in the air for a few moments

while I worked through my options. As I say, most of them concerned getting the hell out of there just as soon as my father turned his back. Evidently, my father had been working on a similar strategy for when he asked me to:

"Pick up those socks would you. My arthritis is playing up again," I complied, only to catch a glimpse of silk flashing behind me in the reflection of my dear mother's picture. My instincts took over and without fully understanding why, I dropped to the floor just as the snare cut through the airspace my neck had moments earlier vacated.

I gasped as shock at my father's attack, and even found time to call him a "dirty bastard" before he was on top of me again, throwing himself at me as the tie whipped free in his right hand. I lashed out with my feet, kicking him in the chest, face and hands, anything I could connect with as I scrabbled backwards across the room, but he was not to be dissuaded, slapping my shoes away and fighting his way between my flailing legs.

"No father! No!" I shrieked when he pinned my torso down with one hand, while stirring his tie with the other in an effort to form a lasso.

It was a bit extreme, my father's reaction, and some might even say Victorian, but I guess as soon as he realised I wasn't the prodigy he thought I was, a quick solution was called for. And when it came to murder, loose ends so often knitted together to form noose ends.

"Please father, wait…"

But my father didn't reply, he merely bore down on me with a murderous intent as he concentrated on the task at hand and I have no doubt he would've wrung the life out of me had my mother not come to my rescue.

In the struggle, I must've kicked the side of the dressing table, for the glass of her picture frame shattered when it hit the floorboards. I sacrificed half my defensive strength to reach into the shards and by some miracle found the glass dagger my mother had thrown me. This in turn quickly found my father's face and I slashed it backwards and forwards until he tumbled away with his hands across his eyes.

"You tyke!!!" he hollered, now beyond fury, and he thrust his hand into the top drawer of his dresser to pull out his old service revolver.

Bullets blasted out the plasterwork behind me as I threw myself at the door, and the landing banisters suffered a similar fate, splintering to matchwood as he let loose the rest of the barrel at his errant son.

It's amazing the decisions you can make in the blink of an eye, but instinct once again forewarned me that I wouldn't make it to the front door if I ran down the stairs – not even if I hurled myself at them headfirst – for my father would have a clear shot at me, so instead I launched myself at the nearest door, crashing through it a millisecond before my father's final .45 did the same.

As luck would have it – bad luck that is – this door shielded a second staircase, though this one led up to the eaves. There was only one way up and one way down from the attic, so I'd be trapped once I was up there, but as my father slung his now empty sidearm and wrapped the silk tie around his knuckles behind me, I realised that my first concern should be with the next few seconds of my life rather than the minutes or hours of whatever future I had after that, because if I didn't get a move on I wouldn't have such problems to ponder for much longer. So I took to the stairs, heading into the low cottage roof and the shadows of the attic.

My father was hot on my heels, scaling the stairs two at a time and intent on cornering me in amongst the cobwebs, but this was trickier than he'd bargained on. See,

the floor of the attic wasn't boarded out up here; my father
had made a start on it several years earlier but contrary to
recent evidence he wasn't much good with his hands and
as such the attic sported only two fixed floorboards, a pile
of planks and a box of nails to show for several years of
good intentions. In place of a floor, the lath and plaster
ceilings of the rooms below crisscrossed beneath the
sturdy joists, ready to suck our ankles through should we
be careless enough to lose a footing. I recognised the
dangers of charging around up here, but I rushed into the
darkness nevertheless, desperate to put as much distance
as I could from my beloved father's cold embrace.

I wobbled across the beams, making for the tiny gable
window at the far end of the attic, but it was so slender, I
wasn't sure I'd be able to squeeze through it even if I tried.
Then again, I wasn't entirely sure I wanted to, what with it
being thirty feet up in the air and above a picket fence. But
it overlooked the road outside and in an afternoon of
increasing desperations, I was ready to start screaming
from windows.

My father took to the beams behind me as I flung the
window open.

"Help! Help! For the love of God help! My father's
trying to kill me!" I sang across the fields, but my pleas
were in vain. We lived half a mile from the nearest
neighbours and while they'd never murdered any young
men themselves, they'd manned the polls for Harold
MacMillan's Tories during the last election, so I wasn't
entirely sure how sympathetic they'd be with my plight.

"Goddamn it boy, be silent will you!" my father
roared, closing in on me with every faltering step.

I made my escape, dashing back across the beams as I
tried to circle around him, only to strike my head on a
roofing truss as my father herded me into a corner.

"Please father, I love you," I tried, seeing if I could

wrong foot the old bastard with that empty gush, but papa was nothing if not a wily old spook when his blood was up and he dismissed my entreaties with a snap of silk.

"You will submit, boy, you will submit. It is your father's will," he snarled, paying himself more than a few compliments on my account there.

"Please father, I won't tell," I promised, and I was serious too. I still had my head in the noose for being there when he'd murdered Juney. I was an accessory after the fact no longer – I was an accessory all the way along.

And that *was* a Capital crime.

"You lied to me, boy. You lied to me about 'the sport' and that cannot be tolerated. You've shown that you cannot be trusted. You've shown that I can not trust you," he bellowed, almost mournfully, as if I'd somehow forced his hand. "You've left me no choice."

He closed in on me some more, straddling the beams as he forced me back towards the window once more.

"The girl! The girl will know," I warned, clutching onto increasingly brittle straws.

"You needn't worry about her," my father assured me. "No one will ever hear from her again once I bail her out of custody."

He was now almost on top of me, but height and age were on my side – or rather, a lack of either – for while my father was forced to stoop like Fagin against the sloping timbers, I was able to squeeze into the angles with a suppleness my father hadn't known since the days of Neville's peace plan.

"You're just making this harder on yourself, boy," my father fumed as he scuffed his forehead and cracked the bedroom ceiling with a careless footfall. "Son of a bitch!"

"Son of a *bastard* more like," I taunted, daring him deeper into the corners to come and get me in the hope he might jam himself against the joists and allow me to make a break for the stairs, but he was no mug my father, and accordingly kept me corralled into the furthest reaches of the roof.

"It didn't have to come to this," my father lamented. "I only wanted what was best for you."

"No you never," I replied, finding a courage to back-chat my father that I could have only dreamt about before he started trying to kill me. "You just wanted me to be like you because you're sick!"

"We're all sick," he replied, almost reasonably. "This whole world is. We lost nigh on half a million good men cutting the cancers out of Europe only to find them on our own doorsteps when we returned." My father drifted a couple of beams to the left, circling around an oak support and neared me by a few more feet. I pushed back correspondingly, but my head was already meeting roof. I was running out of space in which to retreat.

My father continued. "So I do what I can to clean up my little corner of the world. For every whore I kill, I dissuade another dozen of our daughters from indulging in such depravity."

"You are a good *sport*," I sneered.

My father glared at that. "Yes, we call it a 'sport', because it requires guile, cunning and nerve, just as hunting foxes, stags or enemy snipers does, but at the end of the day they are vermin. And vermin can't be tolerated."

"Much like liars," I reminded him, now so tightly crammed into the eaves that I barely had the room to scowl.

"Yes, much like liars," he agreed, narrowing his eyes when he saw what I could now also see – that I had nowhere left to go.

With a drop of the shoulder, my father fell onto all fours and surged at me like a stoat towards a cornered rabbit. I knew I'd reached the ends of all hope; that I was about to feel the sting of death at the hands of the very man I should have been able to rely on, but there was simply nothing I could do about it. I was so boxed in against the joists that I could scarcely even raise a hand to protect myself. I was a sitting duck.

I pushed back against my wooden straightjacket, desperate to at least put up some semblance of a fight, but my hand didn't get within striking distance of my father…

… instead, it went straight through ceiling between the joists I was lying across.

That was it. That was my way out!

I rolled off the solid oak beams praying I hadn't left it too late and landed on the slats and plaster skim a few inches below. The ceiling cracked, but my weight was evenly spread so that the plaster momentarily held.

My father roared with indignation when he saw what I was attempting and raced to snatch me from my flight, but the same roof that had confined me became my saviour as I slammed my feet into the oak trusses above to send myself crashing through ceiling and into unknown.

I barely had time to twist in mid-air before landing on top of my mother's tall boy, killing a clowder of china cats that had lived there in relative peace since they'd stopped being dusted six months earlier. The tall boy itself fared little better, collapsing to its knees to spill me onto the floor just as fast as it could throw me. I slammed into yet more china cats, the ones that had leapt out of my way in a futile attempt to escape me the first time around and was finally rewarded when the tall boy itself dropped on top of me like an all-in wrestler sensing a submission.

As painful as this all sounds – and believe me it was every bit as painful as it sounds – I didn't have the luxury of time with which to enjoy my injuries. My father had told me that during the war many a good man shot through with grape could still fight on when the will was there. And the will was most definitely still there, because that same old salty geezer was suddenly crashing through the ceiling himself, though his descent looked more accidental than by design. His legs came first, flailing like a parachuting pig while his body straked the wafer-thin laths to decorate his sides with permanent pinstripes.

Plaster and dust rained down on me and I braced myself to take his full weight when he landed on top of me, but he didn't pitch up as expected. Instead, he got himself waylaid up near the light bulb as the attic sought to hang onto his middle age spread for ignoring its planks these past six years.

My father kicked violently, ripping jacket, shirt and skin as he fought to drop free and at last I had my chance to escape. I crawled out from under the tall boy and jumped to my feet, racing for the stairs and the front door when my conscience got the better of me.

What was I doing?

I was running from an assault on my life by a homicidal maniac, that was what I was doing?

But seriously, what was I doing?

If I left now I might well get away. I might escape my father, escape the police and escape all this horror to live a long and fruitful life, but what of the others?

What of Shandy?

What of Juney?

What of the girls whose names I didn't even know?

And what of the girls yet to come?

I was in the unique, if unenviable, position of being able to do something about this – but not if I ran. If I ran, I could undoubtedly save myself. But if I stayed to confront my father, I could save others. And who knew, maybe even my own soul.

So, halfway to the front door, I stopped on the stairs, turned back and sprinted up and into the attic once more.

My father was still there when I arrived – just about. He'd managed to claw most of his jacket away from the splinter that had snared it and was now just a rusty nail from freedom. In that instant I knew what I had to do and snatched up the discarded hammer from the dust-covered pile of boards.

My father saw me approaching and struggled yet more frantically, barking at me to desist and tearing all sorts of new pockets in his mid-week working tweed.

"I am your father! I am your father!" he was shouting, as if this counted for anything these days. He held up a hand to shield his head from the dreaded blow, but continued fighting with the timbers as he channelled his mania towards self-preservation.

It was at this moment that I finally saw him for what he was – a pathetic, marauding beast who'd fuelled a lifetime of depravity on the deprivations and disorders of his own formative years. It was sad, but even up until the last day or two, I'd still looked up to my father because of all the obstacles he'd overcome. But it was here and now that I realised he hadn't overcome any obstacles at all. He'd just chosen to take his place amongst them.

With one final yank of cloth my father was suddenly free, but he wasn't about to escape his responsibilities a moment longer. I brought the hammer down, smacking and smashing with all my might until I'd driven several brass tacks into the central joist, pinning to it my father's regimental tie – the one he was still wearing.

"What are you doing?" he choked, suddenly dangling over an eight-foot drop with only six inches of silk to play with.

I tossed the hammer through the hole and watched it clatter into the tall boy below.

"I'm going now father. I'm leaving," I told him. "I should hate you for what you've done, but I'm not going to – because I'm not like you; you or the Reverend. So I'm going to go and I'll leave the Fens Strangler to one last strangling – his most worthy of all."

"No wait, you can't do this. God, help me!" he appealed, but God and I were on the same page as far as this particular lost sheep was concerned, and we bid him adieu and left him to his contemplations.

I don't know how long he clung on to that beam for; a few minutes or a few hours, but his strength would have eventually left him and the drop he'd cheated for more than twenty years finally caught up with him in a snap.

CHAPTER 4:
THE FLICKER OF INTEREST

"That's cold, dude. You killed you own dad," Farny commented.

"No, my father killed himself," I reminded them, knocking my pipe against the drum I was sitting on and digging a match around inside the bowl to scratch out the last of the sticky ash. "I just coppered his tie against a joist. He was the one who actually let go and that's what hanged him, not me," I said. This was admittedly a somewhat sticky legal point but one to which I'd clung to for nigh on fifty years. After all, it's triggering the trapdoor that kills a condemned man isn't it? Not the looping a noose around his neck.

"But couldn't he just take his tie off?" Barry asked, his face a sweet jar of horror and fascination.

"Not able to, not hanging all precarious like that by his fingernails as he was. And he weren't able to pull himself up either because his tie was stopping him from getting over the beam – even if he had been strong enough. No, he was just stuck there, neither up nor down, with gravity pulling at his legs and his necktie tightening inch-by-inch," I painted as graphically as I could, stretching my own neck at the very thought.

"Bullshit!" Tommy finally hawed, breaking the spell I'd cast over his little mates; "I've never even heard of no Fens Strangler."

"Haven't you?" I asked.

"No I haven't. He's making it all up, it would be in all the papers if he'd done something like that," he reasoned.

"It was," I said.

"Well I never saw nothing about it," he insisted.

"Hmm. Well what about Ian Brady?" I asked.

"Who?"

"Myra Hindley?"

"What are you talking about?"

"John Profumo?"

"Uh?"

I continued in this vein for a few more turns, asking Tommy for his thoughts on the Great Train Robbers, Cliff Richard, Stanley Matthews, Bill & Ben and Doctor Beeching's controversial plans for restructuring the country's railway networks, winning a series of gormless gawps until it felt like I was quizzing a confused goldfish.

"Look, I dunno, do I!" he finally snapped before going on to answer his own question by pointing out he was only twelve, not some "fucking dinosaur from the olden days" like *what I was*. "All I'm saying is that he's talking bullshit," he maintained, "that your old man was some sort of serial killer and that you killed him! Why didn't you go to the police then?"

"Well he couldn't, could he?" Ginger chipped in on my side. "Like he said, he would've got the blame for them other killings just like his dad said."

"Thank you Colin, quite right," I said, rewarding him with his real name instead of his optional colour coding.

"Well what are you telling us for then, that's what I want to know, if we could just go to the police and tell them what you've told us?" Tommy demanded.

"I can hear the conversation right now," I told him. "'Excuse me officer, but while we was burgling this old man's house last night, he told us that his dad was a famous mass murderer and that he hanged him. What's that? Yes, that's right, we was burgling his house, why do you ask?'" I hammed, draining the colour from three out of four faces.

"Yeah, we can't do that," Farny agreed, momentarily

muting his mates.

Barry took the lead from his brother, peppering me with questions, though his were the questions of a boy wanting to know all, not a cocky little git trying to pick holes in my story.

"So what happened to your dad, like? Did he die?"

"That he did. I ran away to sea the next day and he was found a few days later. All the papers speculated that he'd gone loopy and hanged himself over this young girl he was having an affair with."

"What young girl?" Farny asked.

"Shandy," I told them. "The press put them together with a little help from Lincolnshire Constabulary and they all figured out she'd either been blackmailing my father or had quaffed his medal for favours received so that when their business came to light following her arrest, he hanged himself to avoid the scandal. Well that's what respectable folks did back then when they were found out to be not quite so respectable as first thought."

"But didn't the police wonder why you'd done a runner? Why didn't they find you?" Barry asked.

"They couldn't," I shrugged. "As I said I skipped the country a couple of days later, working my passage out of their reach on a freight liner sailing out of Southampton and ended up on the far side of the world." I took a blow on my pipe and looked back at myself as I was then: young, feckless and unlawfully ugly, much like the boys in front of me. If only I'd known then what I knew now I would've turned straight back and handed myself into the first Bobby to wander up our gangplank. But I didn't. Much to my regret, I didn't.

"No I jumped ship when we docked in Jakarta, blew my pockets in the bars and knocking shops of that fair city and eventually fell in with the crew of a tramp steamer working their way around the South China Seas."

"What's a tramp steamer?" Barry asked.

"It's a boat," I said. "A cargo boat of no fixed route, it goes where the money is and makes its own schedule." I reached into the darkest recesses of my brain and felt for the name I'd not uttered in some forty-eight years. "The *SS Almayer's Folly*."

Just saying her name again brought back a torrent of memories that whipped me like a Force Eight squall. Horrible images pressed forward from whence I'd buried them many moons ago, unleashed by my utterance of that accursed name to chill my blood and remind me why I was still here to recount this tale: Freddy Bolton's dying screams; Rupak Singh's desperate lunge into the waters; Captain Schmitt's selfless bravery. These images shook me to the core and over-shadowed what had come before and what had come since. But through them all, the worst memories of all were the ungodly howls of Tran Van Khan as he paced the decks and reduced our fine crew to chum.

The lads looked at me quizzically when they noticed I'd turned to stone.

"Are you alright?" Barry asked several times before I finally heard him.

"Mmm? Oh yes, sorry. Just remembering something," I said, as I took another blow on my pipe and lifted my eyes again. "Bad seas they were boys.

"Bad seas."

PART 2:

THE KILLING MOON

The *SS Almayer's Folly* was listed out of Colombo but it hadn't seen the place in years. It was a four-hundred-foot-long floating barnacle sanctuary with rusted masts and a crooked stack in the centre of its deck that belched out blackness night and day.

Her Captain was a Dutchman, or at least that's what he claimed to be, but the mistrust of strangers and Waffen-SS Luger he carried about him at all times suggested an alternative heritage. The rest of the crew were made up of Indians, Thais, Chinamen and No-Fixed-Aboders. There were eighteen of us in all. Freddy Bolton was the only other Englishman on board and he brought me onto the ship when I tried tapping him up on the dockside after I'd done all my silver on brem.

Captain Schmitt wasn't keen to take on another new face at first, not even one as young and as bloodshot as mine, but I guess I won him over when I failed to answer a single question during my interview.

"Running away from something are you boy?" he deduced.

"No, I just... can't go home," I more or less admitted.

The Captain nodded, as if he knew the situation only too well. "I can promise you only hard work and poor pay, " he said, just as my headmaster had done several years earlier after my eleven-plus results had been posted. "These are my terms, take them or leave them."

"I'll take them," I agreed, wondering if I should ask for half my wages in brem, seeing as that's where they were going to go anyway.

"Okay. Go stow your stuff below and sober up. We're casting off in five hours."

*

The Captain was as good as his word; the work was backbreaking in and around port, loading and unloading our payloads, while at sea the mop, bucket and barnacle scraper never left my hands. And it was skilled work too; scrape off the wrong barnacle and we could've ended up at the bottom of the ocean, so I had to get to know her knocks and dinks well enough to run up the side of her in bad weather, but get to know her I did, and little by little I began to earn my good Captain's trust.

Freddy had been on the *Folly* for almost two years and despite being less than twenty-two, he was as salty a sea dog as ever to weigh an anchor. I guess it was only natural that it was to he I grew the closest because of where we were from, but still there was something I didn't entirely trust about him. He was open and jolly and generous with his tobacco, but he had a temper too and could bawl me out over the slightest of things without warning. At nights, we'd lie in our bunks slating the rest of the crew and smoking ourselves to sleep, but rarely would our tattle ever venture near England. I didn't notice this at first, I guess I was just relieved not to be pressed on my own particular problems, but after a couple of voyages I became acutely aware of the lack of personal histories floating about the ship. Of course I wasn't about to rock any boats, least of all the one I was working but it did teach me to sleep with one eye on the door.

And this was what saved my life.

"Coal, get up, now!" Freddy barked as he shook me from my slumber.

I'd only gone off duty four hours earlier and still had the blur of booze in my eyes, so he slapped me across the face and tipped me from my bunk.

"Up!" he ordered.

"What? What is it? Are we sinking?" I asked, this being the one stock question I'd kept asking since joining the crew, betraying the level of confidence I had in my new home.

"No we're not fucking sinking; the Captain's calling general quarters, we're to report to the Boatswain, let's go!" he growled, dragging me out and along the gangway as I was still pulling my boots on.

The night was black and blustery and when we got up top I saw why we were rocking so much.

"We've stopped," I said, looking out across the chop. Freddy didn't reply, he was already a couple of pages in front of me and continued kicking me up the backside until we found the Boatswain surrounded by half a dozen others.

"Boatswain, what gives?" we asked. The Boatswain just nodded out to sea and we followed his eyes until it led us smack bang into another vessel rocking out there in the blackness barely two hundred yards away.

"We almost steamed right over her," the Boatswain spat, releasing a brown globule of chaw to the winds. "Cocksuckers!"

The Boatswain was a Nigerian but he was working hard at being American. He planned to go there one day, when he had enough money, marry himself a couple of white women and find out how dry cleaning worked. This was his dream. But the Boatswain would never realise his dream. Like the rest of us he was doomed to spend the rest of his life emptying his pockets around the ports of the East Sea and hanging socks in the motor room to test his various theories.

"Who is she?" I asked, but the Boatswain just shrugged. Who she was was less important than what she was doing. Smaller than us, possibly half the size of the *Folly*, she bobbed up and down like Davey Jones' dinner table and invited us to come dine with her.

The Captain blew our steam whistle up on the bridge but nothing stirred on the other ship. Not so much as a light burned on her bow. She just bobbed in the blackness, oblivious to the sea, the squall and us.

"She's a ghost ship," Sushanta commented, before pointing out the obvious. "This is a bad omen." Sushanta liked to think of himself as our shaman, a wise man on a ship of the fallen, but Sushanta was prone to the odd tumble himself, as the madams of Macau and Manila could readily testify.

"It's a terrible fucking omen for her crew," Freddy agreed, "but pay day for us."

The Boatswain was less than eager and had seen this sort of thing before. "Pirates; they lure poor greedy fools aboard, skin them alive and take their ships. We have to be careful," he said, pissing out Freddy's birthday cake in the process.

The Captain now addressed the abandoned ship through the loud hailer: "*Sumatran Wind*, this is the *SS Almayer's Folly*. We are a registered merchant vessel out of Colombo. Do you hear me? Do you need assistance, over?"

Nothing.

"*Sumatran Wind,* is there anyone on board? We have medical supplies and food and water. Is anyone there?"

Still nothing.

The Boatswain looked up towards the bridge and the Captain gave the signal he was expecting – if not welcoming. The Boatswain frowned.

"Okay boys, steel up."

We followed him down to the Radio Room and watched him knock the lock off a large trunk he found there to hand out Lee-Enfied rifles. The others had clearly handled guns before but when he handed me mine, I underestimated how heavy it was and dropped it on the Boatswain's boots. The Boatswain pursed his lips, took the rifle back from me and dug into the trunk again.

"Here," he said, handing me a flat-bladed cane knife as a consolation prize. "Maybe you take this instead." As lethal as my machete looked, it would only take a five yard head-start, a step ladder or, say, a Lee-Enfield rifle to get the better of me, which is a sobering thought when you're going up against skin-flaying pirates, so I asked the Boatswain if there was anything else I could have; something I could use from a distance that didn't require any sort of skill. The Boatswain thought for a moment, took the flat-bladed cane knife back from me and handed me a medical kit instead. "You're the orderly now," he told me.

I decided to keep my mouth shut in case my medical kit became a pencil and paper and I was further demoted to campaign correspondent. Instead I quickly rummaged through it for scalpels or big safety pins with which to fight off pirates and followed the rest of the boarding party back up top.

Sushanta reassured me it would be all right as he locked home a *.303* to stoke me with confidence. He may have advertised himself as some kind of spiritualist but he still had a soapy side to himself just like the rest of us. Tattoos up and down each arm told his story, but I couldn't read them as they were in Hindi, so I asked him what they meant and he told me they were the names of the prisons he'd done time in. Several prisons bore stars next to their listings. These, Sushanta smiled, were prisons he was yet to be released from.

We clambered over the side and into a waiting launch, stowing ourselves against the sides as we were winched down to the waves. If I thought the sea was rough while I'd been on board a 6,000 ton steamer, this was nothing compared to the hayride awaiting us over the side.

"Hold onto you brem boys, it's going to be a bumpy ride," H cackled, striking the motor and churning us out into the brine. H was a Burmese opium smoker with an unpronounceable name, so everyone simply called him H. At least, his name was unpronounceable in the sense that nobody had ever bothered trying to pronounce it. I'm sure if we'd all put our minds to it and spent five minutes with him each day learning the shape of his consonants we could've mastered his name within a week, but where was the incentive when he already looked up at "H"? Besides, five minutes was a long time in H's company. Believe me.

Most of the crew only answered to nicknames or ranks. I myself was known only as Coal. It wasn't the greatest nickname in the world, but it never failed to crack up some of my more cosmopolitan crewmates that someone as white as me was called Coal. They might've had a different opinion if they'd looked over now because my frosty complexion had turned a vomit green, as huge great waves came in from all sides to lift us to the clouds and then drop us back into their hollows again.

Freddy grinned like he was riding the loop-the-loop on Blackpool beach and whooped with excitement each time we were thrust towards the heavens until eventually we reached the other vessel. H took us in, hitching rides on the waves that were rocking the *Wind* until we were in sync and close enough to attach our magnets. The Boatswain, Sushanta and Freddy then threw grappling hooks up her side and quickly clambered up the ropes.

Singh went next, along with Najib and Lumpati, and then finally me. H stayed with the launch to safeguard our way home while the rest of our shipmates hung Lee-Enfield's over the side of the *Folly* a couple of hundred yards away to cover any possible retreat.

Lumpati and Singh pulled me up the last few feet then

set off after the others before I'd got my bearings.

The *Sumatran Wind* was grey and full of shadows. It moaned beneath the barracking of the sea and lay in wait to swallow us up lest we forget to watch where we stepped. I clicked my torch on and scoured the decks. There was debris and flotsam rolling between the hatches but no signs of life. Something had happened here.

"Look at this," Sushanta said, shining his torch around the bridge hatch.

We gathered around and saw that a big lump had been knocked through one side of the door and scorch marks charred the surrounding frame.

"Someone fired a distress flare at it," the Boatswain said, and we were fairly happy with this explanation until Sushanta pointing out that they'd fired it from inside.

"Maybe they were drunk," Freddy speculated. I wished I was, especially when Rupak Singh suggested we split up and explored the boat in pairs. As you can guess, there was an almighty clamour not to be the one paired off with the skinny white kid with the plasters, but eventually Sushanta relented and agreed to walk me around the ship.

The Boatswain sent us in the direction of the cargo hold and Sushanta led the way, stock to shoulder and finger to trigger. I kicked the square hatch off the cargo port and shone my torch in to see only bales and boxes. But Sushanta was sharper than me and what he saw confused him.

"Nothing's stowed as it should be. Those crates should be tethered as one, but they are stacked in lines. It doesn't make sense."

I agreed and suggested we discussed this at length back on the *Folly*, but Sushanta was not only sharper than me, he was also more courageous than me and slid over the side and down the nettings until he was standing in front of a wall of crates.

"Come down here. Now!"

I swallowed my fears and bemoaned the fact that I could be killing prostitutes with my dad right now instead of exploring ghost ships as I climbed down to join Sushanta.

"Be careful where you step. Don't touch anything," he advised. We followed the twisting maze of crates and bales around until we encountered the remains of a barrier. It looked as though this barrier had been stacked and shored up from behind with the heaviest crates, but something had dismantled them with ease.

Dismantled them to smithereens.

"Blood," Sushanta muttered, bending over to dab his fingers in a couple of dark spots between the wreckage. Much to my dismay I was able to trump Sushanta with an enormous Jackson Pollock across the back wall, together with an assortment of hair and clothing dumped in a sticky heap by the base of the barricade.

"Oh Jesus!" I retched, but I'd already lost all I'd had to lose in the launch ride over here.

Amongst the blood and bones were a string of pink sausages, or at least, this is what they looked like.

"Intestines," Sushanta said. "Bowls and shit. It didn't like these parts."

"What didn't?"

"Whatever ripped through this boat."

Sushanta raised his rifle to each of the shadows around us and I followed his aim with my torchlight but all we found were more splatters and sausages.

"We're beyond bad omens here," I said.

"Let's get the hell out of here," Sushanta agreed, though he had to say it a couple of times because I could scarcely hear him from the top of the netting as I scrambled back up to the deck.

The Boatswain and Freddy met us up top with similar

stories of carnage and all thoughts of salvage went out of the window as we elected to take the launch back to the *Folly*.

"Wait," Singh urged. "There's more."

Yep, as if the horrors we'd found weren't enough to get us taking pot shots at passing albatrosses already, Singh marked our cards by taking down to the crew's quarters.

"It's wired to explode."

"Explode?" Freddy baulked, backing off a couple of steps as if he wanted to live or something.

"There's enough dynamite behind this hatch to take her to the bottom," Singh confirmed, cracking open the hatchway to show us a crude spider's web of blue and brown wires that ran to a charge fixed to the side of the *Wind*'s hull.

"We left this style of welcome for the Japanese when we bugged out of Rangoon," Singh explained. "But this is a crude effort. No attempt to hide it. Strange."

"Maybe there are more; better concealed?" the Boatswain speculated and sure enough we found another wire linked to a second set of charges strung across the stairwell to the engine room. Actually, we didn't spot it: Lumpati – bless his cotton socks – blundered straight into it, surely dooming the lot of us. But the crew of the *Wind* weren't as adept at rigging booby-traps as Singh had been back in '42, because the chest-height tripwire held fast and simply flicked Lumpati onto his back.

"These guys don't know shit about sabotage," Singh concluded, examining the trip-pins which were driven into solid oak beams next to the charges by a whole inch, making them near impossible to pull out with our bare hands.

"Maybe not. Maybe these bombs weren't meant for men," Sushanta said. "Something else drove the crew to this. Or what remained of them."

"There's nothing here but death," the Boatswain concluded. "Let's go back before we become a part of this voyage." He and Sushanta blew their whistles, summoning everyone back up top and to my immense relief I found we had as many crewmates as when we'd started. Only Singh lingered, searching the stores for rope and joining us five minutes later when we were all hoarse from calling his name.

"We can't leave this ship like this for others to find," he said, dropping a coil of rope into the Boatswain's lap before climbing down after it. He took the line from the Boatswain once he was in the launch and started unfurling it as H took us away. After a hundred yards, Singh came to the end of his line and tied the loose end to the aft cleat.

"Now go, full power," he told H, bracing himself against the hull.

H duly obliged, squeezing the accelerator and taking us away from the *Wind* until the line whipped taut. For one moment we crunched against the weight of that abominable ship, but the launch was just as keen to get back to the *Folly* as the rest of us, and quickly we broke free again, yanking several pins from their oak moorings a hundred yards away.

A thud struck deep within the waves and we looked back to see the first of four quick flashes rip open the side of the *Wind*, exposing her decks to the cold grey seas before the fires had a chance to warm her soul one last time.

"There she goes, boys," the Boatswain said, doffing his cap to show his respects.

The *Wind* lurched onto her side and lay floundering in the waters until she could support herself no longer. Several air pockets blew out her port side windows and at last her bow slipped beneath the waves, up-ending her stern to reveal her static screw. She called to us one last time when the salt waters hit her battery cells, imploring us to remember her name, before sliding beneath the waves to her final resting place three quarters of a mile below.

"Look after her well," the Boatswain commended, replacing his cap and cutting loose the line we were trailing to sever us from our night's work. "Now let none of us speak of this thing again."

That should've been that as far as the *Sumatran Wind* was concerned. We shouldn't have seen nor heard from her again, except in our nightmares. But the sea will always give up her dead.

Just as she'll always find a way to reach those who escaped her cold embrace the first time around.

ii

The weather had blown itself out by the next morning and the sun blazed down to turn the rippling sea into a collage of shadows. I never got over the colours the seas became in weather like this, and imagined monsters lurking beneath the waves whenever a dark square sailed by. I expect I wasn't the first sailor to think these thoughts. But the squares never reared up to flick a fin nor take a bite out of our ship because they were only squares; shoals of fish or banks of seaweed. Or oil. Or simply shadows.

Our previous night's encounter must've played on our Captain's mind because my first task of the day was to check the *Folly's* six life rafts. This was a relatively simple job; all I had to do was fill each raft with water and plug any leaks that sprang. Any idiot could do it, which was why the Captain asked me. The skilled part of the job came with knowing not to fill all six rafts at the same time, but to check them individually, so that at no time would we be sailing around the South China Sea with all our life rafts full of water.

And so it was close to midday and I was just getting started on the fourth life raft when I glimpsed another of those shapes out to sea. I didn't look up at first, because the work was gruelling, particularly under the heat of the midday sun, but the shape registered with me all the same and lingered in my mind's eye just long enough to make me look out for it next time I swung the bucket.

It was still there, just short of the horizon and tickling along with the tidal currents, but this shape looked different to the shapes that had passed by so far this morning. This one looked tangible.

I shielded my brow against the blazing sun and strained my eyes, but the shape was too far away to tell what it was. Probably some flotsam or jetsam that had found the water in the previous night's squall but without a set of glasses I couldn't tell for sure.

I called up to the First Mate who had the bridge and he trained his glasses on the distance, scouring the cobalt swells until he found what I'd spotted.

"Life raft!"

This was our second encounter with another craft in a little under twelve hours, so you didn't need to be an ancient mariner to guess where this particular raft had come from. Sure enough, when we were within a few hundred yards the First Mate lowered his glasses and spoke the words we all feared to hear.

"It's from the *Sumatran Wind*."

It was inscribed on the bow of the little raft, and I cursed my tongue for drawing us to it once again. But it was too late now. One or two of us could've looked the other way and left the raft to her fate, but not a crew of eighteen. We had to bring her in.

On first inspection it didn't look like anyone was on board, but as we neared her, we saw a tiny shape curled up against the bow.

"Steady as she goes," the Captain called, slowing us to a stingray's pace until we were almost on top of her. Najib and Singh climbed down the portside ladder and snared the raft with hooks, while Sushanta, 50ft above, struck the winch and pulled her from the water – lone survivor and all.

"Does anyone else think we should get the rifles before we do this?" I was asking, but Singh just grinned with amusement so I peered in to see what we'd landed.

He couldn't have been more than five feet tall but curled up as he was he looked barely half that. The face was oriental but not Chinese. Possible Thai. I wasn't an expert, though from the wasted state of him, I think even his own mother wouldn't have recognised him. His clothes were tattered and his body racked with scars. I wondered how long he'd been at sea. And what precisely had chased him into the raft in the first place.

"He's alive," the First Mate declared, feeling his pulse and looking around for cheers of joy. The silence was unanimous.

The Captain looked as crestfallen as the rest of us, but there was no tossing him back over board now, so he ordered Lumpati and Ahmed to take our newest crewmate below and have the ship's doctor look at him.

The ship's doctor was a Bengali called Upendra, who rumour had it, had learnt his trade gutting *hilsa* in the Gariahat fish market. An appointment with him wasn't necessarily a green light to keep buying shoes in pairs, so our newest passenger might've been better off taking to the seas again, but he was out for the count and blissfully oblivious to the dangers.

Just as the rest of us were.

iii

I finished my life raft duties after two more hours and thanked my stars I wasn't working a bigger ship, otherwise I'd be able to tie my laces without bending over come the end of the afternoon.

I stowed my rope and bucket, fired a couple of fags off the back of the *Folly* and timed my endeavours to dovetail neatly into dinnertime.

Freddy was down in the Mess already, as were Sushanta and Najib, so the four of us broke bread together, Sushanta and Najib standing on one end, me and Freddy jumping up and down on the other – an old joke, but quite apt. The Mess boys claimed they could only make the best with what they'd been given, and while this was true, what they'd been given two years earlier was seven and a half tons of tinned sweet corn; a versatile vegetable as the crew were to discover and one I'm still passing to this day.

Naturally, it didn't take long before the conversation turned to our newest arrival.

"The sooner he wakes up and we find out what happened to the rest of the *Wind*, the happier I'll be," Freddy said.

"You sure that knowledge will make you happy?" Sushanta asked.

"You know what I mean?"

"Whatever did that to her crew is surely at the bottom of sea by now alongside their bones," Najib ventured.

This time Sushanta stayed quiet.

"What *did* do that to her crew?" I decided to ask, seeing as no one else had even come close to speculating yet.

Three sets of eyes turned to me and stared.

"I don't know, and it does us no good to guess, lest we get so distracted looking for one cause that we miss the other – until it's right behind us."

Najib agreed, though Freddy bet five shillings it was some kind of sea monster. "Bound to be," he reckoned.

The rest of the Watch started to filter in for tonight's fish surprise (and you can guess what the surprise was) before 'Doctor' Upendra finally entered to be confronted by a hailstorm of questions.

"Is he awake yet?"

"Who is he?"

"Where's he from?"

"What happened to the others?"

"What raked his body like that?"

"Can he cook?"

"Oi fuck you!"

Upendra stroked his chin and suggested we retook our seats before beckoning in the person waiting just behind him. As you can imagine, the Mess fell into ear-splitting silence as a now familiar scrawny little wretch stepped through the doorway and regarded us with apprehension.

"It's okay, they're okay," Upendra reassured him, motioning him to take a seat.

The worst of the filth had been scraped off his body and he'd been bandaged with enthusiasm until he resembled a barber's shop pole. A clean set of clothes and an old set of sandals topped off his ensemble and finally he was ready to be reintroduced to the human race.

This was our second mistake.

"Everybody," announced Upendra, "this is Tran Van Khan. He'll be with us until Hong Kong."

Khan was Thai, or at least this is what he claimed to be.

But without papers or documentation it was difficult to tell. At least it was for a European, but the Boatswain sat him down with H for five minutes, who spoke both Thai and French, and that's all it took to dismiss Khan's claims in favour of somewhere rather more combustible.

"He Vietnam," H told us. "He not want to go home."

Still who could blame him for that? Men and machines were pouring in to South Vietnam from both sides of the ideological divide and it wasn't going to be long before the whole region went up like a Chinese chip pan. If I'd been Khan I wouldn't have wanted to go home either.

But this still didn't explain what had happened back on the *Wind*. H pushed the point.

"He say pirates boarded them at night and killed everybody on board. Savages, he say. Very bad killings."

"Very bad killings, huh!" the Boatswain repeated back, chewing those words over a few times before spitting them out along with a glob of chaw. "Must've lost something in translation," he concluded.

"They skinned them? They ate them?" Sushanta put to Khan through H.

"They cannibals," H confirmed, though Sushanta was a hard sell.

"Cannibals this far north? Cannibals who eat raw meat?"

At this response, Khan began to wail, burying his face into his hands and curling up into a ball against the table to make us all feel like heels. At least, almost all of us; Freddy was still urging H to ask him about sea monsters when the Captain entered the Mess and went ballistic at what he found.

"What the hell is going on here? Why is that man out of the infirmary? And why are you all speaking with him? He is under house arrest until we dock at Victoria and not to be spoken to by any person aboard this ship. Do you understand?"

I personally didn't, but then again this didn't prove a stumbling block for the Captain who ordered Upendra, the Boatswain and Najib to take Khan back to the infirmary.

"If it's food he wants, I'll have it brought to you," the Captain told Upendra. "But no one knows what happened on his ship, least of all me. And until I do, he is to be kept under lock and key."

The Captain looked at Ahmed and Freddy and finally posted off a late entry for sensible decision of the week.

"You two; go to the Radio Room and draw side-arms. Then stand watch outside the Infirmary until relieved. No one gets in there, you hear? Or out."

iv

Well, that fairly put the cat amongst the pigeons. Although Sushanta was still concerned about who was the cat? And who were the pigeons?

After dinner, I turned in for the evening, tired and grubby, yet excited to have the cabin to myself for once. As weary as I was, I couldn't let the opportunity slide, so I borrowed one of the Boatswain's dirty books and drifted off to sleep to the sound of baby Jesus weeping for my soul.

I rarely remember my dreams. Some people can recall them in detail, but this hardly ever happens to me. If anything, all I ever experience is a brief nudge from my subconscious at the end of my sleep, which always causes me to wake up confused and slightly frightened. And this particular night was no different. After just a couple of hours a voice in the middle distance asked me if I'd spoken to my father yet and I awoke to hear myself replying that I hadn't seen him in years.

This was only partially true: for while I hadn't seen him in years, my father rarely left me.

The same could not be said of Freddy though. It was well past midnight and he'd not yet returned to his bunk. I found my clothes, then the door handle and decided to go looking for him in case he'd found a bottle he needed a hand with.

The *Folly* by night was a different place to the *Folly* by day. It consisted of the same corridors, the same decks and the same stairwells, but everything looked tighter by night; even the corridors that never saw natural daylight. It was obviously in my head, but it felt as if the *Folly* tensed up each night to guard herself and her crew from the dangers that lurked beyond her lights.

Perhaps this was because I was young and still had an imagination. Others on board, I was about to discover, had lost their innocence many moons ago.

Freddy wasn't at his post outside the Infirmary. Neither was Ahmed. Their absence stopped me in my tracks when I saw the unguarded door and I wondered if I should alert the Watch. But as boyishly naïve as I was, I didn't subscribe to Freddy's own theory that every bucket out of place was the work of sea monsters so before I went blabbing to the Captain I figured I'd better make sure of my facts.

Steeling myself with a deep breath and a fire-paddle, I crept forward stopped to listen outside the Infirmary door. What I'd been hoping to hear was nothing; or at the very least, drunken platitudes and cockleshell karaoke. What I actually heard was grunting; heated, gruff, animalistic grunting.

I should've run, gone to see the Captain via the armoury and leapt off the back of the boat firing two handguns in all directions. That's what I thought I would've done in light of what had happened on the *Wind*, but you never act the way you think you're going to in situations like these. My father, if nothing else, had taught me that.

So slowly I turned the handle and cracked the door ajar just enough to take a peak inside.

What I saw behind the door, my imagination simply couldn't have prepared me for.

Khan was bent double over the infirmary gurney, forced into this unnatural position by Ahmed who had him by both wrists. Khan obviously didn't like this and was pleading with Ahmed to let him go, but Ahmed was oblivious to any protest, helped somewhat by the rolls of bandages that had been tied around Khan's mouth to muffle his cries. Still, if Khan didn't like this, he was probably hating what Freddy was doing at the other end of the gurney.

With socks, trousers and shorts floundering around his ankles, Freddy leaning into Khan with as much enthusiasm as he could muster, again and again, as if trying to nudge him off the gurney using only his hips. Of course, he was raping poor Khan, but at the time I could make no sense of what I was seeing because I had no idea blokes did this to other blokes. It simply wasn't in my encyclopaedia. I mean, why would they? It seemed akin to stuffing bread up one's nose.

Still, as wiltingly stupid as I was back then, I had just enough about me to realize that this sort of thing wasn't quite cricket, so I quietly closed the Infirmary door and took the first few steps back to bed – only to crash face first into the Boatswain, who'd materialised behind me without so much as a sound.

"What's going on here?" the Boatswain demanded.

Here? Here? I liked that. Here there wasn't much going on but behind the door Freddy and Ahmed were twinning the Infirmary with Sodom and Gomorrah.

The Boatswain pushed me aside and threw back the door, just in time to see Freddy rolling about on the floor trying to pull his slacks back up while Ahmed was asking Khan if he was "okay", remembering just in time to pull down his gag to hear the answer.

"Back with you, you dogs!" the Boatswain roared, lashing out at the Entertainments Committee with hands, feet and my fire paddle. He even aimed a kick at me, presumably because he assumed I was a part of this welcoming committee, before snatching Freddy's gun belt away and whipping out his pistol. "You dogs, you filthy pigs of dogs," the Boatswain spat. I guessed he wasn't a dog person. "You have been warned of this before. The Captain will hear of this. You will all forfeit your shares!"

The Boatswain cocked the hammer to demonstrate he meant business and lashed the butt at Ahmed's head as he dashed for the door. Freddy too was soon tumbling out, crashing into me to send us all into a heap in the corridor outside the Infirmary.

"Fuck's sake. This is the exact same prejudice that got me kicked out of Sandhurst!" Freddy complained miserably.

v

Now, as sorry as I felt for poor Khan (obviously not that sorry it could be argued), I felt utterly devastated at my own piss pot of misfortune at having lost my shares and in all likelihood my place in the crew simply by being in the wrong place at the wrong time. But then that's so often the case with misfortune, as we were all about to find out. For I was just scrambling to free myself from Freddy's *coital interruptus* irritations when the door reopened and the

Boatswain hollered at us to get Upendra.

"Bring him here quick, you've bloody killed him, he's dying!" he screamed, ruining what was left of my night – if not my life. See, even out here, the authorities took a dim view of piracy on the high seas, particularly Freddy's specialist brand of piracy. Kangaroo courts had been called for less.

With that thought burning in my brain, I leapt to my feet and sprinted for the next deck without waiting for the others, only too aware of the fact that he who brought the news so often got to write the headlines. So I banged on Upendra's berth, then raced around looking for him in the Mess, Radio Room and Passenger Suite, eventually finding him sailing fags at the new moon on the horizon.

"Doctor Doctor, Freddy and Ahmed have killed the dink." I might've been sexually naïve, but I was well up on my casual racism at this age.

"What!" coughed Upendra, throwing his last butt overboard and haring back through the hatches until we found a cluster of concerned rubberneckers standing by the Infirmary door.

"Get in here now!" the Boatswain shouted, but Upendra just froze when he saw the mess awaiting him and turned to the Boatswain in despair. And I can't say I really blamed him. Khan looked to have deteriorated a hundred-fold in the last few minutes and was now almost grey in colour, dripping with sweat and shaking from head to foot as seizures ripped through his battered and buggered body. He reached out a hand towards Upendra, as if appealing for release from the agonies, but Upendra was a merchantman hack, not a relative of the Almighty's and he just guppied with indecision.

"Morphine!" the Boatswain prompted, so Upendra pushed his way towards the medicine cupboard, dug a key out of his pocket and poked it about in the lock until the doors swung open. Syringe met bottle met needle met arse but Khan's condition didn't improve one jot, reeling from the needle and arching his back to cut a blood-curdling scream at the ceiling.

"Grab his arms," the Boatswain yell, summoning us in to take a limb and pin Khan down as he thrashed about on the gurney and shook the last few vestiges of life from his frail frame. The Boatswain stuffed a splint between Khan's teeth to stop him from biting his tongue off while the rest of us urged Khan to "let go", "stop fighting" or in Ahmed's case "run towards the light", but Khan wasn't going anywhere – especially not with Ahmed again – and if anything, seemed to grow in strength.

"Fuck me!" Freddy swore without any trace of irony when he got a whack in the nose, and after only a few seconds, I noticed all five of us had our feet off the deck in our efforts to pin Khan down.

"Er does anyone else…" I started but I'm not sure if anyone did because at that moment Khan bit his splint in half and roared like a lion into the Boatswain's face.

If I hadn't tumbled back in fear at this point I would've no doubt ended up like Freddy, flat on his back against the corridor wall with Khan's footprint colouring his face. But Freddy got off lightly next to Upendra and Ahmed, both of whom were hurled across the Infirmary and into the medicine cabinet as if they were no more than sacks of silk.

The Boatswain was already running for the door when Khan rolled off the gurney and blocked his path, a feat I'd not have thought possible earlier that evening but Khan had found an extra three feet from somewhere and now towered over the panic-stricken Boatswain like a baying cobra.

Before our very eyes, Khan's girth burst out to match his new-found height, ripping muscles from malnutrition

and sinew from scrawn. His skin turned nea: r
bubbled beneath the surface as coarse black
out the length and breadth of his body.

The Boatswain made one last despe
freedom but he was dead before he knew it, splashed
across four walls by a set of claws that sliced through bone
and cartilage as if they were blancmange.

"Fuck's sake, come on!" Freddy screamed, grabbing
me by the collar and dragging me back up the corridor as a
black and bloody paw the size of a pitchfork fizzed past
our eyes to slice the air before us. Ahmed and Upendra's
screams chased us through the ship as Khan tore them to
chum and a shot rang out to silence the horrors, if not
Khan's roars, making me wonder if the shooter had
scoffed the bullet himself.

Inevitably, doors began opening along the corridors
and ruddy-eyed shipmates barked at us to explain
ourselves, but we had neither the time nor the inclination
and simply urged them to do likewise and run for their
souls.

We burst out into the night and sprinted for the stern
before discovering, much to our dismay that we'd run out
of boat. It was either the breaststroke for a couple of
hundred miles then up and away again when we hit the
Philippines or an urgent rethink.

"The Captain," I wheezed.

"Guns!" Freddy sort of agreed.

We legged it to the Wheel House and found the
Captain ordering the intercom to tell him what was going
on. Alas, the intercom could only respond with agonised
screams as Khan rampaged through the lower decks.

"Guns Captain, we need guns!" Freddy demanded,
winning startled looks from the Captain, the First Mate
and Erik at the wheel.

"What's happening down there?" Captain Schmitt

ₚeated, this time directing his question at us.

"No time to lose. It's coming!" I gasped, barely able to catch a breath. "Guns."

"What's coming?" the First Mate insisted, failing to appreciate the urgency of the situation.

"Khan!" Freddy hollered, as if this somehow qualified as an explanation, but there was simply no time to explain. "Guns now!"

As intriguing as this all was, Captain Schmitt was saline enough to know that there was a time for explanations and a time to start shooting, so he whipped out and cocked his Luger and barked at the First Mate to break out the rifles.

Me and Freddy went with the First Mate to the Radio Room where Kaluu almost blew our heads off when we opened the door.

"What's going on? What's happening?" Kaluu implored, a popular question of the night but none of us answered, probably because none of us could. Instead we weighed ourselves down with enough guns and ammunition to stop a thunderstorm in its track and left Kaluu to send out an SOS to anyone who might be listening.

"Lock this door and don't open it for anything," the First Mate told him. "Good luck."

I still didn't know how to use a Lee-Enfield rifle but I figured I'd rather face Khan with a weapon I didn't know how to use than a box of plasters I did, so Freddy gave me a quick tutorial and showed me where to stick the bullets and which end made the bang, and that was enough for now.

Back at the Wheel House, the Captain had been joined by half a dozen others and they all had stories like mine, if not Freddy, who it could be said was closer to Khan than most.

"It's an animal!"

"It's a monster!"

"It came at us like the devil!"

"We didn't stand a chance!"

"What was it?" someone asked, so I repeated my assertion that it was Khan.

"He turned into that thing before our very eyes."

The crew turned to us. Silence.

But only for a second.

vi

Intercom screams filled the Bridge as Khan plundered the remnants of the sleeping quarters below, until the Captain snapped at us that it didn't matter what it was, all that mattered was getting it off the ship.

"Get to the Wheel House," the Captain shouted into the intercom. "We have guns and ammunition and we can protect you. Get to the Wheel House now!"

The Captain turned and told us to take up positions overlooking the decks and shoot anything that emerged from below we didn't recognise as a friend.

"Schnell!"

The Wheel House was elevated above the main decks and could be accessed by two flights of steel steps on the port and starboard sides. Me, Freddy, Lumpati and H spilled out against the starboard rail, while Sushanta, Najib and the Captain did likewise on the port side.

Beneath us, I felt the boat lurch eastwards and pick up speed. The First Mate had been ordered to make for help and to hell with the consequences. A hundred and sixty nautical miles away bobbed enough men and machines of the US Navy start a small war – which I think was the general idea – so the First Mate pointed us in their direction and set about turning the *Folly*'s read-outs red.

"Don't panic fire," Lumpati whispered when he saw me shaking. "One careful shot will serve you better than three frightened bangs."

I took a deep breath and tried to steady my nerves but all I really wanted to do was curl into a ball and cry myself to sleep.

That was when it started.

Gunfire crackled from the port side bow and I heard Najib and the Captain shouting at someone or something to come towards it. I don't know if it sensed a trap and fled in the other direction as a consequence but a moment later a shape darted between several container stacks about fifty yards in front of my field of fire.

I disregarded Lumpati's advice entirely and shot off two quick rounds with absolutely no idea where they went, but I felt better for doing it all the same and quickly chambered another. H told me to hold my fire and directed the starboard lamp towards the container stacks, sweeping the beam from shadow to shadow until we saw something make a break for it again. I let off another bang but H knocked the barrel of my rifle away to kill a passing wave.

"Don't shoot," H scowled, before shouting to whoever was out there, "Up here! Up here!"

The beam once more fell upon the movement, but it wasn't the monstrous apparition of Khan we saw darting between the container stacks but that of Rupak Singh.

He ran from stack to stack, wide-eyed with madness and caked in all that was left of our shipmates. He'd seen first-hand what we'd only tuned into on the intercom and now he could hardly draw a breath for the terror that bore down upon him. Lumpati joined H and called to Singh, but I was too dry to pitch in. Not that it would've done much good anyway; Singh wasn't listening. Something else had his focus and it was tracking him amongst the stacks.

"This way Singh, this way! We'll cover you!"

Out of the corner of my eye, ten yards from Singh, I saw something else moving. I couldn't make it out at first, because it was as black as the very night itself, but something was down there creeping amongst the rocking shadows and circling our startled shipmate. I squeezed my eyes as tight as I dared in an effort to penetrate the gloom but the silhouette was always somewhere else other than where I was looking.

"It's behind you, Singh! It's behind you!" I finally concluded, sending Singh spinning this way and that, desperate to move, but paralyzed with a fear of making the wrong decision.

Again I shot into the darkness, this time sending a *.303* slug into a bulging black shadow just beyond Singh's left ear. Once again I hit only decking, prompting yet another rebuke from H, but this time I knew I was right to shoot.

"It's there, it's in the shadows. It's behind him!" I insisted.

Freddy took me at my word and opened up with his rifle, plugging each shadow with a shot to the heart, and Lumpati pitched in too. H let go of my barrel and blasted a couple of silhouettes of his own and before long all four of us were scouring the deck around Singh, searching for flesh and blood amongst the steel and tin.

Singh finally realised where his best hope lay and made a break towards us – only to have his path blocked by a huge savage shape that reared up out of nowhere before him.

Khan's appearance took my breath away; he seemed to have grown even larger than our first terrible encounter, standing a clear nine feet tall and as broad as a barrel of rum. His thick black coat sucked in what little light surrounded him so that he appeared to have no form at all, just mass – mass and two great arms that stretched out like the skeletal branches of long dead trees.

H and Lumpati were emptying their mags into Khan, but Khan barely batted an eyelid, he simply flicked his head and roared with indignation, baring a row of blood-flecked fangs to snort his contempt.

Singh screamed one final farewell and lunged the only way left open to him, straight over the starboard bow and into the forbidding waters.

"Nooo!" Lumpati screamed, dropping his rifle and grabbing a life jacket to hurl to his compatriot, but Singh was gone, swallowed up by the swells and in no mind to fight them.

Khan now turned on us, furious to be denied his sport and intent on satisfaction. His snout wrinkled up to bare those terrible yellow incisors and then he dropped onto all fours –

– and charged straight for us.

We responded with a volley of shots but this didn't deter Khan a jot, and he was upon us in the blink of an eye, snapping and slashing at our ranks as we fell back in a panic. Lumpati's head spun clean away from his shoulders and almost kissed me as it sailed past, while H was dumped into a pile of his own intestines as he fought to find the beast's bulls-eye with his final shot.

I'd been nearest the Wheel House door so I'd had the space to tumble back into, but this would've normally have counted for nothing – Khan was that fast. But I've always been lucky with my friends and I had the remarkable good fortune to be with the one man on earth who Khan most wanted to reacquaint himself.

Freddy Bolton.

Khan leapt on Freddy's back as he tried flinging himself over the side, pinning him to the steel decking with his five-inch talons and screaming into his face with a ferocity that made his previous furies seem like petulant sulks.

"Help me! God help me Coal!"

Khan shot me a glare as if to say, "don't even think about it", so in the interests of fairness I afforded Freddy the same level of help I'd given his bedfellow earlier that evening and scuttled for the sanctuary of the Wheel House.

The First Mate and Erik dragged me inside and spun the lock to seal the hatch while Sushanta and Najib did likewise to the portside access. Captain Schmitt had decided to get stupid with himself and try sneaking up on Khan from the other side of the Flying Bridge, so I chalked him off without even waiting to hear his screams. But they'd come. Of that I had no doubt – just as soon as Khan was done with Freddy.

My randy ex-bunkmate had not stopped howling from the moment Khan had pinned him to the deck, but they were still screams of terror, not pain, telling me Khan was intent on enjoying this kill.

"For the love of God, help me! Help meeee!!!" he implored, but what could we do?

"Put your fingers in your ears," Sushanta suggested, which was as good a plan as any so I jammed my fingers into the side of my head until all I could hear were the sounds of my own exhaustion and the crashing of my heart. Sushanta elected to hear things through, and I was able to monitor my ex-bunkmate's progress from the expressions Sushanta pulled. I don't know what Khan did to the *Folly*'s resident romantic – and frankly I don't want to know – but from the looks on Sushanta's face, I'd say he gave every bit as good as he got.

A sudden, almighty crunch against the steel door sent me sprawling across the deck. The six-inch glass porthole shattered under the next blow and Khan stuck his snout through the hole to howl a storm into our souls. The First Mate blasted away with his sidearm, hitting Khan in the face, before sending the next two slugs rattling around the Wheel House to chase up from pillar to post. Khan seemed unfazed and continued pounding the hatch with all of his might, while both the First Mate and Sushanta peppered his snout with lead.

Eventually Khan moved away, though it was a purposeful lumber of a creature changing tactics rather than that of a beast beating a retreat.

"What the hell is that thing?" Erik asked. Again nobody answered. And not just because nobody could – but because Khan never gave us a chance.

The steel door may have withstood all that Khan could throw at it but he soon saw he'd have more luck with the glass windowpanes that fronted the length of the Wheel House. A narrow walkway ran just beneath it and Khan now stepped into view looking larger and hairier than a Highland beauty queen.

The five of us backed against the far wall and for one terrible moment, Khan simply stood studying us through the glass as if we were prime cuts in a butcher's window. He wrinkled his snout into a perverse smile and snapped his jaws a couple of times, as if to bite the very air between us, then he swung one of his great claws and shattered the glass into a thousand silver shards. Khan bound straight in, hitting the deck along with the glass and he went for the First Mate.

The rest of us rushed to escape, tumbling out of the portside hatch as a foursome, but only three of us hit the bottom step, Najib having been snatched back into the Wheel House by one of Khan's loose claws. I barely heard the screams before the hatch splashed with blood and the carcass of Najib was hurled into our path, almost as if

Khan was expressing pique at our impertinence. Still you know what they say; when the devil's got you by the tail, never offer him your hand too, so we ploughed on into the night, stumbling across the rolling deck as the *Folly* now crashed through the waves in a blind arc.

I looked over my shoulder to see the enormous shape of Khan leaping from the Wheel House to land at a canter just ten yards behind us. He was utterly unstoppable and I knew at that moment, just as surely as a condemned man knows when he sees the rope, that I was going to die. I tried to find the courage to die well, urging myself to about turn and go down fighting, but my strength had deserted me; all I could do was brace myself for that dreaded blow.

Erik was the first to fall, gobbled up in an instant without Khan even having to break his stride. He shrieked just as all the others had shrieked and was snuffed out in a heartbeat. It sounded quick. I hoped it was quick. I hoped mine would be quicker.

I hoped Khan hadn't seen me at the Infirmary.

I hoped I'd be spared what Freddy had endured.

I hoped…

Sushanta had no intention of going out with such ease and darted between the stacks, weaving this way and that, through a maze of narrow runs to put some distance between himself and the beast. I simply followed, unable to think of my own plan and determined to fuck Sushanta up in the event he looked like getting away without me.

As it happened, Khan was less manoeuvrable in these cramped confines and so by some miracle we were able to put the merest of hair's breadths between ourselves and our snarling foe so that by the time we emerged from the stacks we had the luxury of almost a full four seconds to consider our next move.

Naturally Sushanta led the way, sprinting to and then scurrying up the aft mast like a squirrel running up an Oak.

I tried to follow but this time I couldn't. Try as I might, I simply couldn't pull myself up the smooth white pole. I guess Sushanta had spent his childhood shinning up coconut trees for his supper while I'd spent mine lying next to an electric fire reading *The Adventures of Tintin* while I'd waited for the old man to get back from the chippy.

Khan burst out of the stacks and stumbled against thin air for a few seconds before finding his balance. He roared at me once more with a ferocity that stripped the skin from my face, before charging for the kill.

I was about to flee – where? I had no idea – when I suddenly saw Sushanta's shoes at the bottom of the mast. Given the situation it was an odd thing to notice, but then it occurred to me that they were down here while the man himself was up there – which of course was how he'd climbed the pole. It was suddenly so simple.

Unfortunately I barely had the time to straighten my hat, let alone kick off my shoes, so I did the only thing left open to me and fled aft, hoping salvation would offer itself once more, only this time a bit more glaringly.

No such luck. I reached the back of the boat with desolation to spare and found myself cornered alongside a tattered Ceylonese flag. Khan slowed when he saw I had no place left to go and he stretched out his arms to prevent me from making a break for it. Once he was sure I was hemmed in he began closing in on me, slowly and carefully, determined to enjoy my anguish to the full. It was a deliberate act of a beast conscious of his actions.

"Wait," I decided to try, wondering just how much this fiend could understand. "Wait, I'm on your side."

Khan snorted derisively, smacking his lips as if he was savouring the fear in my voice.

"Wait, I know where there's food, lots of food!" I tried again, "all you can eat," but Khan clearly wasn't a fan of sweet corn either and simply flexed his claws, as if sharpening a collection of carving knives over a prime cut.

"Wait, please..." I tried one last time, knowing that this was my last throw of the dice. "I... I *love you*!"

The things we say when we're about to die don't have to make sense and more often than not they don't, they're usually just noises for our own comfort, but for the merest fraction of a second Khan faltered, possibly out of sheer confusion. He looked at me and blinked, so I seized this lifeline and went with it all the way, holding out a hand towards Khan and drenching him with my sincerest smile. Khan continued to glare with a sadistic bemusement and I wondered if I'd made a break-through, like Daniel in the lion's den, that by reaching out to Khan in such a way I'd somehow tamed the savage hunger that drove him on his murderous rampages. Of course, this all happened in the blink of an eye, but it happened all the same and I was just wondering how best I should stave in the little fucker's head when he was human again when Khan took a swing at me.

That was the moment – that was when I knew I was dead. It was a terrifying feeling, but if life has taught me one thing it's that even the final half a second of your life is still life.

And in life, anything can happen.

Khan's hind suddenly blistered with gunshots knocking him sideways and into the stern, though these weren't one or two rounds from a Lee-Enfield, these were 600-rounds-per-minute spat out at close quarters from a Thompson submachine gun. Captain Schmitt, who was looking surprisingly peachy all things considered, had seen how ineffective our *.303*s had been against the beast and had dashed back to grab the heavy artillery. The Captain finished off the clip in Khan's back and side, then ejected the magazine and slammed home another to begin hosing him down once more.

I seized my chance and scrambled across the deck, dodging Khan's flailing talons and the Captain's stray .45s until I had a man with a machine gun between myself and certain death.

Despite the Captain's heroic efforts, I knew it was only a temporary reprieve and much to my shame I'm afraid I didn't stick around to help him, despite owing him my life. I simply ran for it, legging it for all I was worth and kicking my shoes and socks off as I went.

I shouted back at the Captain to do the same, that he couldn't kill Khan no matter how much he shot him, but I didn't linger to see how my advice had gone down, I simply leapt at the aft mast and scurried up it until I almost knocked Sushanta off his perch. He was roosting on the mast's top mount, a small crossbar onto which were coupled the ship's antennae and the flaghoist lines. It was a precarious perch with just one castaway up there; two were going to test its strengths to the limits.

To my relief (and to Sushanta's immense credit), he held out a hand and pulled me up, swivelling around to allow me to straddle the other side of the crossbar from him.

"Use your belt to strap yourself to the mast," Sushanta suggested.

I did as he suggested but my more immediate concerns were for Khan, not our wobbly perch.

"What if he climbs up here?" I asked.

"If that happens, undo your belt again," Sushanta replied, "and try to land on your head."

vii

From our vantage point we could see Captain Schmitt fighting it out with Khan. He would sprint from cover to

118

cover, ejecting magazines as he went, then turn and unload the whole of the next clip into the shape tracking him across the decks. A brilliant white muzzle flash would light up everything within twenty yards of the Captain, including the bulging black outline of Khan, who seemed to get closer with each passing strafe, before once again darkness would descend.

It was a valiant effort, but one I knew to be doomed, simply because the Captain couldn't buy himself a yard of thinking time. He was running out of ship and ammo. And he was running out of both fast.

"What shall we do?" I asked Sushanta, my voice cracked with fear.

"What would you like to do?" Sushanta replied, calm as you like as if this were a sunny afternoon of shore leave and we had brothel brochures to peruse at our leisure.

"I don't know... something... anything," I struggled, as the Captain rattled sparks off the containers directly below us.

Sushanta put a hand on my shoulder and spoke in barely a whisper. "Each of us has a destiny to fulfil; we have ours, and the Captain has his."

I think I knew what Sushanta was getting at; namely, keep your mouth shut in case the monster hears us up here, and I found it hard to argue with a man of such strong convictions. I guess I was just feeling helpless at watching the Captain thrash around in ever-decreasing circles after he'd offered up his life for mine, but Sushanta was right; what could we do other than die alongside him?

Not much.

And so, to my undying shame, that's exactly what we did.

Not much.

"*Motherfucker!*" the Captain screamed as he spat a final fireflame across the decks, before slinging the Tommy

Gun for his Luger.

Pitiful individual cracks now rang out in place of the staccato drill that had ripped the night apart, but this was not enough to keep Khan at bay and in the fog of gunsmoke below the blackest of shadows now rushed at the Captain and swallowed him up in an instant.

There were no more sounds after that. No more gunshots. No more psychotic howls. And no more Captain Schmitt. Sushanta and I were all that stood between Khan and another ghost ship.

Neither of us said anything for an age, we just stared out across the inky black seas and held on to the mast while the screws took us wherever they felt so inclined.

As I'd said before, Sushanta regarded himself as a man of faith. I don't know which particular flavour he practiced – whichever forbid him from doing heavy lifting in port the First Mate once reckoned – but Sushanta remained an anchor of reason and tranquillity on our sometimes rocky voyages, no more so than at this moment. I looked at his strong noble face and was glad it was he I was to share this final ride with, rather than any of my other ex-crewmates, God rest their wretched souls. Sushanta glanced back and nodded sadly, either because he understood the solace his companionship was bringing or because he was weighing up how best to dangle me should Khan make it this far north.

"He is the wolf," Sushanta finally whispered. "Part man, part beast, unleashed upon this earth by the moon."

I glanced starboard and noted the full moon now a quarter of the way into the sky.

"You know this sort of thing then?" I asked. "From your folklore and stuff like, I suppose"

"No, but I saw that film with Lon Chaney and this seems to be the same sort of thing," Sushanta replied, forever confining my veneration of the orient to Leyton.

A sudden growl somewhere beneath us caught both our attentions and we froze. Slowly, very very slowly, I turned my eyes towards the deck and squinted into the gloom.

Both the sea and the *Folly* were bathed in a silvery blue that reflected off every stack, rail and ripple. Beyond the moonlight though, beneath the surface of the water or between the stacks, the darkness was complete – blacker than death itself.

Somewhere in amongst these shadows, Khan growled again. It was a low rattling howl of a beast asserting his claim to lands fought for and won and it told us he knew we were still within earshot, if not precisely where. The decks fell silent as Khan snaffled and snuffled beneath our feet, but for the life of him he couldn't pick up our scent. I guess he had only himself to blame for this, as the decks and more or less every surface were splattered with carnage to such an extent that he'd lost us in the stench.

A stack of drums tumbled over as Khan stepped up his search, then a steel container was ripped apart, but Khan got no closer for all his ferocity, and each time he howled it was angrier than the last.

And yet we ploughed on through the waves, our turbines turning far below with no sign of a reprieve until they must've glown red against their labours. The *Folly* couldn't continue slogging its guts out indefinitely, but what could we do? Neither me nor Sushanta could make it to the Wheel House to ease her engines, and Khan couldn't care less either way. Like Sushanta and I, our beloved ship was at Khan's mercy.

I wondered what would happen if we came upon a reef or outcrop of rocks. We'd crash obviously, maybe even capsize, but what would happen to us? Khan wouldn't suffer so much as a scratch, not even if we went through a supertanker's screws, but me and Sushanta would be unseated and left to his mercy. I tried not to think about it but decided, should disaster appear on the horizon, to unhook my belt, wrap it around my neck and step off to join my father.

Yet still we ploughed through the waters unmolested.

I lost all track of time after an hour or so and to my disbelief, even somehow fell asleep despite Khan's screams below. It wasn't a physical sleep of rest and recuperation, because every muscle remained clenched against the terrors of what might be, but a trance-like hibernation of a mind doing all it could to protect itself from insanity.

I don't know how many hours passed, but pass they did and eventually it was left to Sushanta to yank me back to the awful reality I'd fought so hard to leave. I blinked a few times to get my bearings, before focussing on Sushanta.

He was smiling.

Why was Sushanta smiling?

Had he gone mad or something? Or had he just remembered Lou Costello smacking Lon Chaney over the head with a mop?

Sushanta pointed behind me and his smile broadened. I turned to scan the horizon, but could see nothing. No ships, no islands, no clouds nor even stars. There was nothing there. I was just about to ask Sushanta what he could see that I couldn't – an invisible rabbit with a tray of drinks perhaps – when all of a sudden I realised what he was smiling at.

The horizon.

We could see it.

After a night as black as pitch, we could make out the line of the horizon because the sun was just beyond it and it was colouring the skies in the east.

Our night, all long and horrifying and eternal as it was, was almost at an end.

"Will Khan turn back into a man again?" I whispered, barely daring to hope.

"We shall see," Sushanta replied, casting an eye down at Khan as he stood by the portside bow and staring out at the approaching day himself. Khan snorted his distain then let out one final roar, before slinking off into the ship to prepare for the day ahead.

Sushanta unbuckled his belt from the mast and slipped it around his waist.

"And so now it is our turn," he said.

viii

We gave it an hour or two and only climbed down once the sun was on our necks. The first thing we killed was the *Folly*'s speed, easing her engines until she slowed to a gentle chug.

I watched over Sushanta with a Lee Enfield while he wiped what was left of the First Mate from the dials and checked to make sure we weren't about to explode. My faith in guns was less than wholehearted after the night's events, but the rifle's weight gave me a much-needed boost nevertheless. Still, if Khan were to emerge from below, and by that I mean the big hairy Khan that nobody liked, I'd be up that mast again before Sushanta heard the clank of stock hitting deck.

Most of the dials had been smashed, so it was hard to gauge where abouts we were, but Sushanta calculated we'd probably covered 50 miles the night before, in a north-easterly direction, putting us somewhere between a hundred to two hundred miles off the coast of Vietnam.

"North or South?" I asked.

"Why, are you choosy where we land?" he replied. It was a fair point.

123

The radio room had not been spared either, the door having been smashed off its hinges and the valves and bones that had sheltered within shredded with a wanton fury. I wondered how much Kaluu had managed to get out before Khan had silenced him. I wondered if anyone out there had heard him. And if they had, what they were doing about it. Tearing out their pages from their communications books and throwing them overboard if they had any sense.

"This is deliberate," Sushanta reasoned. "Intentional. He did this to silence us. This beast is more than just an animal."

Sushanta brushed the loose fingers from Kaluu's Webley and motioned me back down the corridor.

"Now let us go below."

The bowels of the ship were quiet but for the hum of the engines. By day there'd be a hustle and bustle of bodies rushing backwards and forwards down here, and by night, there'd be the distant echo of snoring and the occasional clatter of glass on tin – but this morning, the morning after the night before, there was nothing.

Bucketfuls of black blood coated the steel decking like oil and pooled against the bulkheads. Some places were sticky underfoot, some slippery, but all of it clawed at my throat like a petrified scream. Inside the cabins was worse. Arms, legs, heads and bones were strewn. Most looked as if they'd been taken apart pretty quickly, and some as if they'd been revisited for a chew. Indeed, all we found of Upendra was one of his legs. Khan must've liked the Doctor after all.

Along with the entrails were deep gouges in the wood and steel work. We guessed that Khan's claws must've done these, but to leave that kind of damage without breaking off in the process was mind-boggling.

"Let's get the hell out of here; take one of the life rafts

and go. Let him keep the *Folly*. Fuck it!"

"If he is what I think he is, our best hope is to get him while he's at his weakest, not throw ourselves to the mercy of the waves." Sushanta replied.

Nothing more lurked for us in the crew's quarters, so Sushanta spun the hatch at the far end of the gangway and took us down into the engine room. It was as hot as hell down here, more than usual, and in places the engine housings were near impassable. We swept as much of the terrain as we could, poking nooks, crannies and spider's webs and sending the odd slug into bundles of filthy rags lying in between the pipes, but after twenty minutes of searching we came up empty-handed, so once more we pressed on, through the next hatchway, down the next stairwell and into the Holds.

Most of our stores were packed with bales of cotton and sweet corn, the first we were transporting to Hong Kong, the second we were slowly feeding to the fish. There were dozens of places Khan could've hidden down here if this had been his intention, but to our dismay, Khan proved a little more proactive than that and a shot rang out the moment we stepped in Hold three. I was a little slow taking cover because I'd thought it was Sushanta who'd fired the shot so that Khan's second bullet rattled off the barrel of my Lee Enfield and knocked me flat on my back.

"Fuck!" was all I could think to say, not least of all when I saw the third finger on my right hand was now missing just below the knuckle. Khan gave me no time to savour the pain though as bullets skimmed and clattered off the bulkheads all around me forcing me to throw myself through a curtain of four-inch chains to get beyond his deadly hail.

Sushanta's rifle spoke up in my defence, blasting the epicentre of Khan's muzzle-flashes with a volley of its own to send Khan tumbling from his perch. The walking corpse we'd picked up the previous day now hit the ground like a panther and raced away with an agility that beggared belief. Sushanta did his best to put a dink in Khan's gait, splintering the air behind him with a volley of *.303*s, but I was in no shape to fight.

"He's coming your way!" Sushanta yelled, forcing me back to my senses.

Khan's scrawny form ducked between two crates ahead, so I blasted the next gap in his path, hoping to ambush him, but Khan's reactions were like none I'd ever seen. He dropped out of my line of fire and rolled on his side to send two shots back in my direction before I'd even realised I'd missed him. The first of these shots hit the crate to my right, sending a shower of matchwood into my face, and my agonised recoil somehow saved me from his second.

How was this fair? A werewolf who was good with a gun – what chance did we have?

I scrambled over the decking as Sushanta covered my retreat, emptying his magazine into everything within a five-yard radius of our unwanted shipmate. I hurled myself through the hatchway and hung my rifle around the jamb to return the compliment, but Sushanta wasn't for running. Despite Khan's fleet-footedness, Sushanta was determined to have this out with him before the night swung the balance against us again. He raced away to get the drop on him and more shots rang out followed by a volley of obscenities in a language I didn't recognise. I don't know how I knew they were obscenities; maybe they weren't. But to me most oriental languages sound that way when barked over gunfire.

One final crack signalled the end of the fighting but Sushanta continued to holler and rant. I listened for another thirty seconds before silence descended over the

Hold. I shouldered my Lee Enfield and kept it trained on the hatch but nothing emerged.

"Sushanta?" I whispered, but the only sounds to reply were the holding chains as the boat's motion tinkled them against one another.

"Sushanta?"

I hated giving away my position, but my bravery was almost spent and I couldn't stand the thought of being left alone with this inhuman beast, even in his human form.

"Coal?" a voice whispered just beyond the hatchway

"Sushanta, is that you?"

"Don't shoot."

Sushanta waved a dirty white rag to double-check we were both on the same hymn sheet then stepped into view. His side was red with blood and he half-staggered half-hauled himself through the hatchway with the air of a man defeated.

"Help me Coal! Help me back to the surface."

I was reluctant at first, fearing to put down my rifle, but Sushanta assured me it would be okay.

"He won't come after us. Not now."

"You got him then?"

"No," Sushanta shrugged, wincing as I looped an arm underneath his shoulder. "Khan lives."

I hauled Sushanta up top again and sat him down against the portside rail. His blood looked rich and ruby against the dried out smears from the previous night. I picked up my rifle and peered through the hatchway to make sure we weren't being followed, but Sushanta again said that Khan wouldn't be coming.

"He'll not try to kill us by day, it's too dangerous for him. He'll sit tight and wait until the night comes, then he'll look for us."

"But, the gun…"

"He was defending himself, not trying to kill us. He

wants to live as much as we do and he knows we must come for him by day. He was ready for us, but he'll not seek trouble, not while he can be hurt. He'll wait us out."

"How do you know all of this?" I asked.

Sushanta pulled his hand from his side and took a deep breath as he examined his leaking abdomen.

"It's what I would do. He's a survivor. Has been for many years I expect. He has been here before."

"So what's the plan?"

"The plan?" Sushanta huffed, raising an eye towards the heavens. "All we can do is deny Khan his sport."

I wondered how we could do that, then realised what Sushanta meant when he dug out his Webley.

"Are there any plans that don't involve us blowing our own heads off?" I asked.

"I cannot move and my strength will leave me before this evening. I cannot climb and I cannot fight. Better for me to take the long road now than leave myself to be picked apart by the beast."

"I notice there's lot of you in this plan. What about me? What am I meant to do after you do yourself in?"

"After me?" Sushanta shrugged, "the gun is yours." He thrust the barrel under his chin but I jammed my thumb behind the hammer as he pulled the trigger, saving Sushanta but killing my thumbnail as the firing pin split it to the pink.

"Fuck!" I yelled, snatching the gun from Sushanta and prising my thumb from its works.

Sushanta begged me for the gun but I tossed it overboard, partly to make a point and partly out of rage at finding myself two fingers down already.

"You're condemning me to an agonising death. I cannot escape his wrath," Sushanta insisted.

"You said it yourself," I mumbled through a mouthful of blood, "he won't come for us by day. We've got a few hours yet. And I need you."

"And when the night comes?"

"If we haven't got Khan by then, I'll blow your fucking head off myself."

ix

We spent the first couple of hours catching our breath and taking on food. I hadn't much of an appetite and Sushanta could barely keep down a mouthful of biscuits but we were both in need of sustenance more than we desired it.

After three hours of rest, I felt almost human again and doused my head in cold water to rinse the remnants of fog from my senses. My fingers didn't really hurt, except when I jabbed them unexpectedly, which I seemed to do about every thirty seconds or so, but I could just about get by if I did most things with my left.

Sushanta had been right about Khan. He made no attempt to gatecrash our brunch and had probably been grateful for the downtime himself. But this was merely the eye of the storm and we knew it. As the ship's shadows swung from portside to starboard I was reminded that our time was quickly slipping away and that Khan would soon be on the claw again.

"So, what's the plan?" Sushanta croaked, his face five shades lighter than mine despite the head start his parents had given him.

As it happens I'd had a few thoughts. The first of these involved loading up a life raft with all the biscuits and brem it could hold and taking my chances in the open seas, but there was something I didn't like about this plan. And not just the slow and lingering death part. No, I didn't like it because it meant letting Khan off the hook. And as my strength returned, so did my anger. Of course I wasn't stupid enough to be tempted into another fight, but neither was I of a mind to chalk off our adventure as one-set all and honours even. Khan had to meet his maker. And as long as I was on the same boat as him and the sun was in the sky, that was a possibility.

So what could we do?

The first thing we could do was keep him away from us for as long as possible so I peeled the First Mate's keys from a pile of rotting nastiness I found up in the Wheel House and went about locking down every hatchway, duct and grating that would still close. I even ventured into the ship as far as the Engine Room, securing fire doors and portholes between Khan and the outside world. Some locked, others I jammed with fire axes and furniture. I didn't know how long I could imprison him below: certainly not indefinitely. But every minute I delayed him was another minute I survived.

When it came to the outer hatches, I wrapped the handles with chains and locked them off with securing bolts. I even pulled the acetylene torch from the maintenance stores and welded the hatches into solid steel plates that Houdini himself would've had the Dickins opening.

Khan was a different prospect though.

I topped the whole lot off by winching several steel containers from the stacks with the deck hoist and dropping them in front of – or in some cases, on top of – the hatches that opened out onto the decks, so by the time the sun dipped its toe in the west I couldn't see what more I could've done – except kept my promise to Sushanta.

He'd not moved all day, so you could argue how much help he'd really been. But I can be a calculating little cuss when I have to be and Sushanta's continued breathing reassured me that Khan hadn't doubled back while I'd been barricading the bulkheads. As awful as it is to admit

Sushanta was my canary.

"Kill me. Kill me now!" he demanded when I went to see how he was. "It's almost night. You gave me your word."

But I had no intention of leaving myself all alone in this ship and so I told Sushanta I had a better idea. "I'll put you beyond Khan's reach."

Lifting Sushanta as gently as I could, I lay him into the life raft nearest the stern and began lowering him into the waters. We were only travelling at a couple of knots, but the raft's bow skimmed and rolled off the swells all the same before the sea took a hold of him and pulled him away from our hull.

I walked the rail around to the stern and watched Sushanta slip into our backwash before tethering his raft to our flagstaff. I'd played out 70 yards of rope, figuring even Khan couldn't vault that far, and left Sushanta with enough blankets, bread and brem to see him through the night.

Blue skies turned blood red as the sun made way for the moon and I knew I didn't have long so I gathered up as much ammo, bread and water as I could carry, then shinned it up the midships mast to perch for the night.

The last few rays of sunlight flickered on the horizon until the shadowy seas finally snuffed them out. From that moment the only light to be seen was that of the moon, hanging high above my head like the dinner gong of Damocles.

I locked and loaded my rifle and set my senses to terrified, but for ages I heard nothing but the sounds of the sea and the wind in the riggings.

An hour passed, then two. Three came and went and on and on we ploughed towards midnight, before eventually a sharp crack roused me from my stupor. Catastrophically, it was the sound of my Lee-Enfield hitting the deck when I'd succumbed. It was down there now, somewhere in the blackness and by the sound of it in several dozen pieces. I wondered if I should go back down and find another but a dull thundering coming from beneath the decks told me my preparation time had come and gone.

Khan was coming once more.

X

Despite being locked three decks below, Khan's roars sounded horrifyingly close. Each howl would be accompanied by a thunderstorm of blows that rattled the *Folly*'s rivets in their holes and knocked a few hundred barnacles from her bow. Occasionally Khan would switch his focus from one part of the ship to another, whittling his way towards the surface cabin by cabin.

After about an hour or so, Khan punched out a porthole in the side of the hull to get at the fresh sea air beyond. There was no way he could squeeze through it, but he was at least able to poke out his head and vent his insane rage up towards me in dolby stereo.

I tried to distract myself by squinting down at the glimmering seas and at Sushanta's raft bobbing away in the waters. I wondered if he was still alive, and if so, what he was making of the cabaret.

Khan disappeared from the porthole and went rampaging through the lower decks again while I tried to pick out the time on my wristwatch. It was almost four. The sun rose at six. If my barricades could hold Khan for another two hours I'd have the luxury of a whole other day to mess with the next of his tomorrows.

I crossed what fingers I still could and used all of my Christmas wishes up at once.

*

Things had been silent for an hour now. Either Khan had given up or he'd punched himself stupid. I dared hope for the latter, but would've settled for the former just as long as it meant another thirty minutes of peace because it was now half past five and I was agonisingly close to having made it through another night.

I'd polished off the last of my food and drank and peed all but a cupful of my water into the South China Sea from a great height. Now I dropped my backpack into the blackness and rolled my shoulders with relief. It was good to be free of that. It was good to have avoided Khan all night. And it was good to know that soon I would be enjoying some much-needed sleep.

All things considered, there was much to be cheerful about.

The engines were still chugging along and I wondered how long they'd have to chug before we made landfall. If it happened during the day, I could aim the *Folly* at nice rocky outcrop and take the life raft to safety. Khan trapped below in a sinking ship, his world ending inch-by-inch, was a thought that had kept me going through the night and I wondered if I should make a serious attempt to study the Captain's charts. Even if I couldn't make head nor tail of them, Sushanta might know what to do, so I looked once more to check his raft was still attached to the aft and found there was good and bad news on that front. The good news was that it was still there and it was still floating. The bad news was that there was an enormous lumbering black shape currently squatting in it, grunting with satisfaction and crunching down on the remnants of my former shipmate.

Khan had got out!

The initial shock hit me like a freight train, but this terror was tempered by the fact that Khan was otherwise engaged, polishing off the contents of the raft as if he hadn't eaten for weeks.

And there was another softener to the blow.

He was *off the ship*!

He must've gone over the side of the *Folly* and hauled himself along the tow-rope to dine alfresco, handing me an unbelievable opportunity.

But only if I was quick.

I all but fell out of the riggings and landed in a crumpled heap next to my backpack. Khan was still out at sea, licking the empty raft with his back to me and none the wiser he was about to go it alone. At this moment and from this distance I could now appreciate how truly immense he was. His coat was thick and shaggy, particularly dripping wet as it was, but it was still not thick enough to hide the knotted sinews that rippled the length of his monstrous body. I was so mesmerised by the spectacle of this unworldly beast that I had to remind myself I'd get an uncomfortable close-up if I didn't get a move on.

I grabbed my supposed sailor-hitch and yanked the free end to release the knot, but nothing happened. My own fault, knots have never been my strong suit and I hadn't thought to tie this one so that I could release it quick, so try as I might the knot held fast, tightened into an impenetrable lock thanks to a night of boat-dragging. My only hope was to cut it free, but this was easier said than done when I didn't have anything that even resembled a knife.

It was at this moment, when hope was once more wrestled away by despair that Khan turned around. He spotted me in an instant, gnawing at the knot and kicking the flag with frustration, and he roared to tell me I'd been rumbled.

Khan dived into the sea just in front of the life raft

and began hauling himself along the rope, hand over claw, and towards me.

I realised I wasn't going to bite through the rope before Khan had bitten through me, but I simply didn't have the time to get a blade. I was up a tree with monkeys and dogs both out to get me. Khan was now halfway back and surging through the *Folly*'s backwash as if it were a babbling brook. I looked around for any sort of sharp edge, but found nothing. The only thing I did find was another Lee Enfield rifle, and I wasted a few precious seconds wondering if Lee Enfields came with bayonets attached, before it occurred to me I could just shoot the rope in two.

"Shit!" I said, chambering a round and drawing on the flagstaff.

"Rhrrrrrrrrrrhhhh!" Khan replied, as he hauled himself from the waters and up towards the deck.

I fired the first shot, missing rope and boat altogether, and merely winged the knot with my second. The fact that I couldn't shoot a static target from less than an inch away hardly filled me with confidence and I continued blasting away, missing knot, line and pole as the rifle jumped about in my arms like a pneumatic drill. My only shot to find a home did so into Khan's shoulder, enraging him further still and he stormed the last few feet towards me to swipe me with his talons.

"No!" I screamed, stumbling back and dropping the rifle where I'd found it. The final round ignited in the chamber and the bullet cut through the air and into the heart of the knot with the sort of precision I could only have dreamed of. The knot instantly relinquished its grip on the flagstaff and dropped Khan towards the fizzing waters directly over our props. He might have been able to take a few bullets, but surely even Khan couldn't withstand a mincing. Alas, I never got to find out. Khan snatched at the rudder housings just before he was sucked into the wash and he held onto them for dear life, half in and half out of the water, roaring at me with defiance and starting back up the stern.

I couldn't believe this was even possible. The side of the ship was flat steel, but Khan smashed the hull with his enormous claws, puncturing enough of a handhold to haul himself up as if he were carving out his own personal ladder.

I shot at his hands, hoping to dislodge a finger or two, but it soon became clear that tying knots wasn't my only deficiency, so I flung the heavy wooden stock into Khan's face and took to my toes.

Khan vaulted the last few feet over the rail and was after me in a flash. I darted into the maze of the container stacks and lost him long enough to buy myself a few options. I could either run for the Wheel House and shoot myself with one of the rifles I found there, jump overboard into the sea and drown, or run for the Wheel House, grab a rifle and then jump into the sea and shoot myself as I drowned.

Decisions decisions!

Annoyingly, there was a fourth option also open to me, though this one meant gambling my gizzards against Khan's claws. The sun was now just peaking over the horizon, spelling the end to another night, and with it came the frustrating glimmer of hope. Khan had barely a few minutes left in his present state. If I could outrun him just a little longer, my pursuer might just end up outrunning himself.

With this in mind I chanced the only other way that was left open to me and ran off the open decks and into the bowels of the ship.

The portside coke hatch had been twisted back during the course of the night, so I threw myself through it and slid down the coke chute headfirst into a jagged pile of pain. But Khan was determined to have my soul dripping from his chin before this night was out and launched himself after me like Cerberus.

I scrambled over the coke pile and through the coke house doors, tumbling blindly into boiler ducts as Khan slammed into the shovel hatch just behind me. This was quite a misjudgement for him and untypical of everything I'd seen of him thus far, making me wonder if the fading moon was already beginning to sap his agilities. I didn't linger to find out though. I pushed on past the motor room, through a hole ripped out of the side of the engineer's workshop, past the diesel tanks and down towards the stores.

That's when I realised where I was going. I was being corralled back to Khan's lair thanks to my own barricades. All other routes back to the surface remained impassable. The only path open to me was through the hatches smashed by Khan during the night, meaning I would soon be cornered in the beast's own retreat with no hope of escape.

But Khan was slower than before – noticeably slower. Where before he'd cut through the ship like an unstoppable force of nature, he now limped and stumbled the same as I did – a deflated version of the monster I'd come to know and abhor. He was still the same terrifying spectacle, but now I was able to keep my distance, and through the narrower confines of the ship, even outpace him.

Khan's powers were leaving him. Soon he would be as vulnerable as I.

Unluckily for me, not soon enough.

I ran through the next hatchway but found the following hatchway sealed. I looked around for another way out, but saw there were none. All other hatches had been sealed from the outside and a sign on the wall told me where I'd pitched up. 'Hold Number Three', it read, like a blank death warrant waiting to be filled in. This was the end of the trip.

The air was heavy with the smell of death and the floor crunchy with tiny bone shards. Crates and bales had been smashed to smithereens and one corner of the Hold had been designated a latrine. Finger bones and gnarled ribs protruded from the congealed mess and I suddenly realised why Khan had stayed down here all day while I'd been battening down the hatches above. He'd been stuck on the bog all afternoon dealing with the consequences of his murderous appetite. I looked at those jagged ribs and took some comfort from the fact that my knobbly knees would at least bring a few tears to the little fucker's eyes when he sat down with tomorrow's crossword.

Khan roared at me from the only open hatchway but it was a lacklustre roar of a monster way off his game. I stumbled back all the same, slipping on a discarded Luger and landing flat on my back in Khan's effluence. Khan moved in for the kill, so I rolled through the shallow end and scrambled across the hold, determined to avoid his affections for as long as possible. That was when I found the only *other* way out of the Hold.

Through the porthole in the side of the ship – the one he'd roared through the night before.

Khan might not have been able to squeeze through it when he'd tried, but I was a skinny nineteen-year-old and willing to leave great chunks of myself behind trying.

I jumped up onto a crate and threw both arms through the circular porthole, diving headfirst out into the sunlight beyond. The jagged glass that lined the rim gouged my sides and threatened to cut me in two, but this was as nothing compared to the searing agonies that shot up my leg –

– when Khan bit me!

His fangs clamped down on my flailing ankle before I could fall out of the ship, and bones and cartilage burned with Hell's fires as he crushed them together in a single bite. I screamed as if my soul was escaping past my tonsils and tried to yank my foot free, but Khan's claws closed around my leg and he began to pull me back into the ship.

I held onto the hull and refused to be reeled in, resolved to lose the leg before I lost the fight and I lashed out again and again with my free foot until I connected with something squidgy. For the briefest of moments, my ankle came free and I was able to tumble out of the porthole and escape the worst of deaths. I doubt I would've been so lucky had the moon not been on the wane, but these were the breaks, and some might argue I still had it all to do, seeing as I was now out of the boat –

– and bobbing upside down in the open ocean a hundred miles from land.

xi

I had only seconds to think and for once I used them well, righting myself in the waters and snatching out at the side of the *Folly* as it surged on past, grabbing – by the grace of a God not yet done running me through the wringer – the hoist chains I'd dropped Sushanta into the sea with. I'd not winched them back in because I'd always figured on lifting him out again. Now, they were my last slender grip on this life and I held onto them with what little strength I could muster.

There was nothing left of me. Nothing but pain, but I hung onto the chains as they dragged me through the waters and implored myself to move. If I stayed where I was, I would've probably passed out after another few minutes and dropped into the big sleep without ever realising it, but I'd come too far for that.

Not here. Not like this. I'd simply been through too much to chuck it in now, so I started to climb.

Now I won't pretend it was easy. And I won't pretend the black fins in the water behind the boat gave me an added incentive, but working hand over fist and cursing the Almighty every inch of the way, I managed to drag myself up out of the water and up the chain's links.

It sounds impossible I know, particularly from the position I'd found myself in, but youth, fear and a precious toehold can sometimes be enough. Of course, irony had played her part, as I would later discover, but I gave it little thought at the time.

After the most energy-sapping hour of my life, I finally reached the winch arm and looped a leg around it. A few deep breaths and I slid down the arm until I crashed into the deck. I landed on my shattered ankle, and this, combined with the inhuman expectations placed upon my body put paid to me where I fell.

The sun crystallised the salt against my skin to burn what was left of me to a frazzle. It might have even finished me off had a bank of high clouds not blown in from the south to shield me while I slept. But typical of this voyage, these clouds were far from benign and during the course of the afternoon they blew in a squall to buffet the *Folly* and shake me from my slumber.

I awoke to decks awash with rain and great waves sailing past our rails on either side, throwing the bow sideways against their peaks and troughs.

I hauled myself to my feet, testing my weight on my game ankle and finding to my surprise that it held – though it let me know all about it and no mistake. The *Folly* was floundering out of kilter, pitching ever more starboard as huge grey rollers turned her around on her keel and the weather was only getting worse.

I dragged myself towards the Bridge, clinging onto the rails for support, and clambered up the steps on all fours, eventually righting myself against the Captain's wheel. The front windscreen was gone, and the rain lashed in to make my job more difficult, if that was possible. I'd not steered a ship before, not even a pedalo, so I had no idea what I was doing. I knew you had to steer into the waves in order not to capsize but I wasn't sure how to do this. I turned the wheel, but nothing happened; the bow ignored my requests and continued to take its orders from the seas.

I figured we needed more power to match the force of the waves, but none of the switches seemed to make a jot of difference. The *Folly* had chucked in the towel even if I hadn't.

At that moment a rolling wall of water crashed across our bow from the portside, swamping our decks and threatening to push us to the bottom. The wave continued along the ship, smashing through every porthole and funnel and almost knocking me back out the way I'd crawled in, but I held on with grim determination and eventually saw the bow surge up through the surf once more.

The next wave wasn't so massive, but it still threatened to fill our pockets with seawater if I didn't get us moving, so I crunched dials and threw levers, but the chug-chug-chug of our engines was no more, in its place only the roars of Mother Nature and the crunch of steel on steel. The *Folly* was dead in the water.

Another wave knocked us sideways, sending us careening into a second roller that swamped us from starboard. The deck disappeared beneath all this water and I waited to taste the torrents, but once again we came through it, rising to coast the next few peaks and floundering into the beyond.

I'm sure the Captain would've said they didn't build them like they used to but the truth was I had a hand in my own salvation. See, by barricading the hatches as I had, hardly any water made it below, so no matter what we crashed through during the storm, we always rose up again to crash straight through the next, like a cork in the surf.

I hung on to the wheel, throwing it this way and that even though it did no good, but heartened by the endeavour anyway. In fact, I was just starting to allow myself the extravagance of confidence when an almighty crash to the stern once again snatched all hope from me.

The aft mast came down.

It was the obvious weak point and was washed from the decks by fast-moving wave that ripped across our stern. But worst was yet to come. The cables that spanned the two masts refused to break, so the forward mast bent towards the sea and tumbled over the side when the next wave sheared it from our decks.

My sanctuaries were gone.

I stared at the decks and at where they'd used to be as I tried to take in what this meant, but it was too much. My last hopes were gone. Now even if I survived the storm, I would not be able to survive the night, not now I was within Khan's reach. This was a disaster, the worst thing that could've happened bar finding out that there was an eternal After Life – and that this was it.

I was sunk.

I couldn't tell the time, the skies were too black for that, but I figured we had only an hour or two of daylight left.

But what to do?

What could I do?

I was all in, dead in all but name and once more thrown to the wolves – or moreover, the wolf. I simply couldn't see a way out.

But then it occurred to me. There was one way out and it was my last and only option.

I had to kill Khan. And I had to kill him now.

xii

The storm was still wailing, though we'd come through the worst of it, with the waves now dropping back below the railings. The damage to the *Folly* had been considerable, with half of the containers washed out to sea and two of the remaining life rafts smashed beyond repair. There was now only one left, although even this one had its shortcomings, being that it was stacked full of rotting arms and legs. I couldn't understand how this had happened but then it struck me.

Khan was packing to leave.

The little sneak had decided his time on this ship was at an end, so he was fleeing the scene of his crimes in the hope of making land or chancing upon another vessel.

We'd come full circle.

His putrefying picnic was intended to sustain him for a few days adrift, and anything he didn't eat he could simply pitch overboard at the first sign of stack smoke. It was perfect.

I wondered how many ships he'd got through so far. And how many more there would be to come. It was then that another thought struck me.

Khan didn't know I was back onboard.

He couldn't. He'd seen me jump from the porthole and could've only drawn the obvious conclusion because he wouldn't be bugging out if he knew he was leaving me behind to tell tales. He must've missed me climbing back up the winch chains. It was an understandable mistake, but a mistake all the same and it handed me gilt-edged opportunity. Working quickly, I hobbled to the maintenance shed, grabbed a crank brace and returned to drill three small holes in the bottom of Khan's life raft. I stuffed these with oily rags and concealed them with his cargo, then I put everything back as it was before slipping away to hide. If all went to plan, Khan would put to sea and get a hundred yards from the *Folly* before he realised his socks were getting soggy. But by this time it would be too late; he'd be too far from the ship and suddenly up to his neck in open ocean. And in these infested waters, you really didn't want to find yourself thrashing away alongside sixty pounds of assorted fresh meat.

I chuckled to celebrate this unexpected good fortune, only to go and spoil things when I slammed face-first into Khan as he was leaving the Shelter Deck with the Boatswain's torso under his arm. Khan rubbed his head and vented his frustrations, barking a chorus of "bings" and "bongs" at me to damn me for my persistence.

"You said it, corky," was all I could reply, hurling the crank brace into his face and racing to find something to kill him with.

Khan fled over the Boatswain's chest and back into the ship. I hurried on after him, collecting a fire axe and swinging it at his back whenever I got close enough.

Which was surprisingly often. Khan seemed to be as invalided as I. I guess he had the ability to soak up everything you could throw at him at night, but his body still had to pay the price the next day. Not the ultimate price though. Nothing he sustained seemed to threaten his mortal coil, but he still looked as though he could use a night off.

"I'm gonna kill you!" I screamed, launching myself down the steps and after Khan as he ran into the shadows. Most of the lights below had shorted out, but a couple of emergency reds had come on to turn everything a sickly monochrome.

I swung the axe as Khan ducked into the boiler house, only to knock myself sideways with a blast of steam as I hacked through one of the cooling ducts.

Khan seized the opportunity to grab a crowbar off the wall and flung it against my rotten ankle. I howled with despair as pain ripped me to the DNA, but somehow I found the strength to respond, thrusting the axe head into his face to knock out the last of his smile.

Khan cried with anguish. He wasn't used to fighting at close quarters in his scrawny state and he clearly didn't like it. He could feel pain. He could feel fear. And he could be flattened by anyone bigger than the ship's cat. He really wasn't a day sort of person.

I pushed myself to my feet with the axe and thrust it at Khan's chest but he tumbled out of the way at the last moment and scrambled towards the air vent on the far bulkhead. If he made it I'd have no chance of following him and I'd lose him to the ship once more. And that couldn't happen. Not now that he'd seen me alive.

I went to swipe him off the wall, but the axe was embedded in the deck and I had no strength to pull it free. Khan saw his chance and looped both arms into the conduit and kicked his legs to wriggle inside.

He was getting away! My last hope was slipping from my clutches.

I leapt at his trailing leg and just managed to snag a foot, pulling him part of the way back, just as he'd tried to do with me only hours earlier. But Khan grabbed something inside the conduit to stop me from dragging him out and we ended up hanging there in deadlock, him half in the pipe, me half on top of him.

What could I do? I couldn't bite him as he'd bitten me. I couldn't savage him and eat him and squeeze him out in a great big sticky mess as he had a mind to do to me later, so what could I do?

If I'd had a gun I could've popped him nice and clean. Bang, job done. Or a knife, I could've cut open his belly. But I had neither of these things. Just an axe I could no longer lift and a rapidly failing grip. So I reached for the one weapon that was still within my reach and slammed it into the small of his back with all of my might.

My crowbar.

I stabbed it in point-first, driving it through Khan with everything I had until the clank of steel on steel told me I'd run him through.

Khan screamed like a steam whistle, flailing and lashing out at me as I stirred the bar into his back, but this was the moment I'd dreamed of and I'd show him as much mercy as he'd shown my pals. Thick black blood splattered my arms and face and ran down the walls to leave us both writhing in a slick of gore, but Khan would not succumb. I gave the bar another sharp yank and was eventually rewarded with the crack of his spine as it split in two. Khan's legs fell limp, but his wailing continued and I was just wondering what I had to do to kill the bastard when a carpet of bristles burst out along the length and breadth of his body to complicate matters.

xiii

I let go of the crowbar and stumbled towards the hatch as Khan sprouted out all over. I'd seen this happen before and as mesmeric as it was, I had no one else with me to soak up the claws so I doubled back towards the top decks as fast as my injuries would allow.

I heard Khan crash and smash his way out of the now tightly fitting conduit, and land with a thump on the boiler deck. He roared a catalogue of savage promises after me but I dared not look back; I simply staggered on in confusion and terror until I realised I'd taken a wrong turning.

I was in the Engine Room.

This was a calamity because unlike the boiler room there was no way out of the engine room. No second hatches. No air vents. No portholes or trap doors – just one hatch in and one hatch out. If I was truly determined, I could climb into the diesel tanks and feed myself through the carb's to be blown out of the stack as exhaust smoke but this was truly the only way out.

Khan hauled himself into the hatchway and filled the Engine Room with a scream so furious it almost restarted the pistons. If I'd had a breath to lose Khan's fury would've taken it away, but as it was all I had were white-hot spiders of fear streaking across my body at the knowledge of what was to come.

But Khan just wobbled in the hatchway without coming for me. He was hurt and hurt bad. He'd had to drag himself here by his front claws and it was now that I saw his hind legs were useless. The damage I'd done *little* Khan had finally put a dent in *big* Khan's stride. The realisation that I'd condemned this monster to a lifetime of plundering boats with wheelchair access heartened me just a decimetre, but it did nothing to help me directly. For even without the use of his legs, he still had me cornered, and he had a whole nine hours stretching out in front of him with which to extract his revenge.

Freddy's suffering was nothing compared to what I would know.

Khan crashed his claws into the steel deck between us and hauled himself towards me for the start of a very long kill.

I backed into the corner and braced myself for the

unbraceable, only to crack my head on a diesel valve behind. The sharp pain jolted one last idea into my head so I yanked the rubber hosepipes that connected the engines to our reserve tanks and spun the little red wheel to spray fuel across the Engine Room. Khan saw what I was doing and went for me before I could get the cloud ignited, forcing me to delay the inevitable as I ran around looking for a match.

No joy; I had not a lighter nor a match nor a bowl of Lumpati's sweet corn Dhansak with which to set the place ablaze and all too soon a set of black claws raked my shoulders to send me crashing into the bulkhead.

"Mother…!" was one half of my final sentiment, but the rest was stolen when a whoosh of heat filled the confines thanks to one of the soldering guns on the wall hitting the deck to toss that missing spark into the fray.

Whhhhhooooppppppppp!!!!!

I knew I couldn't escape this, not from a werewolf with a grudge in the blazing engine room of a ship with its fuel tanks ablaze, my fate was sealed, but if this was to be my curtain call, at least I'd taken Khan with me. And this wasn't my nobility speaking, I was just being a bad loser. Khan was going to burn. Or possibly drown. Or maybe – if I was lucky – both.

And I'd at least hastened my own exit from this world too. The fires burned with a ferocity and I reeled as the skin stripped from my face. My blood boiled and bones cracked the length and breadth of my body as I squirmed in the heat of the inferno, but to my dismay I remained horribly lucid throughout, burning to death and knowing every second of it.

After an eternity of indescribable agonies my mind started to fog and at last I made peace with my fears, although the pain remained, only much more intense, tightened in the pit of my stomach like a knotted ball of cramps, the likes of which I would've killed to be free of.

Khan saw that I wasn't quite dead and pounced to finish me off, swinging both claws at me to ravage my carcass before I was too crispy to carve, but he didn't manage to land a blow. With lightning reflexes I parried his blows and even more unbelievably grabbed a hold of his arms so that he couldn't strike me again. I held him there as he barked at me with a furious thunder before I realised I could understand what he was saying.

"You will not rise to challenge me!" he was bellowing, though these weren't his actual words, just the underlying meanings behind his savage roars – but I could understand them all the same. "I will destroy you!"

What the hell!

I was genuinely confused.

I could understand Khan's roars? I could hold back his colossal strength? I could climb the winch chains when half dead with only eight fingers? I could walk on my shattered ankle?

And I could survive this suffocating inferno?

Of course, the reason I could do all of these things was obvious, but it simply hadn't occurred to me until I saw the hand I was holding Khan's arm with. It was as immense and as gnarled at Khan's, grey to the skin and layered in a coat of coarse hairs with five-inch talons at the end of each of its four remaining digits.

I too had changed into the beast.

I too was now one of Khan's kind.

Khan himself was clearly having a day to forget and my transformation to stand square to him was clearly his worst fears realised.

"You filthy cheese skin, you have no right to these powers. You are not worthy," he complained, as if this was chief in my list of concerns. "I am ten-fold your superior! I have reigned since before you were born!"

I have to say I've known Speak Your Weight machines who could insult a man better than Khan so I roared into his face to go fuck his mother's stink-hole – causing Khan to blink, almost as if to say "there is such a thing as going too far you know, old chap" – before launching him across the engine room and into the flames.

The powers by which I threw Khan away made me feel so tremendous and if I hadn't stopped myself I would've clattered across the room and ripped his arms from his sides, cracking his bones and sucking the marrow from their splintered canals. But something halted me; a voice, deep down within my shackled soul told me to forget about Khan and worry instead about the reserve tanks and that yellow curtain of flames which was about to lick the diesel inside.

The time had finally come for me to leave the *SS Almayer's Folly*.

And leave her fast.

Khan was still scrambling to escape the flames with his useless legs but I had no such problems, launching myself through the hatchway as if on springs and bounding along the corridors to burst out onto the boat deck beneath a blood red moon. The storm had blown itself out and the glare of that great orb charged me with a strength I could scarcely comprehend.

I'd never before felt so alive and howled my eternal devotion to the moon's wondrous power but a sudden crack from below reminded me of the power 600 gallons of diesel could unleash when cooked under extreme pressure, so I charged the stern on all fours and took a running jump over the back of the *Folly*.

The waters rushed up to greet me and all at once I was submerged in their icy depths, but the cold didn't bother, nor did the thought of what lurked within these waves; I just swept my limbs through the currents and resurfaced thirty yards from the ship.

"A curse on you!" Khan barked at me though the shattered porthole in the side of the *Folly*. "A curse to follow you from this day forth, to sit upon your house and tarnish your…"

Unfortunately I never got to hear the rest of it for at that moment the fuel tanks ignited and the *Folly* disappeared behind a blinding flash of light.

Where once there had been a complete boat, all that remained were two burning ends, and all that had sat between them rained back down to splash the waters one last time before joining the *Sumatran Wind* at the bottom of the sea.

Which just left me, all alone in the dark, with not so much as a life vest to cling to.

I may have been an inhuman beast of colossal savagery but I still had a mortal soul. I was still afraid of death and all that the devil held in store for me so I struck out for shore, swimming due west with a strength that didn't falter –

– for eight long hours.

By the time the sun peaked over the horizon, I was standing in a mangrove swamp, shaking salt water from my coat and eating the arse out of a turtle I'd caught flapping in the surf. Nothing had, nor ever has, tasted as good as that stinking ripe reptile and I stripped her to the shell, beak, flippers and all, before slinking off into the jungle to find a tree under which I could rest for a much needed sleep.

I was alive.

I was on land.

And soon I would be human again.

Now I just had to get home.

CHAPTER 5:
OPINION IS DIVIDED

"Oh what, so you're a fucking werewolf now, are you?" Tommy hawed, looking around my basement in pantomime amusement and snorting derisively. "What a load a' bullshit!"

"I wish it were, kid, I really do. But Khan had it right and I have been carrying this curse for almost fifty years now," I shrugged, blowing on the faded embers of my tobacco and supping on the flavours this released.

"What, so you like, change at night then, when there's a full moon, an' all that like?" Barry asked, his eyes so wide they should've dropped from his sockets by rights and rolled underneath the sofa to look up at me from the floor agog.

"Sometimes," I told him. "Not often these days I'll admit. It fades with age, but in the right conditions, when the moon is at its fullest and the blood is pumping, then yes I do become the beast."

"Well I ain't seen you about," Farny reckoned.

"And just as well you haven't," I assured him. "I don't leave this house when I transform, I lock myself in the basement and wait out the night ripping at the walls. I've built this prison well, to withstand a lot of abuse – and noise," I reminded them, "because if I ever got out, God help all those that crossed my path."

I let that one hang in the air, like the silvery grey plumes from my old shag, before nodding in the direction of the basement door and the fresh lacerations which it adorned.

"What, you did those when you were a werewolf?" Ginger said, his face a collage of horror and fascination.

And acne.

I nodded, a stern, yet approving look of a man confirming a secret.

"Did he fuck!" Tommy countered. "He probably did them getting this sofa down here."

"Those aren't sofa leg scratches, sonny," I reassured him. "Go and take a butcher's if you like."

Tommy narrowed his eyes contemptuously and refused to rise, as if by doing so would somehow admit his gullibility. But Barry and Ginger on the other hand had no such qualms and were over there in a flash, tracing their fingers along the parallel three foot long scars that ran the length of the reinforced steel plating and reporting back that they did indeed appear to have been made by something other than furniture (that said, Tommy had been right about one thing, my sofa had been a right vicious bastard to get down here).

"There's only three scratches to this one," Ginger observed, picking out a particularly long set of lines that ran from right to left.

"And there are only three fingers on this here hand," I explained, holding up my right hand for them all to see.

Barry, Ginger and even Farny all gasped at the sight, but Tommy just rolled his eyes.

"Is that where Khan shot you in the gunfight?" Barry asked.

"It is. It never grew back, not even when I change. Khan had that much of me at least."

"This is such bullshit!" Tommy squealed, unable to stand it any longer. "He probably did that at work or picking his nose or something."

"But the scratches…" Ginger pointed.

"He's planned this, don't you see. He did them himself and he's trying to shit us up. He's just a stinking scarecrow with a load of old bullshit stories, that's all." But

Tommy didn't have the ears of the basement, which is understandable really. I was offering these boys serial killers and werewolves while all Tommy was offering them was a liar. And what self-respecting twelve-year-old didn't want to believe in werewolves?

"He said it himself," Tommy continued to rally when he saw he wasn't winning the argument, "he was a hundred miles out to sea with no idea where he was, but somehow he just manages to swim back to *facking* shore, just like that. It's all bullshit."

"You're right," I confirmed. "I was a hundred miles off shore with no idea where I was – at least I was when I was human. But as the beast, I have senses a bloodhound can only dream about. It's why we go on such rampages, you know, the smell of the meat drives us insane with hunger. But it also meant I could smell land from many miles away, so I knew which way to swim. That first morning I made it to a small island, the first of a chain of uninhabited islands that straddled the East Sea so I was all right. Then, I spent the next two nights in the water swimming from island to island until I eventually reached the mainland, just south of Dà Nang."

"Where's Dà Nang?" Ginger asked.

"It's in Vietnam," I educated them.

"You know, like in the films," Farny outlined further.

"Er, yeah, that's it," I kind of agreed. "Only this weren't no film, it was a real war, with soldiers and casualties and terrible battles. Awful it was."

"Oh here we go, he only fought in the war an' all," Tommy scoffed.

"No, not that one I didn't. But I did encounter a couple of platoons of foot soldiers that first night when I was the beast. On both sides as it happened. So at least my contributions to the Vietnam War were balanced."

I looked down, to make clear my memories of this

particular incident weren't for public consumption, and instead went on to explain how the moon had completed its cycle the night after I'd arrived, so that I was able to pass myself off as a human for the next 25 days, handing myself in to the first patrol I encountered and getting a ride back to Saigon when I'd convinced them I was a dotty young missionary out doing the Lord's work. Or at least I had been until my congregation had been attacked and killed.

"NVA or VC?" a lieutenant barely older than me asked, shoving a map in front of me so that I could point out where all this had happened.

"I didn't see, they hit us so quickly," I sobbed. "But we were ambushed around about here," I pointed as vaguely as I could, giving him a couple of hundred square miles in which to go looking for someone to shoot.

"It's okay Padre, you hang in there. We'll get you home, no problem. This is no place for you. We'll get you back to Australia, you see if we don't."

"Huh?"

In Saigon, I was fed and clothed and repatriated by the British Embassy. They fast-tracked me through the process when they found out I was the son of a VC winner and to my amazement there were no coppers waiting for me when I landed two days later at London airport. A couple of plain clothed inspectors did drop by to see me after a week, so I told them I'd run off to sea after a huge row with my father and I hadn't even known he was dead until I'd been told in Saigon. The inspectors bought this, hinting that they had a certain idea what the row was about ("Went out in his car a lot at night, did he?"), but they pressed no further and after barely twenty minutes decided to close the file and say no more about it. "No point besmirching a man when he's dead, no matter what he's done. That does no one any favours," the senior inspector reckoned as he rose to leave. I'd already found my father's scrap books missing when I'd returned to the cottage a week earlier but neither inspector ventured to mention anything about them, so I nodded to show I understood, but that was basically that.

I was a free man.

Free of my dad. Free of the Strangler. Free of the police and free of suspicion. In fact, if it hadn't been for this murderous curse I'd brought back from the east with me I could've probably led a happy and normal life.

"And you've been a werewolf ever since?" Barry asked.

"That I have. I sold the cottage in King's Lynn and moved up to the Highlands of Scotland into the middle of nowhere so that on full moons I could roam the mountains without fear of bumping into anyone. But I always would. Whether they be a camper or a botanist or a farmer or a hiker, I made a lot of kills those first couple of years before I finally managed to get a hold of this thing. That's why I moved to this house, and this shitty little neighbourhood, because it was the only place I found that had a basement in the time I was looking. So I bought it quick and lined it with steel before the next full moon could unleash my terror upon this world, and thankfully it has held. Since then I've done my best to lead a good life and keep myself to myself and I've been here ever since."

"My chin is *soooo* itchy," Tommy complained, rubbing his face until his cheeks glistened, but none of the other boys paid him any attention. I had them in the palm of my hand and they were in no rush to jump off. A case in point; I'd forgotten to lock the basement door behind myself, and if they'd had a mind to Barry and Ginger could've made a bolt for it and I would've stood no chance of catching them. But they didn't. Instead they just came back down the steps, retook their place on the sofa and urged me for more.

"So, you can't die then?" Barry asked. "That's what they say about werewolves, isn't it? That they're immortal."

"I ain't immortal young man. And frankly I'm glad of it. No, I can die and one day I will, just like any other man," I promised him, then thought to add, "especially at the hands of another beast as ungodly as myself."

Barry, Ginger and Farny all sprang to attention. Tommy groaned at the ceiling.

"Oh for fuck's sake, no more, please!"

But there was more. Much more in fact. Because the worst was yet to come for poor young and accursed John Coal.

PART 3:

THE BLACK SPOT

It was the summer of 1975. I'd been home for about ten years and had worked hard to carve out the best life I could under the circumstances. I'd bought my bungalow, adapted the basement, taken a hold of the monster within and had even managed to fulfil my mother's most ardent wish for her only son and got myself a job –

– as a travelling sales rep.

It wasn't the best job in the world, or even the most lucrative, but it got me away from the nine-to-five and I enjoyed seeing different parts of the country. I'm not the most sociable person as a rule, but I can talk a good game or hold a smile for up to five minutes at a time when I'm showing a client where to sign, so I didn't do too badly. To be honest, it would've been hard to have been crap at the job because the product more or less sold itself.

Sandpaper. That was my main account. I went from town to town, doling out free samples to hardware stores and workshops and demonstrating the extraordinary durability of our sheets to anyone who had an unbuffed stick at hand.

"Up to twenty-eight per cent longer lasting than the best high street brands," I used to tell them across their counters. "These sheets actually save you money if you order in bulk."

Load of bollocks of course, but who can accurately remember how long a sheet of sandpaper normally lasts? But people were happy to order a batch of the stuff for four new pence a sheet (please allow 48 days for delivery) because sandpaper's just sandpaper at the end of the day and who really cares where the bloody stuff comes from [eventually] just so long as it's cheap enough and doesn't tear like a sheet of soggy bog paper the first time you run it over a splinter, so I made a respectable living from my travels and rarely ended a week with an empty order book or belly.

But there was one week.

I was in Lincolnshire somewhere and I was lost. I was trying to get to Louth, but Lincolnshire County Council must've run out of money after sticking up signposts on every street corner for Lincoln itself and poor old Louth got overlooked. "Well, who wants to go to Louth anyway when they can come to Lincoln?" Lincolnshire County Council probably reasoned, and with some justification, except that I had an appointment with a new timber merchant on the Louth trading estate and I was keen to keep it.

I had a map with me of course, but I'd managed to lose the A16 just south of Hundleby and was now inevitably on one of the 37,000 roads in Lincolnshire that led to Lincoln.

"Oh for Christ's sake!" I grumbled, stamping on the brakes when I realised I'd missed yet another turning.

It was getting late, almost three o'clock in the afternoon, so I didn't want to double back and risk missing my appointment looking for the A16 again. So instead I made the mistake men all over the world make when they're lost, late and desperate – I asked a local for directions.

He must've thought it was his birthday or something because I got the complete works – the inside knowledge, the secret short cuts and the best place to stop for pie, chips and pint along the way. Naturally, none of it involved anything that could even vaguely be described as a main road.

"Nah, steer clear of them A roads, boy, not if you're going to Louth, not from here, like. Just cut down that turning a hundred yards back until you see a big flintstone wall, then take the next left, as if you're going to Skeggy, but don't – go left instead. You can't miss it, there's a pub on the corner called The White Horse or The White House or something like that, a little further up. I don't know, I don't drink no more. Gave it up in '53 and haven't had a drop since. And you know what, I don't miss it in the slightest."

"This is all incredibly helpful," I told him, my knuckles turning white against my Cortina's steering wheel.

"So just back there then on the left. You see it? Back there. You'll be in Louth in forty-five minutes, you will."

But I wasn't. Of course I wasn't. An hour later and I was still driving around in circles looking for flintstones on the advice of Barney Rubble and wondering how I could've been so stupid. And as a mark of just how lost I was, even the signs for Lincoln disappeared after a while.

I stopped next to a field of swaying wheat and spread my road atlas out across the roasting bonnet of my hot car. The sticky breeze immediately attempted to fold it back up again and hungry horse flies joined in to assault my good humour, dive bombing the back of my neck until I was swinging punches and screaming vengeance against the AA, my lying guide and the crew of the *Enola Gay* for dropping their payload 6,000 miles off target.

I screwed the map back up, dumped it across my roasting backseat and stepped on the accelerator as I was still climbing into the car.

It was now getting on for half past four and the timber merchants were only open until five. I couldn't miss my appointment, not after spending the whole afternoon touring hedgerows and lanes, no matter how green and pleasant the surroundings were, so I kept my foot to the floor and flicked my windscreen wipers on in case any locals crossed my path.

I was going too fast. I knew I was going too fast, but we always think we can get away with these things at the time – but we never can. The curve in the road came at me faster than I came at it, but I barely had a chance to do anything about it. Before I'd even lifted my foot from the accelerator I was crashing over a grass embankment and watching in horror as a fence post leapt from the ground and darted straight towards me to shatter the windscreen in my face.

I held up my arms to cover my eyes and felt the front of the car drop into a ditch but the crunch I was expecting never came.

Only silence. And darkness
And then nothing.

ii

I don't know how long I was out for but when I climbed from the car I could tell it was no longer afternoon, it felt more like early evening.

I'd come to a dead halt against the far side of an overgrown ditch and the inconvenience aside I felt thankful for the thick foliage and mud I'd managed to find. A little to the right and I would've wrapped myself around a big old oak that didn't look as if it could take a joke.

I brushed myself down and counted my limbs, relieved to discover I still had two of everything, then slipped a Rothman between my lips to take the sting out of the fresh country air.

I'd missed my appointment. I was only too aware of that, and now I was stuck in the wilds on a blissfully hot evening with only a suitcase of sandpaper to see me through till morning. It was going to be a memorable night, for sure.

No cars passed in all the time I'd been standing on the embankment and none had come by in all the time I'd been snoozing in the ditch either. Or if they had, they must've been Darwinians. I realised my only option was to start walking and hope to blunder into a passing tractor or a pub before nightfall but no sooner had I taken a step than I kicked an old stone marker nestling in the long grass bearing the name 'Long Fenton' and an arrow which pointed across the road to a dirt track on the other side. It hardly sounded like a metropolis, but at least it hadn't read 'Lincoln 64 miles', which was something at least.

I nipped across the road and started along a wooded track, scarcely believing anyone could get a bike down here let alone a car, but this was deepest, darkest Lincolnshire I had to remember. There were tribes in the Congo who could've come here and flogged mirrors to this lot if they'd had a mind to.

The air was clammy and the breeze barely a waft. A long hot afternoon had turned into a long hot evening and the setting sun was perfectly framed by the arcade of overhanging branches so that its rays followed me all the way down the dusty trail until I encountered the first of several neat cottages nestling against a wooded hillside. A little Norman church lay just beyond them, surrounded by three or four dozen lichen-covered graves of long dead Lincolnites and just beyond an adjoining stone wall the place I'm sure most of the churchyard's residents would've much rather been – a pub, 'The Black Fox'.

I counted amongst the other buildings on this street a village store, a community hall and a repair shop, all of which were closed, which was a pity as I could've probably sold two out of three of them some sandpaper. Instead I settled for buying myself the first of several much-needed pints and headed into the pub.

The gang was all here, with ruddy-faced morons

harring and hawring against a backdrop of good-natured bestiality accusations, while a rosy-cheeked barmaid giggled from the pumps as if she didn't quite understand, despite sporting an enormous pair of community tits that looked as if they were on first-name terms with every callous in the village.

Then I stepped through the door.

Fourteen faces looked at me as if I'd just climbed out of a spaceship, so I quickly checked my reflection in the door to double-check a fence pole wasn't still sticking out of my face, before asking if it was okay if I came in and got a drink.

"Of course young 'un. You come in and make yourself right at home," confirmed a jovial old soak, as he stepped back to make room for me at the bar.

The rest of the pub weren't so convivial and welcomed me with open gobs, while the rosy-cheeked barmaid simply juggled her tits in front of a trio of pumps to let me know the specialties of the house.

"A pint of Best?" I settled for, only to crash for a second time that day when I reached into my pocket and pulled out nothing but a fluffy lining. "Bollocks!"

"Looks like young 'un's forgotten his brass," the jovial old bandleader deduced.

"It must have fallen out my pocket when I climbed out of the car," I said.

The old boy gave me a wink, then turned to the barmaid. "Can easily be done. Mary, put the young man's tipple on my slate."

I put up a token protest, but was ready to chin the first of them who tried to take it back from me and instead supped deeply, sinking into its frothy head until I'd drain all but a splash and wiped my eyebrows with malty satisfaction.

"Thirsty huh?" the old boy concluded.

I told the bar hangers about my crash and crummy afternoon in general, and so they bought me another pint and urged Mary to make me a cheese sandwich in the name of charity and prepare the guest room for the night. This shook a few knowing chuckles from the locals and a mischievous smirk from Mary, telling me her good deeds stretched to more than cheese sarnies but I tried not to notice.

"Don't bear thinking about," one yokel commented.

I relented to placing myself in my hostess's capable hands, as I'm only human (most of the month), and even a bed that bounced across the floorboards all night long was preferable to the back seat of an upside down Ford Cortina, so I lifted my glass and toasted my sponsors.

"Gentlemen, your health."

"You'd best concern yourself with your own there, boy," they advised me and as quickly as that I was one of the gang, complete with slaps on the back and insinuations about my sexual orientations. And all without having to stick my hand in my pocket either. Oh yes, when I'd tumbled into that ditch, all things considered, I'd fallen on my feet finding Long Fenton.

"You from the big city are you?" one of the chaps asked.

"Lincoln?" his mate qualified.

"Norfolk," I replied.

"Norfolk?" they all cooed. "You're a long way from home ain't ya, chum?"

"Travelling salesman," I told them.

"I see. We thought you might be one of them there scientists from the Ministry like," the old boy said.

"Not unless it's the Ministry of Sandpaper," I reassured them, then thought, "What scientists?"

"Up here to open the new fertiliser plant, just over the back there. Finally finished it last week, they did. Been buying up land all over the borough for their roads and facilities. Bought my old barley field for a packet," the old boy smiled, like a magic bean vendor returning from market with four tons of prize Friesians.

"Nope, sorry, that ain't me," I shrugged, promising them I was no "scientist, minister or shoveller of shit".

"We're all shovellers of shit, my friend," the old boy assured me with a wink. "We just don't all use a shovel, that's all."

"Too true. Too true."

Me and my new pals chuckled the night away, Mary looking thinner as my liver grew fatter, and I would've probably ended the evening happily falling off my bar stool and into her bed if it hadn't been for the arrival of a latecomer to our revelries.

"Why *hallo* there young Brian, found some brass down the back of your sofa finally?" the old boy chuckled.

Young Brian didn't look that young to me, he looked about forty, but then that's so often the way with these rural types, all that heavy lifting and toothpaste dodging turns boys into men before the rest of us. Brian was probably nearer my age, late twenties or early thirties, but he had twice the muscles I had, most of them in his brain, and hands that could've sanded down a flight of banisters quicker than my best sheet of extra coarse.

He took one look at me leaning up against the bar of his local in my fancy big city suit and bell bottoms, and he swallowed the wasp he'd come in chewing.

"Who's that?" he asked, not to me, but to the jovial old soak who'd been so accommodating all evening.

"Chap from out of town," the old soak toyed, "here to sample our fine Mary's wares."

The reaction this provoked, not least of all from me, when I brought half a pint of Best up through my nose, triggered much amusement all around and was obviously the intention. Brian stood there scratching his thoughts and scowling in all directions before settling on me as the easy mark.

"That right is it? You here to tap up my intended?" he asked, his voice deceptively squeaky.

"No no," I spluttered, clearing the last of my pint from my airways so that I could speak up as to my own intentions. "I just came in for a drink, that's all."

"A drink is it?" Brian surmised. "Long way to come for a drink from Lincoln, ain't it?"

Fuck me, did any of these bozos even notice the stars at night, or did they all just assume they were Lincoln's all-year-round Christmas decorations?

"From Norfolk, actually young Brian," the old soak corrected him, presumably because the notion of Mary being banged by someone from Norfolk was even more heinous than the notion of her being banged by someone from Lincoln. I decided to keep to myself the fact that I'd once visited London.

"Norfolk? You're a long way from home, boy," Brian told me. "Best you were getting back there before it gets dark I suggest."

This was almost comical, and if it weren't for the fact he could hang me up by the horse brasses if he so desired (although only on moonless evenings) I would've told him to go stick his head in a cowpat. But two things quickly became obvious; firstly, that Brian was a man to act first and think never. And secondly, that far from being one of the gang as I'd so foolishly assumed, I was actually the gang's sport and they'd hung bells and whistles all over me knowing full well the village baby would be popping in for his dream feed before chucking out time.

"I crashed my car on the main road at the end of the track. It's upside down in a ditch back there. I'll not get it out tonight," I explained.

"How very convenient," Brian postulated.

"Well, not really (you great fuckwit)," I half replied (and half thought).

"So you reckon to be staying the night do you?" Brian growled.

"Mary's got the guest bed all made up for him," the old soak laughed, twisting the knife in both our guts further still.

"What guest bed? She ain't got but one bed in the place!" Brian fumed, and the whole pub duly fell about, none more so than Mary, who I now saw was the sort of woman who liked to keep her fiancé on his toes – perched outside her bedroom window while a succession of dirty salesmen hung out of the back of her.

"Wait, they're all winding you up," I tried in vain, but Brian was beyond reason and probably rarely needed one in the first place.

"Out you go, my beauty," he snarled, grabbing me by the lapels and bundling me through the front door and out into the street.

Behind me, I heard the old bastard who'd started all this off laugh with delight and call, "Time gentlemen, please!" to universal merriment, before Brian hurled me into the dust. I curled up into a ball of expectation, but to my surprise Brian didn't follow my tumble up with his hobnail boots. Instead, he simply tottered over me in triumph and advised me to let that be a lesson to me.

I cautiously uncovered my head and looked up at him.

"What, when I crash my car in a ditch in future, I should just bleeding well stay there rather than go looking for help? Is that the lesson you're talking about?"

"You know 'ee only too well," he confirmed, making about as much sense as cutlery at his and Mary's wedding breakfast.

I clambered to my feet when I decided it was safe to

do so and looked around at the lengthening shadows. We were bang smack in the middle of dusk and the sun was barely visible through the trees. It wouldn't be long before the thick blanket of night had settled across the entire village to secrete the track back to the main road. "How far is the next village?" I asked, sensing Brian might have less of a problem with this question than most.

"Four mile, just follow the lane through the village and keep to the left and you'll get to West Ullerton af'er a while," he said, bidding me a fond faredy-well and heading back into the Fox to reclaim his prize.

I knew it could go either way, but I couldn't resist getting in one final dig about Lincolnshire's famous northern hospitality and sure enough it pickled Brian's ears enough to get him backing out of the pub again.

"I'd watch what you say about Lincolnshire, my friend. You're a long way from Norfolk up here, you'd be advised to remember that," he said.

"I'm a long way from fucking West Ullerton too in case you hadn't noticed. And I've had a crash today. But don't you worry about that, mate. I'll just head off and try to find some village I've never been to in the middle of nowhere before it turns pitch black, in the hope there might be someone *there* who can help me in my hour of need. But you enjoy your pint, mate. Nice one. Cheers."

I don't know what I was expecting from Brian – a pricking of the conscience or a swinging of the fists so that I could justify whacking him over the head with the brickbat I had secreted behind my back, but my dig provoked an altogether more unexpected reaction.

Brian reached into his pocket and dug around for some keys, then nodded down the street to a battered old truck parked next to the church and said:

"Okay then chum, I'll give 'ee a lift."

iii

I guess Brian had a soggier side to him than I'd given him credit for. Or perhaps deep down, inside that throbbing T-bone he kept between his ears, he knew he was Long Fenton's dancing bear to everyone else's pointed sticks. He knew it. But he couldn't help it. Maybe he even knew there was nothing between me and Mary, but simple face meant he had to run me out of town all the same. After all he was "young Brian" to the rest of the gang. And what self-respecting barnyard brawler liked to be patted on the head by their respected elders?

"I appreciate this," I conceded, as we weaved our way through the wooded lanes and out towards the wide-open fields that spanned the countryside between Long Fenton and West Ullerton.

"Don't mention it," Brian mumbled and coughed, clearly uncomfortable to find himself on speaking terms with a man he was more accustomed to launching into streets.

"Seem like a lot of wankers back in that place," I tossed into the conversation. Brian glanced my way but said nothing. He simply changed gear in agreement and pushed on into the setting sun.

A minute or two out of the village, we came to a shiny new wire fence that circled a huge industrial eyesore every bit as shiny and new as the fence was, but in all the worst possible ways. Silos and towers stretched away from the plant across the open fields, connected to each other by a series of gleaming pipes, and a wide concrete access road cut across the lane we were travelling as if it hadn't even noticed it was here, to head up the hill towards where I assumed the main road would be.

"The fertiliser plant?" I deduced.

"Damned thing," Brian confirmed with a scowl, making me wonder just how many scientists one barmaid could bang anyway. "I dunno why it had to come here. Why us? Why now?"

"Got to go somewhere I guess," I told him, not really caring, just heartened by the fact that there was pain in young Brian's life.

"Then why didn't it go elsewhere?" Albert Einstein ruminated, scarcely watching the lane in front of him, so fixated was he on the county's newest fertiliser plant.

"What's so bad about it? I mean, it might be a bit of a monstrosity for sure, but it'll mean jobs."

"I got a job thank'ee very much. Or at least I had until that damned thing came here," Brian fumed. He went on to elaborate a little, about how he'd had the manual labouring market all sewn up for as long as he could remember, working for every farmer in the district and dictating his own terms so that he was never short of offers or brass. Few of the young men born in Long Fenton seemed to want to stay here beyond short trousers (and who could blame them) so the population was growing older as Brian's mattress was growing fatter. And things would've probably continued this way until eventually one of the old buzzards fell off their perch. And who would've been in a prime position to buy out their smallholding then?

Oh yes, Brian's future had been looking very rosy indeed.

At least it had until a fertiliser plant had chosen this forgotten little backwater to set up shop. And when it opened its industrial-sized wallet, it solved everyone's problems in one foul swoop.

Well, almost everyone's.

"You could always get a job at the plant," I reassured

him. "Work your way up; one day even be manager."

"I don't want to work in no factory!" he snapped back. "I like to feel soil beneath my boots; sun on my face. I work the land with these here hands. And I wanted to work my own."

Brian swallowed his anger and glanced in the mirror at the receding plant. It was clearly upsetting for him to talk about so I pressed him further to pass the journey.

"One man's setback is another man's opportunity. Remember that (when you're shovelling shit for two peanuts a day, knuckleheaded, ha-ha-ha!!)," I reassured him (mentally laughed my socks off at).

I was just starting to relax at my own recent misfortunes and enjoy the ride to West Ullerton when we rounded the next corner and found ourselves right back where we started outside The Black Fox again.

"What the buggery…" Brian gawped in confusion, his brow seeming to jut out even further than usual with every passing minute.

"You took a wrong turn perhaps?" I ventured with a sigh of frustration. I'd already been looking forward to flogging my sob story to the regulars of West Ullerton and Brian's taxiing was costing me valuable drinking time.

"I couldn't have, there ain't no wrong turning. It's a straight road all the way through."

"Maybe the plant moved the road when they were laying their own," I hedged.

"But I recognised it all the way. It ain't changed none," Brian denied, annoying me with his objections when he'd clearly taken a wrong turn somewhere, unless it was a circular road and everyone in Long Fenton simply changed the signs and swapped hats whenever Brian was out of town.

"Well we've taken two lefts somewhere," I insisted, but Brian wasn't having it.

"But I didn't!" he was adamant, "look, I'll prove it," and off we went again, back up the same street, along the same road, past the same plant and around the same bend...

... only to end up at exactly the same place again.

Outside The Black Fox.

In Long Fenton.

"This ain't right," Brian said. "This ain't right at all."

"No," I agreed, sensing the hardware shops around this way must make a fortune flogging Brian elbow grease and sky hooks all year around, "this indeed isn't right."

One of the old boys stepped out of The Black Fox and pointed himself in the direction of the outhouse, so Brian asked him if they'd changed the road over since last week. The old boy scratched his head and asked Brian if he thought he should be driving this late and in his condition, which Brian duly took out on the gears of his truck and away we went again, off up the street, out of the village, into the sticks and past the plant.

At this point Brian pumped the brakes and studied the road ahead before moving off again.

"This is the road," he insisted. "This is the road to West Ullerton."

"It's the road we've taken twice already," I pointed out.

"I know it is!" Brian snapped. "But it goes to West Ullerton."

"Are you a betting man, Brian?" I asked, figuring I'd need some cash tonight wherever I ended up.

"That tree, I used to play in it as a nipper," he said, pointing at a big old oak across the road from the plant. "And them there, them line of hedges, they back onto Ronnie Earlcott's farm. I helped cut them only two weeks ago."

"I don't doubt it," I shrugged, hoping I hadn't

somehow ended up on Lincolnshire's least subscribed tour.

"Well these things are on the road to West Ullerton."

"Then they are presumably on the road to Long Fenton too?" I pointed out.

"Are you saying I don't know my own county?" he huffed.

"Not a bit of it, just pointing out that they may've rejigged the road around the plant to make way for construction traffic. They sometimes do that, you know, and often you can barely spot the seam," I told him, although this last bit was a complete load of old twaddle, but I tried to make it sound as if I knew what I was talking about. An old salesman's habit.

"I recognise this road," Brian maintained, finally putting his foot down again.

"And so do I."

I also recognised The Black Fox when we screeched to a halt outside it once more, and the look of bemusement on the old boy's face as he came back from the outhouse tugging his zip.

"You boys having fun, are yee?" he asked.

"Not so you'd notice," I replied before Brian had a chance.

Brian now had the steaming hump and took to the road again before the dust cloud of our most recent arrival had even settled. This time however we drove out past the plant, turned left onto the new access road and followed it out to the west see where it took us. The neat black road carved a tarmac corridor through the wooded countryside and ran as straight as an arrow; so it came as something of a surprise, even to me, when we cleared the crest of a rise, only to find ourselves right back in Long Fenton once again.

"Okay, now that is weird," I finally admitted,

wondering if the hippy surveyor had used a kaleidoscope to set this road out instead of a theodolite.

"D'you believe me now?" Brian demanded, but I didn't know what I believed. I certainly didn't believe that the fertiliser plant had deliberately relaid all the roads in the area to lead back to Long Fenton as some sort of marketing strategy, no matter how much fertiliser they were hoping to shift, but something was certainly amiss.

"How is it that we've driven out of the village one way, only to arrive back by another?" I asked, lighting a thought inside Brian's head that manifested itself as the grinding of his gears and the spinning of the steering wheel until we were heading out of the village in the opposite direction. Strangely the road was unrecognisable heading in this direction, as roads often have a want to be. But this was different; different bushes, different trees and different ditches lined the route to the ones we'd passed coming the other way, but somehow we still managed to enter Long Fenton at exactly the same point, pulling up outside The Black Fox as surely as a couple of goldfish encountering the same plastic galleon time and time again.

"What have 'ee done to us?" Brian finally barked, turning in his seat to lay his fears at the feet of that most fearsome of country slubberdegullions – the stranger.

"Whatever's being done, pal, it's being done to me too," I promised him.

We set off another three times and each time took a different road, in a different direction and a different turning once outside of Long Fenton, and each time we ended up back outside The Black Fox until finally I'd had enough.

"Alright, stop the truck, I'm getting out here!" I demanded, when we were outside the village for the umpteenth time, at where I reasoned to be the furthest point from The Black Fox.

Brian pulled over, so I wrestled with the door handle until I was free, and bid Brian a fond fuck off.

"Where yee going, boy?" Brian asked.

"Back to the main road. I'm going to hitch a lift from there," I said, looking about to get my bearings.

"To West Ullerton? Main road don't go to West Ullerton," Brian told me.

"Neither does this one," I reminded him. "Long Fenton's that way and that way," I said, pointing the way we'd come and the way we were heading. "So I'm going that way."

Brian followed my finger across the fields to a crop of trees that ran south away from Long Fenton (hopefully) and into the distance.

"The main road," I said, slamming the truck door and slinging my jacket over my shoulder, "it should be over there by my calculations."

"That ain't be the main road," Brian corrected.

"Would you be awfully insulted if I didn't take your directions?" I asked, adding "you turnip-headed twat," just to season the sentiment.

iv

The night was lingering in the wings, just waiting for the moment of optimum inconvenience to drop its blanket across the land, so I pushed on while I still had the dusk by which to see, across the fields, up the banks of the rise and into the trees.

The darkness smothered me once I got beneath the leafy canopy, but I was sure it would only be a matter of time before I stumbled across the main road. If there's one thing you get serving at sea it's a good sense of direction. Winds, clouds, stars and of course, the moon, they can all help when you're trying to find your way home, except of course when you can't see them, as in this case. But I checked the trunks of trees for moss and lichen with a match every now and again to ensure I was still travelling south and after twenty minutes entered a small clearing.

The night had done nothing to blow the humidity from the crick of my neck, despite the breeze in the leaves, but what was slightly more disconcerting was the lack of the normal summer sounds. I'm a country boy by upbringing so I know how a July night is supposed to sound. Crickets chirp, owls hoot, flies buzz.

But not tonight.

Tonight, other than the breeze in the trees, there was nothing. Not even a gnat whirring about my ears.

I stopped and listened for as long as I dared but all I could hear were the sounds of my own breathing and the rustling of foliage. Where were all the insects? Where were all the birds?

All at once, I wasn't sure I wanted to know the answer to these questions so I picked up the pace and continued up the slope, up towards where I was sure the main road would be, and away from this Godforsaken backwater.

A sudden loud crack over my shoulder had me jumping out of my shoes and whirling in all directions to clout whoever had just snuck up behind me but there was no one; just the wind, the trees and the night.

I studied every shadow and challenged my imagination to find the perpetrator, but nothing emerged so I swallowed my fears and continued across the clearing.

I'd not got two paces when a loud rustling had me changing direction with a fright.

I was now aware of something in the tree line. I couldn't see what it was and I couldn't hear what it was, but I could sense it was there all the same. I stopped and stood in the middle of the clearing trying to pinpoint whatever it was, but I simply couldn't get a bead on it. And I've got unnaturally good senses too, what with the blood that courses through my veins. So I cupped my ears, strained my eyes and even sniffed the air, but whatever was out there moved like a shadow in slippers and hid just beyond the corners of my eyes.

"Hello?" I tried to call, but my voice was as parched as the land. "Is anybody out there?"

Nobody answered. I took little comfort from this omission and decided to change tact.

"I've got a gun. And it's loaded. I'd rather not use it, but… I'm a spy (obviously a very secret one) so don't sneak up on me or I might not know you're only playing about," I warned whoever was out there, adding. "And I'm licensed to kill."

I could've also mentioned I was a werewolf but the truth was more preposterous than the lie. Besides, it was my week off, so I plunged a hand into my pocket and tried to make out that I was not a man to be messed with.

A voice.

At least that's what it sounded like. Whispered in the darkness, no louder than the breeze, it spoke a language I didn't recognise and laced every sentiment with a cruel hiss.

I backed away from the trees with my gun wilting in my pocket and lost what little heart I'd had.

A second black shape darted between the trees a little way off to my right, but froze stock still the moment I looked at it. The figure stood hunched between trees and showed no sign of fear when I hollered at it in paper-rage. I braved a couple of steps and struck a match, only to almost wet myself with relief when I found it was merely a fallen branch curled up to almost standing height, with knots and twigs for features.

But it had moved, I was sure it had. The shadow had

moved. I'd seen it – sort of.

A second sudden onrushing behind me had me leaping six feet to my left and flicking matches in my defence, but they lit up nothing but empty air and a few tinder dry clumps of grass where they fell.

It was all in my head. It had to be. The night was playing tricks on me. That was all.

But I wasn't prone to paranoia. I'd been cast away to the outer limits of human endurance too many times before to let simple shadows get the better of me. There was definitely something out here –

– something foul.

I decided to return to Long Fenton as fast as I could and spend the rest of the night at The Black Fox come what may. To hell with Brian, to hell with those Flower Pot Men who'd made merry at my expense and to hell with any tits I might bump into during the night.

All I wanted was not to be out here in the darkness anymore.

And possibly another of those cheese sarnies if they had any left.

I tried to remember the way I'd come but fear had cost me my bearings. Was it straight on across the clearing and left? Or back through the trees and to the right? When the voice murmured its evil thoughts once more just beyond my left lobe I realized it didn't matter just so long as I ran, so that's what I did, fleeing through the night and every overhanging branch in this county as lean and twisted shapes fanned out behind me to now give chase.

It felt like a hundred shadows following close behind, reaching spindly arms and grasping at my collars and every now and then I would see something darting between the trees to rip through a ray of moonlight.

Voices – lots and lots of voices now spoke up in excitement; whispers and grunts, cackles and snarls, like the babble of malevolent children taking delight at pulling the legs off a particularly juicy spider.

If ever I've been more scared in my life I'd obviously done well to bury the memory for I could barely draw a breath to extinguish the flames that burned deep within my chest. I simply ploughed on, stumbling headfirst over tree roots and rocks, rabbit holes and divots, until I fell out of the treeline and tumbled into the yellow grass of Ronnie Earlcott's fallow field.

I picked myself up and continued running, daring to glance over my shoulder for just the briefest of seconds and instantly regretted it when a dozen spectral sprinters burst from the treeline to chase me across the field.

They moved like nothing I'd seen before, seeming to glide across the rutted terrain like skaters on ice. They closed the open ground between us in seconds and threatened to swallow my very screams but a blinding flash of light immediately vanquished every shadow around me and knocked me on to my face.

"You back already then are you boy?" chortled the most beautiful voice I'd ever heard as a truck door swung open the other side of a barbed-wire fence.

"Brian? Oh for fuck's sake. Please help me, take me back to The Black Fox? Please, please, please!" I implored with all of my soul.

"That, my old beauty," he said with great satisfaction, "is something I reckon I can just about manage."

v

I spilled all to Brian on the drive back to Long Fenton; the shadows, the voices and the chase, and while he didn't entirely buy everything I was flogging he was unsettled enough with his recent circumnavigations to hold his cynicisms in check.

Not like the rest of the gang in The Black Fox. Oh no, they laughed down my every tremble.

"Shadows out there is it? 'a course there's shadows out there, boy, it's bleeding night-time, or ain't yee noticed?"

"'fraid a the dark is you, son?"

"Leave a light on for him, Tony. Will-o'-the-Wisp be after him."

"Ha-ha-ha-ha, good one, Dicky."

"Fucking wankers!"

Brian stayed uncharacteristically quiet throughout the inquisition, unsure which side of the bar to unfurl his bedding. On the one hand he had just driven around in circles trying to unsuccessfully leave a village he'd grown up in and presumably knew as intimately as the top of Mary's head. But on the other, I was an outsider, and a flashy books-smart townie at that, with white collars, polished shoes and fingernails that didn't need trimming back with an angle grinder so he was clearly conflicted. In the event, Brian sided with the arseholes he knew rather than the arsehole he didn't as that seemed the least complicated furrow to plough despite all the misgivings that were clawing at his eyebrows.

"Don't know his elbow from a stick in shit, that one," he contributed to the collective assessment, winning guffaws and chuckles all around to cement his return to the fold. "Scaredy cat city folk, what are they like?"

"Never seen a shadow before, hey boy?"

"Not a shadow that runs," I reasserted. "That can chase you across a field," but they weren't having any of it, insisting I'd been running from bats or clouds or Zulus or something.

"Ha-ha-ha-ha, stupid townie."

Still, I'll say one thing for them, they were only too

happy to buy a man a few drinks while they insulted him, so I was able to steady my nerves with a couple of warming shots and a never empty pint pot, although The Black Fox's resident ring master, who's name I came to learn was Richard – Dicky to his friends – had scoffed the last cheese sarnie while I'd been racing with goblins across Ronnie Earlcott's field, as he liked to put it.

"Fraidy-cat townie!"

"What a dick!"

Brian, having re-established his place amongst the ranks of my persecutors, now eased off, either because he knew in his heart there was something genuinely strange going on, or because he found it harder than he thought ripping the piss out of someone he'd carouselled around the county.

"Time gentlemen please!" Mary eventually called, ringing an old brass bell at an hour that was closer to first knockings than last orders.

I still had nowhere to sleep and all talk of me spooning the night away with Brian's missus had been dropped once the gang had a new gag to knock about. Not that there was any sort of opportunity for that anymore. Brian kept himself between me and Mary at all times and had even waited until I'd slipped outside to splash my shoes before going to the toilet himself, so I might not have known where I was staying, but I most certainly knew where I wasn't.

I finished my drink and stood in the road outside The Black Fox as the rest of the gang bid each other a fond faredywell and stumbled home to their comfy warm beds. Old Dicky was one of the last to emerge, sporting a nose he could see his way home by and he gave me a formal, if slightly awkward, nod when he saw I had no place to go.

" 'night," he said, looking away before I had a chance to catch his eye and snag his couch. I watched him waddle up through the main street and take a dirt track into the trees and I wondered if I should go after him and emotionally blackmail him into putting me up. I probably could've, but I was too drunk and proud to beg these people. If they couldn't offer I wasn't going to ask, preferring instead to sleep rough; to make the meadows my bed, the grass my pillow and the stars my nightlight.

And of course, the shadowy ghost monster things my bunkmates.

"Shit!" I said, realizing I'd forgotten all about them. A night of bumpkin baiting and a bellyful of beer had jarred the experience clean from my head to leave me standing next to a church yard full of long shadows as the lights inside the pub suddenly went out.

"Hang on!" I called, taking to my toes to catch up with my chief tormentor before he could drop a front door between us. "Hang on, mate, I've got a favour to ask."

Up and down Long Fenton the lights were going out. I knew if I was so much as a second late, Dicky would have his shoes off and be feigning snoring from behind the front door as loudly as he could until I went away so I belted it up the high street, along the dirt path and up to the gate of the large thatched cottage at the end of the path, only to stop dead at the sight that met me.

Shadows swarmed all over Dicky's cottage: over his roof, his walls and his garden. They tugged at his windows, dug into his straw thatch and climbed on top of his chimney as they probed his home for a way inside, but Dicky himself was oblivious. Through the kitchen window I could see him eating a sausage roll as he examined the pots and pans on the hob for signs of edible leftovers, while jet-black hordes scurried up and down and around and around the brick and flint walls of his home.

I was frozen to the spot, unable to move for fear of

betraying my presence and yet compelled by the sheer spectacle of these ghostly apparitions. They were more or less human in form in that they had two arms, two legs and a head, but no other discernable features I could see. They were simply black, like shadows, like holes in the night, devoid of substance or detail, and that much more horrifying for it. They moved with an inhuman agility and clambered over the walls and roof as though they had nothing to fear from granite and gravity. And more than once I saw two of the figures blend as one as they scrambled over each other, only to then part as three or four in opposite directions.

I don't know how long I'd stood there at the gate. It could've only been a matter of seconds although it felt like an eternity, but now I became acutely aware of a pair of eyes staring at me.

It was Dicky.

He'd finally spotted me through the kitchen window and didn't look at all happy about it. I tried to signal him to get out of the house but what I sent obviously wasn't what was received because as seamlessly as he could, he strolled over to the light switch and flicked the kitchen lights out.

The shadows immediately went frantic, racing around the cottage and slipping through any crack they could find as though they were gaping doorways.

I watched with horror as shapes swarmed in behind the glass of every window and all at once there was a horrified scream from the pitch-black kitchen as Dicky was sucked from this life...

... and dragged kicking and bleating into the next.

vi

"They're here! They're here! They've got him!" I yelled at the top of my voice as I sprinted back along the high street and towards The Black Fox.

Curtains twitched and lights clicked back on but I didn't check my stride once, not until I'd got to the pub and was banging on its doors until my arms burned in agony.

"Open up! Open up! For the love of God, open up!"

Why I'd returned to the pub, I couldn't tell you. If these ghostly shadows had been able to slip through the keyholes and cracks of a two-hundred-year-old private residence, a three-hundred-year-old public house wasn't going to offer that much more security. I guess it was just instinctive. I'd spent most of the evening here in relative comfort and contentment so it was natural I should return to a place like this when the chips were down. Besides, if you must be snatched from this world by a horde of unstoppable shadow monsters intent on erasing you from existence, lying across the bar of a country boozer with your head under the optics was as good a place as any.

"What is it? What's all this racket about?" Brian snapped from behind the door as the sound of slippers and stairs gave way to bolts and chains.

"They're here! They're here!" I repeated breathlessly, pushing my way past Brian as soon as he had the door open and making a dash for the hard stuff.

"Oi, get back here!" Brian objected and all at once Mary was there too, doing what she could to wrestle a bottle of Cinzano from my face.

"Don't you understand, they're here. The shadows are here!" I repeated, backing away from behind the bar as voices approached from outside.

"He's barmy," Mary concluded. "Get him out of here."

Brian dragged me out from behind the bar but stopped short of slinging me into the street. Instead he plonked me onto a bar stool and poured me a glass of scotch as Ronnie, Tony Potter, Nigel Whatsisname and half a dozen other regulars turned up to take advantage of the re-opened pub.

"What be all this fuss about?"

"It's the young 'un. He be gone potty."

"No, it's Dicky," I spluttered, quaffing my scotch and gasping at the burn. "They've got him."

"Who's got him?" Tony asked, nodding at Mary to prompt her to break out a few more glasses.

"The shadows he says," Brian relayed.

"The shadows?"

"Load of nonsense," someone at the back dismissed, though I noticed he didn't leave us to it once a bottle was uncorked.

"He's playing games with us he is?"

"At this time of night!"

"No games," I insisted. "They took Dicky. They were waiting for him when he got home. He's dead!"

"Dicky's dead?"

"What's that?"

"He says Dicky's dead."

"Who says?"

"The young 'un."

"What you done to him, boy?"

"What's happened?"

"Any ice at all, Mary?"

"No no no, it weren't me, it was them. You'll see, the shadows," I warned, but all at once temperaments began to flare and accusations started flying across the pub until

Mary suggested the obvious, that someone went up to Dicky's cottage to check it out for themselves.

Which is certainly one way of stopping a heated conversation in its tracks.

Silence – ear-splitting silence.

All those old boys who'd taken so much pleasure pouring piss and wind all over my evening's traumas now took one enormous collective step back at the chance to dust off their own spines for inspection.

"Come on guys," Mary exclaimed, "someone's got to go up to Dicky's place and take a look for pity's sake. He might be hurt."

"Well, er… it's not that I don't want to, only I did tell the missus I's only be a second or so…" said one of the bottlers at the back as he quickly necked his free nightcap and slapped his feet off into the night.

"Actually, I'd probably should be going too," came the general consensus.

"For buggery's sake!" Brian eventually growled, grabbing Ronnie Earlcott, Tony Potter and one or two others who were trying to make a break for the door before they found themselves conscripted into Brian's army. "We'll go up there to check he's okay. So grab what you can and meet us in the street in two minutes."

Brian grabbed a double-barrelled shotgun from over the bar and filled it with shells from a box next to the cash register. He stuffed another couple into his pocket and bundled me out of the pub and up the street to rejoin the rest of the reluctant posse, who'd all raided their garden sheds for the war ahead.

"You stick close to me, boy," he told me.

Ronnie Earlcott didn't seem to have made the final five, for reasons known only to Ronnie Earlcott, so after a few minutes of waiting we pressed on up the road, up the dirt path, and up to Dicky's cottage, all the time with Brian

189

unsure exactly who to point his shotgun at. Me or the shadows.

The cottage was quiet and covered in flickering shapes, but these shapes were merely a line of nearby poplars filtering the half moonlight onto Dicky's thatch. The five of us stood by the gate for several seconds scouring every inch with torch-beams while Brian worked up the courage to call to him.

"Dicky! Dicky, it's Brian. Are you all right in there? Dicky, it's us!"

I looked for Dicky at the windows, hoping beyond hope that Mary and Brian were right, that I'd lost my marbles or had drunk too much this evening or had taken a bump to the head when I'd crashed my car or something. Anything. Anything other than what I knew to be the truth.

But Dicky didn't appear.

The cottage remained in gloom and nothing stirred, only the breeze in the trees and the silhouettes of Dicky's poplars dancing across the silvery thatch of his roof.

"They were there, I swear it," I whispered. "They were all over his cottage. But they… they…" I tried, but trailed off when I struggled to understand for myself what they did, never mind describe it to somebody else. Instead, I settled for a less involved explanation. "Then they… they… got him."

"Sound like a load of hokey to me," Colin Foster grumbled, though he failed to follow this up with any voluntary investigating of his own despite being the local magistrate. Instead, he just holstered his hoe, bid us all a final goodnight and headed back down the track to his own cottage before we were able to determine otherwise.

"Shouldn't one of us go and knock on his door," Jack Turner-Green suggested, twitching his yard broom at Brian and then the loaded shotgun he was carrying to give us some sort of a clue as to who he was thinking about.

Brian dillied, while the rest of us dallied, until he eventually let out a snort of frustration and pushed open the gate and headed into the breach. The lads covered him with their Ever Ready torches in case of trouble while I kept my eyes on the windows. Brian got to the door and took a deep breath. He rapped on the knocker two or three times then legged it back to us as if playing Knock Down Ginger.

Nobody answered.

"Maybe he's asleep," one of the lads suggested hopefully, but even the most conscientious of Brian's objectors had trouble buying that one with any level of conviction.

"Maybe he's out."

"Maybe he's up in his field."

Maybe. Maybe. Maybe.

Brian was sent up to knock again and despite three more loud raps on the knocker, nothing stirred inside the house.

Brian shone his torch through the letterbox and then through each of the front windows until he saw something on the kitchen floor he didn't like: pots and pans, cups and plates, knives and forks. There'd evidently been a struggle and now Dicky wasn't answering. Ghosts or no ghosts there'd been shenanigans afoot and no mistake.

Brian came back and shoved the shotgun in my face.

"Okay boy, now why don't you tell us what really happened before I blow your chuffing head off. Where's Dicky? What have you done with him?"

The boys turned on me, their accusations as blinding as their torchlights, though none shone brighter than the end of Brian's shotgun.

"I swear, honestly, on my life, I haven't laid a finger on Dicky. It was them... ... ... oh God!" I tailed off as the poplar shadows on the roof now started clambering down the sides of Dicky's cottage and towards us.

"It was what *them*?" Brian shook me.

I simply pointed.

"*Them*."

They lads spun as one but the instant they did the shadows disappeared, but only from Dicky's roof. They reappeared all around us, in the trees, down the dirt track and underneath the hedgerows, only this time I wasn't the only one to see them.

"What the bleeding buggery…"

"They's moving."

"They's all around us."

"Mary Mother of Joseph…"

The lads backed off and tried to catch a glimpse of what had started stalking us on all sides, but each time they shone their torches at the shadows, they simply melted away like quick silver, only to reappear elsewhere a moment later.

"Let's get the hell out of here!" Jack Turner-Green finally resolved, turning and bolting right through the rest of us as if we were bulrushes to be shoved aside and trampled. The shadows grew closer: twisted black fingers reached through the undergrowth to snag our loose limbs, while twisted black voices whispered hideous conspiracies to fan the flames of our terrors.

"Oh God…"

The rest of us now made a run for it, stumbling back down the dirt track and towards the high street, flashing our torchlights in all directions to clear the path of shadows, only to create infinitely more as their beams were refracted through a thousand leaves of foliage.

Brian and I were younger than the others, but even we couldn't keep pace with the old timers out front. I guess a sudden invitation to dine with the Devil can be a great leveller for most. Jack Turner-Green was a particularly sprite chicken, jettisoning slippers, yard broom and torch as he galloped for deliverance, but the shadows had him fixed in their sights and they weren't about to go hungry.

A huge black hole suddenly swept across the path from right to left, snatching Jack in mid-stride and wiping him from this earth. I heard his screams but he was gone before they were and nothing remained, save for the snap of air that collapsed back into the space he'd once occupied.

"Oh Jesus, they've got him!" Tony Potter screeched, pulling up sharply for fear of blundering through where his friend had just been.

"Keep moving! Keep going!" Nigel Whatsisname urged, slamming into the back of Tony and shoving him forwards, but it was too late; a gnarled outline stretched out a twisted claw and swiped Nigel clean through the midriff. Nigel shrieked and for a moment lost every spot of colour before splintering into a million sizzling ashes.

"No!!" Tony howled, but he too was gone before he could utter another vowel, swallowed up by the night to leave only a wisp of sulphur in his wake.

Which left just me and Brian. The shadows now moved in for the kill but Brian wasn't the sort of man to go under without a fight, no matter how utterly futile the gesture was, so he levelled the shotgun and blasted the onrushing black air as if it were solid.

For a moment the whole of the forest was lit up by the powder charge leaving the barrel and Brian and I were once again alone in the forest. The shapes returned with the night, but they seemed further back than they had been before and Brian shot again, sending lead pellets and sparks in all directions as he started emptying his pockets through both barrels of his 12-bore.

"Go go go!" he shouted as he shot and so without

fully understanding how we'd won our reprieve, we ran for our very souls.

We reached the end of the track a few moments later and tumbled out of the trees and onto our faces on the high street. Torch beams soon bathed us in white light and we looked up to see the whole village had turned out to see what all this fuss, nonsense and gunfighting was all about.

They would soon know.

vii

"Is that you shooting up there, young Brian?"

"What happened? What's going on?"

"Have you seen my Jack? Was he with you?"

But Brian was far too busy scrambling to his feet to answer any questions and I wasn't that much freer with my time either.

"Run! Run for your chuffing lives, they're coming!" Brian was at least generous enough to share this with his fellow Long Fentonians but they didn't take heed; they just stood there staring and gawping at us as we sprinted back to the brightly lit pub, scratching their heads and wondering what on Earth could be coming down the track that would make them want to run for their lives.

Screams.

"Holy Jesus, look at that?"

"What the hell..."

"Oh my God...!"

They didn't stand a chance.

I looked back, just for a moment, and saw a sight that'll stay with me for the rest of my days – and no doubt long beyond. An army of darkness swarmed out of the dirt track and from the trees on either side of the road and gobbled up the villagers as if they were blades of tinder grass caught in the updraft of a forest fire.

The villagers tried to run – they tried – but you simply can't outrun pure evil. Not without a good head start anyway. Charcoal phantoms to the left, to the right and from above dropped on them from all sides and snatched them asunder, reducing them to forgotten memories as the villagers tumbled in on each other.

Brian slotted the last two cartridges into his gun and gave the night both barrels, winning us a few more precious yards with which to make it to the pub, and we bowled wide-eyed Mary flat onto her backside as we bundled on past her, slamming the door in our wake and flicking on every light that we could find.

Ronnie Earlcott and three or four others were already inside with their feet well and truly under the table and they blinked in sync as we killed the mood lighting in favour of dazzle.

"What's happening? What's going on?" Mary tried once more, but we were not inclined to answer any questions a short spell of inactivity would answer just as emphatically. Instead we pushed the old boys out of their seats, upturned their tables against the windows and stacked chairs against doors until we had nothing left to stack.

"Brian, please just tell me, what's happening?"

"They're gone. They're all gone!" Brian finally shouted, stuffing shotgun shells into his pocket and knocking the head off a bottle of brandy to empty across two dirty glasses. We knocked them back in unison and wondered how we were still alive to see the terror in our hearts reflected back in each other's expressions.

"Who's gone?" Ronnie Earlcott asked.

"All of them," I told him. "Everyone who came with us. Everyone who's still out there. Everyone!"

The old boys still didn't seem to be able to take it all in, but none of them poo-pooed our ghost stories any more, not even the Parson, who it seemed spent more time in here than he did next door.

"Jack Green? Tony Potter? Jim Reynolds? All dead?" he sought to clarify

"Dead?" I replied, staring at the glass shards in the bottom of my brandy. "I ain't sure they got off that lightly."

Mary stared at us, her mind simply unwilling to accept the situation.

"Don't talk daft," she chided us. "It be too late at night for tomfoolery such as this."

But no one was laughing, least of all Mary when she saw we weren't joking.

"Oh sweet mercy!" she eventually broke down.

"How? What's out there?" Arthur Wilkinson asked.

I left it to Brian to answer, and he put it better than I had done earlier that evening, using just one word. "Darkness."

A couple of the old boys went to the windows and peaked out but reported nothing at the battlements.

"That's cos I's got the outside lights on," Brian said. "I don't think they likes the lights."

"Maybe they can't get through it," I went one better. "Like shadows, perhaps they can't live outside the night."

Brian nodded enthusiastically, showing his approval for my theory probably because it gave us some kind of an edge against these demons. Whether it was true or not was another matter, but they'd been held back by our torches and scared off by the shotgun flashes so there was definitely something to it.

"Mary girl, did you leave the bedroom light on?" Brian checked. "Mary?"

Mary snapped out of it after a little finger clicking and

stared at Brian.

"Did you leave the bedroom light on?"

"I think so. Do you want me to turn it off?" she replied, demonstrating just how much she'd been listening these past few minutes.

"No, in fact I want you to turn on every light in this place. And grab every lamp and torch you can lay your hands on. For tonight, this pub becomes a beacon against the night."

We did as Brian said, edging our way around the pub and turning on each light we found, but it was cautious work. We couldn't just walk into a dark room and flick on a switch because of what might've been lurking in there, so we walked a candle in front of us, holding it outstretched to ward off any waiting shadows as we felt for the sockets. And just as well we did; more than once I entered a room only to see an inky great spider race across the ceiling and out of a crack in the window to escape my candle's glare. There was no passageway nor stairwell we could take for granted.

Once The Black Fox was shimmering like a Skegness Penny Arcade, we reconvened in the bar to plan our next course of action. Old Clive stared out of the window near the snug. He still hadn't seen what was besieging us and was keen to do so, pressing his face to the glass and wrapping the curtain around himself to take a peek into the darkness outside.

"Watch yourself there, Clive," Brian advised when he saw what the old fool was doing, but when the curtain fell back Clive was gone.

"What the hell? What's happened to him?" Bob Sellers gasped.

Brian just shrugged. "He's gone," was all he replied.

Needless to say, none of us went anywhere near the windows again. We just hugged the bar towards the back of the saloon, too afraid to move, too frightened to sit still.

"The way I sees it, we just gotta get through to dawn, that's all," Brian reckoned. "What time it get light these days?"

"Sun peek up about half four," Arthur said. We checked our watches. It was almost two o'clock now, so all we had to do was sit tight for another couple of hours then presumably we'd be all right.

'Presumably' being the key word.

"You reckon there'd be anyone else left in the village?" Ronnie asked hesitantly, his mind finally turning to family and friends.

"I don't know. But if there are, I hope they've figured them out like what we have," Brian said.

"But what have we figured out?" Mary questioned. "What the hell are them things out there?"

Silence.

After a time Brian decided that one of us should set ourselves up as the resident expert on the subject and saw himself as the natural candidate for the position. "Them be shadow monsters," he told Mary with a newfound air of authority, neither illuminating her nor setting her mind at ease with his insight.

"They are a sign from God," the Parson predictably concluded, who I noticed, was called Pongo by everyone else, even to his face. Under normal circumstances I might've had the courtesy to call him Reverend or ask him his real name, but these were not normal circumstances so I called him Pongo like everyone else; something that clearly irked him at first, but what could he do when there were more spiritual things to get panicky about?

"No Pongo, they're death. And they're here for us all, even you."

We spent an unpleasant little half hour debating the nature of Brian's shadow monsters and got no closer to any answers. No one had ever seen nor heard of anything like them before and Pongo was adamant there was no mention of the phenomenon in the village chronicles housed next door in the church. They seemed to have come out of nowhere.

"What time is it?"

"Just gone half two. Only a couple more hours to go," Brian replied, almost allowing himself a small sigh of relief.

"And you're sure we'll be safe when it gets light again?"

"Pretty much. We're still here and we're safe. Them things ain't tried to get in since we switched all the lights on. Light's the key," Brian said with mounting confidence.

And that was when it happened.

That was when the electricity went out.

viii

A jaw-dropping, freight train of horror plunged through my heart as a prelude to my death, but I still managed a couple of semi-coherent thoughts, such as wondering if it had been the phantoms who'd pulled the plug on us. The truth was rather more incredible than that though, if somewhat less sinister.

"Oh my God!" Mary squawked. "The meter! It needs a shilling."

"What! You stupid bitch! Why didn't you top it up you dozy fucking…" But before Pongo could finish his sentence, a sickening demonic chorus struck up outside as our persecutors babbled their excitement at our sudden accessibility.

The old boys dug into their pockets for coins or knocked over and smashed the optics as they groped around for the cash register, but I knew from past experience that we barely had time for a short prayer, let along enough to stick a shilling in the meter, so I snatched the bottle of brandy off the bar and threw it against the nearest wall.

"A match! Quick, a match!" I shouted at the others, knocking drinks and fags and ashtrays onto the floor as I scoured the bar for a light.

Brian came to the rescue, striking a match and holding it aloft thinking I intended this to ward off our attackers, but there was no time for an explanation so I snatched it from his fingers and hurled it against the brandy-soaked wall.

A whoosh of heat and blinding flash immediately filled the saloon, and in that instant a dozen sable figures poised at our elbows recoiled against the flames. Mary instinctively dived behind the bar to escape the phantoms, but unfortunately she jumped into the one place that was sheltered from the glare and before I could call at her to get out of there, she was already gone.

Brian howled in despair when he saw what had happened and it took all of mine and Bob Seller's strength to hold him back from going on after Mary. When he finally realised it was futile, he drenched the floor behind the bar with cognac and tossed a second match on after it.

"God be with you Mary," he said, choking back the tears as a flash of yellow flames engulfed the spectres that lurked behind the pumps.

The fires chased our phantoms from the pub but this was only a temporary solution at best. Brian grabbed the last few bottles of flammable booze, but there wasn't enough to keep the darkness at bay until dawn and the heat was already popping light bulbs to ruin all hopes for restoring the electricity.

And that wasn't all.

The flames now leapt from cushions to curtains,

pictures to chairs so that as the blaze spread around the saloon our sanctuary proportionally shrank. Quickly the heat became too much to resist and after only a few more minutes we were crouching in the entrance of the pub as flames and smoke licked the licence above the doorway, curling our hairs and tanning our necks.

"Can you see them?" Brian shouted over the roar, staring out into the night at the blackness that surrounded us. "I can see them. There, they're all around."

I followed his gaze across the street and saw just beyond the flickering halo that surrounded The Black Fox, our tormentors waiting patiently for the flames to blacken to ash.

"This thing won't burn for another two hours," Brian said, edging a couple of inches further out into the street as the smoke thickened to a choking cloud of soot. "We'll have to make a run for it."

The reaction from the others was one of dismay, especially from Pongo, who was now crossing himself with such regularity that he was in danger of wearing his fingers down to the knuckles, but Brian was right and we all knew it. We couldn't stay here. And we couldn't retreat back into the pub when the flames began to recede. We'd be through the floorboards and into the cellar as soon as we set foot in the place. We had to find somewhere new to see out the night.

"The church" was the obvious suggestion, and the closest building to our current position. The glare from fire was almost reaching its walls, especially now that the top windows of the Fox were blowing out, and Pongo sealed the deal when he told us that some fifty candles still burnt inside the chapel as part of last Sunday's harvest festival thanks giving. That was the good news. The bad news was that we had to get there first. And the headstones that lay between us and the church steps cast ten feet shadows across the overgrown cemetery, like some kind of shadow monster sanctuary. It was going to be a battle every step of the way.

"Give me a hand to collect some sticks."

For all Brian's previous bullish behaviour, I had to say one thing for him; he was one of life's fighters. Where I sensed the others would've probably lain down and died, Brian simply refused to give in without knocking someone or something's teeth in. I was glad to finally have him as an ally and I sensed that, if it ever came to it, he'd be the sort of chap who'd throw himself on a grenade to save his friends.

That is, if his friends didn't push him on it first.

We pulled a dozen sticks and batons from the burning window frames, and tied them together to form crucifixes. Brian doused them with his last remaining bottle of cognac and Pongo blessed each cross before we ignited them and stepped out into the darkness looking like a delegation of Mississippi Morris Men.

Brian had the aforethought to grab one of the torches before it had been lost to the fire and he led the way, flashing its beam across every dark crevice and into the trees to scare away any lingering ambushers.

Once beyond the full glare of the pub fire we clustered closer together, keeping our backs to one another and holding out our crosses to form a circle of light through which the spectres could not penetrate. We inched across the road like this, minding our feet and watching each other's backs until we reached the churchyard wall.

"Leef rieht raef" the voices whispered to each other in the darkness. *"Yeht eelf, tub yeht tonnac epacspe!!"*

I'd been all around the world and I'd heard all manner of peculiar languages but I'd never heard anything like theirs. It wasn't human. But as with so many foreign tongues, you didn't need to know the lingo to understand the subtext. Their intentions were only too clear.

"Woh yhtrow era yeht fo eht ssenkrad!"

"Be gone!" Pongo tried to command, but his voice was cracked and hollow. The spectres cackled their response and danced ever closer to our ring of fire, taking great delight at the Parson's lack of conviction.

Brian meantime was peeking over the wall and sweating on the shadows that awaited us. He waved his cross around and zapped them with his torch, but like the heads of the Hydra, they seemed to multiply with every flashing rake.

"Burn them out!" I urged, the flames of my own wooden hex slowly dying to a blink.

Brian tossed his cross into a clump of tinder grass that bedecked the final resting place of some lucky old soul who'd already met his maker, and the whole lot went up like a belated cremation. The blaze raced through the yellow undergrowth, forcing all the shadows crouching behind the lopsided headstones to flee into the surrounding trees, so Brian and I jumped over the wall and dragged a reluctant Pongo with us as he had the keys to the church.

Obviously we were now standing in fire, but this was preferable to the alternative and we hopped and skipped through the roasting grasses, chasing them through the churchyard until we stumbled upon a flagstone path.

Behind us, Bob, Arthur and Ronnie dallied over their leap from the frying pan for so long that they missed their chance. The grasses that would've singed their ankles but protected their souls burnt out after only a few seconds and the residual smokes now doused their crosses so that suddenly they were standing on the far side of the wall clutching blackened window frames tied together with leather belts.

The spectres made their move, gliding in from behind the graves and dropping out of the trees to surround Ronnie, Arthur and Bob on all sides. There was no rush, no desperate lunge from the shadows; they had the three of them for dead and they took their sweet time over this, feeding on their terrors and prolonging their agonies for the sheer sport of it.

"Oh sweet Jesus, help us please!" Arthur bellowed above the pitiful wails of the others, but even if our Lord and Saviour could hear him above the delirious hissing of their abominable assailants, he clearly didn't fancy his chances and all at once the darkness engulfed the trio.

"God no, Billy! Get out...!!" Ronnie shouted as the shadows lapped over them, which made no sense to us, but then again none of this did. Perhaps it finally did to Ronnie. Perhaps he now knew why all this was happening. Because we sure as hell didn't.

The grasses were still burning around our ankles, so Brian grabbed me and Pongo and we ran the last dozen yards up to the church steps. Pongo got the key in the door at the third time of asking and we fell inside as the shadows retook the churchyard, smoking headstone by smoking headstone.

Brian slammed the door and bolted it, presumably just to pass the time, and the three of us backed up the aisle towards the pulpit where the cloth covered altar creaked under the weight of five carrots, a manky cauliflower and four-dozen candles. It had either been a lean year for crops or a great year for candles.

I flicked on a nearby light switch and a couple of 60 watt bulbs warmed to a glow to take the silt off the pews, but the church was still steeped in gloom. Up in the ceiling I could see our constant companions moving backwards and forwards, crawling over the beams and around and around the stained glass windows, watching our every move, but unable to come any closer because of the candles.

Brian flashed his torch up towards them, briefly scattering them to the cracks and crevices of the 800 year-old roof until I grabbed his hand to stop him.

"Better to have them where we can see them, than to have them where we can't," I reasoned. Brian thought about this for a couple of flickers then clicked off his torch. As quickly as they'd fled, they sidled back in to reoccupy the eaves, moving as silently as satin on glass and circling as closely as they dared.

"What are you?" Pongo finally asked the phantoms. "What do you want with us?"

They didn't respond; they just slithered and crawled over each other in a perpetual circuit, biding their time as our candles burnt down to milky pools. And they had some time to wait. These candles were fat white columns of wax. They'd burned since last Sunday and were only halfway through. They would easily last another two hours.

But then what?

This was the thought that now occurred to me. What did we do when the sun came up? We'd been so preoccupied simply trying to make it through the night that we hadn't even given it a thought.

"We'll get the bejesus out of here," Brian reckoned. "Get as far away from this damnable place as possible."

This sounded like a sensible plan – in theory. There was only one problem. We'd already tried that half a dozen times the previous evening.

ix

Something was holding us here. Something had stopped us from leaving. Long Fenton was a goldfish bowl with rounded sides that we could not see beyond and it had something to do with the shadows. Of that I was certain.

But what?

Pongo had spent the best part of the last hour ripping through the town chronicles for some sort of clue as to who they were but there was nothing like this anywhere in all the volumes; a few fires, a couple of harsh frosts and a man who'd been hanged for eating the proctor's daughter, but that was all. There was simply no precedent.

"Even if we make it to daybreak, if we can't leave this place we'll be right back where we are the next night," I told the others.

"But, we'll just cut across the fields or summat. We'll just go anywhere."

"I tried that, remember. We'll end up walking in circles until nightfall just like we already did."

"But, surely if we just walk in a straight line?"

Pongo reached the end of the last volume and read aloud the line that had been scribed there as recently as last week.

"*Fertiliser plant work finished. Opening soon. Richard Deekings to cut the ribbon.*" He closed the book and removing his glasses. "That was to be today. We were to have a party to mark the occasion."

"Well some of you's was, not I," grumbled Brian, still unable to bury his hatchet in spite of all that was happening. Now that was commitment to a cause for you.

And then it occurred to me.

"Do you think this has anything to do with that?" I asked, voicing niggles I'd been carrying since all this weirdness had begun without being able to put my finger on exactly what. Brian was predictably onside straight away.

"Yeah, them fuckers. They'd done been poisoning our minds or summat with their unnatural chemicals!"

"Possibly," I considered, although I still couldn't see the business angle. "But I don't think this is all in our heads. I mean people are actually dying out there."

"Or maybe we just think they are," Brian put forward.

"If you believe that, then do be my guest and blow out the candles, mate," I told him, to which Pongo jumped up in dismay.

"No please Lord, don't!"

"I ain't about to," Brian reassured him, glancing up at the increased swirling overhead as if the mere mention of blowing out the candles had stirred their black blood in their black veins – if indeed they had either. "But if it ain't in our heads, what then?"

"Perhaps it's some sort of secret government weapons programme they're cooking up. Test it on us lot before spraying it on the Russians, that sort of thing," I suggested. "Or maybe they're from outer space."

"Outer space?" Pongo repeated.

"Yeah, like from Mars or somewhere," I said. "I mean, for all we know this could be happening across the entire world, not just here. It could be an invasion from space."

"Flying fertiliser plants over from Mars?" Brian asked, unwilling to consider anyone else to blame now that I'd mentioned the fertiliser plant.

"No I don't mean the aliens are from the fertiliser plant, I mean..." I started to explain, only to be interrupted by a fourth voice from the far end of the nave that saw me almost stacking it across the candles.

"You can't hide from something in the light," he said from the gloom of the baptistery, drawing all eyes, natural and unnatural upon himself. For a moment I couldn't see who'd said this, but then he spoke again and stepped forward. "You can only blind yourself from the truth."

When he stepped into the light I saw that he was a

little red-headed boy, aged no more than about eight. Brian and Pongo seemed to know him at once and stared in open-mouthed horror, their expressions a mirror of one another's.

"Alex? How is this so?" Pongo finally asked.

"How do you think?" Alex replied, taking another couple of steps towards us until he was only a few feet away. His appearance was dark, darker than it should've been, as if he was a mere projection shone against a burnt figurine.

"Are you real?" Brian barely dared to ask, his voice a whisper in a quake.

Alex blinked. "As real as you are."

"Who is he?" I asked, aware that I was a chapter or two behind the others as far as Alex was concerned.

"It's Alex," Brian replied, recapping the facts so far.

Pongo went a little further with his explanation. "Alexander Earlcott, Ronnie's son," he said as if introducing the two of us at a village fete. Alex turned to look at me and Pongo added, "He's dead".

A few years earlier Alex had been playing with matches in the hayloft of Ronnie's summer barn when he'd started a blaze that engulfed himself, his four-year-old cousin, Jacob, and four horses in the stables below. He had been warned about playing with matches time and time again but fire was his fascination. He simply couldn't help himself. This is how everyone knew what had happened despite finding only cinders and ashes and their shoes outside. It had been a tragedy that had tipped Ronnie over the edge and one of the reasons he'd sold his land to the fertiliser plant with barely a backwards glance; no one to hand it on to – too painful to keep. And once Ronnie had sold up, the others had quickly followed.

That had been four years ago. Yet here he was, standing before us large as... well, perhaps not life, but he was here all the same.

"Are you a ghost?" Brian asked the obvious.

"Are you?" he replied.

"What do you mean? I don't know what you mean. Alex, please just tell us, what's going on?" Brian pushed, figuring if anyone knew, a spooky long dead arsonist kid might know.

"Don't you remember?" Alex simply said.

"Remember what?" Brian replied.

"Remember what you did?"

Brian looked at me and Pongo for clues, but we had no more answers than Alex. "What did I do?" he asked once more.

"You will remember," Alex told him. "When the time comes, you will remember what you did."

Alex now looked at me and stared without blinking. "You are John Coal."

"You know me?"

"You shouldn't be here," he said. "This is not your destiny."

It was an odd thing to say, but then again he was an odd boy. In an odd village. Invaded by odd shadow monsters. But it did get me wondering if there was an angle here I'd not explored.

"Will you let me go then?"

"I'm not holding you here, John. You are the only one who is doing that."

"How am I doing that?"

"By not leaving," he said.

I was caught in two minds as to whether to say a rosary for him or put him over my knee and spank him back to the grave but in the end I bit my tongue and pressed the point.

"And how exactly do I leave?"

"The same way you arrived. It is your way back," he

said, which was just gobbledegook designed to frustrate me no doubt. I'd tried every route out of here the night before, including the track back up to my car on the main road and I'd ended up standing in the centre of Long Fenton every single time.

"Alex," Pongo now said, stooping to rest on one knee in front of him.

"Yes Pongo?" he replied with the merest hint of a smirk. Even in death Pongo would be Pongo. Good to know that even shadow monsters had a sense of humour. The Parson composed himself and asked the question he had to ask.

"Are you with God?"

"Are you?" came back his inevitably evasive reply.

Pongo thought about this and mentally flipped a coin. "Yes. Yes, I am."

Alex thought otherwise. "Those with God do not seek answers. They already have them."

Alex's smirk now broadened to a thick malicious grin and he laughed a childish laugh. In a night of heart-stopping horrors, it was probably one of the most horrifying.

Then there was a blinding flash and Alex suddenly burst into flames. He screamed in agony as he burned in front of our eyes and his death howls went on for an unbearable eternity until he stopped stock-still and glared at us in a fury.

"I burn! You all *buuuuurnnnnn!!!!!*"

A gust of hot wind knocked us onto our backs and Alex disappeared into pall of smoke as his angry squall raced around the church, knocking over pews and ripping the light fixtures from the ceiling until he finally hit the alter...

... and extinguished every candle in the church.

x

We were plunged into darkness and flat on our backs for the taking, but Brian had foreseen the oncoming trickery and was ready for the onslaught, cutting through a swarm of descending demons with his Ever Ready scythe and bellowing at the blackness to bring on its worst. But Brian couldn't protect us all. Not with a single beam. And it was too late to relight the candles and too blustery with Alex still racing around the place to strike a match. If we stayed where we were we had just seconds to live so I ran. Blindly. Anywhere. More or less in hope than expectation. I ran.

I crashed over pews, knocked into stone pillars and slipped on carrots as howls of alien derision rang out all around me but I didn't stop. Not for a moment. Not for a second. Somewhere far behind me Pongo was going out with a few lines from *"The Lord is my shepherd"* which was his prerogative but I wasn't about to lie down in green pastures for anyone, let alone the bungling lookout who'd let this many wolves into the paddock, so I entrusted my soul to my own two feet and thrashed through the darkness until I clattered into the front doors. There was no time to think, barely enough time to act, so I yanked back the bolt and pushed open the doors, only to be dazzled by the first few blistering rays of dawn. The sun was only just poking up through the trees behind the smoking shell of the pub, but it was enough to obliterate the shadows at my elbow and flood the nave with light.

Brian battled his way through the spectres and towards me but Pongo was all out of fight and consumed before he could lie to himself that he would *"fear no evil"*, leaving just me and Brian to discover what the new day had brought.

"We made it! Buggered if I know how but we made it, by fuckery!" Brian puffed, clutching his sides and looking back at the inky hobgoblins as they hissed their indignation at us from inside Long Fenton's God forsaken house of worship. "We bloody done made it."

We stayed on the church steps for another hour basking in the sun's early glow and watching the shadows recede all across the village. I had hoped the new day might've banished the shadows entirely but they lingered in the trees, under bushes and in the chapel behind us, watching us from the murk and biding their time for when they next had the run of the streets. Well I wasn't about to hang around that long. I had eighteen or so hours of daylight to figure out what Alex had been getting at and I planned to use every last one of them to escape this accursed place or at the very least die trying. There had to be a way. I just had to find it.

"We'll take my truck, head out on the Ullerton road and then hike up to Tom's old windmill. It be the highest point around and looks out across the whole country. If there's a way out, we'll see it from up there," Brian reasoned, rising to his feet and offering me his hand.

"Okay," I agreed, "let's go."

We walked through the charred grounds of the churchyard and flashed Brian's torch under the wheel arches of his battered old truck until we were satisfied we weren't carrying any unwanted passengers, then set off.

The route looked different in this early light and I dared get my hopes up that something might have changed in the night. It had – but in a way neither me nor Brian could've foreseen. Not even in our worst nightmares.

Just beyond the village the road was blocked by a staggered queue of traffic. It looked as if the entire population had tried fleeing, only to be stopped in their tracks some unseen obstacle. What's more, the ground was littered with dead. They lay in the road, filled the ditches or sat behind their steering wheels, stone dead with their feet on the pedals of their stalled vehicles.

We got out of the truck and stared at the decaying tailback, horrified and confused at the grim gridlock ahead. What's more, we knew the dead on sight

"There's Dicky Deekings," Brian pointed. "And his missus. And Arthur, and Ronnie, and Colin. What the hell's going on here?"

We walked the length of the devastation, feeling pulses and checking each body, but they were not only dead, they were cold and dead. Whatever had happened here had happened some time ago.

"But they were taken by the shadows, we saw 'em," Brian said. "Why did they bring 'em here? Like this?"

None of the dead looked as if they'd been savaged by beasts or burned in any way, other than having the life snuffed out of them. Their lips were pale and their eyes glassy, and a couple had sick down their chins, suggesting some kind of poison was responsible, but nothing like this had happened the previous evening. It didn't make sense.

Brian gave a short howl when he found Mary, lifeless as all the others, in a tangle of thorns opposite her car. It looked like she'd fallen into them while trying to flee and died caught up and terrified amongst the barbs. Brian cut his face and shredded his hands pulling her free, but he seemed oblivious to the pain. He just cradled his one-time intended in his arms and rocked back and forth saying sorry over and over again as the tears rolled down his cheeks.

"Brian, she's dead. We have to leave her," I said, adding, "she won't mind," when he balked at the suggestion.

"She was my baby," Brian explained, and it was clear

that he dearly loved her; despite knowing the whole village child-minded for him whenever he was in the fields.

"We've got to go," I just said again, holding out my hand for him just as he had for me back at the church.

Brian insisted on finding a blanket to cover Mary over with, but settled for a tarpaulin when he couldn't find any blankets. He plucked a couple of wild flowers for her hair, kissed her on her cold dead lips and said a sad farewell. Then he got to his feet.

"That be done then," he said with a renewed grit between his teeth. "Now let's get out of here."

We walked to the head of the line of cars and found Pongo's old Morris Ten wrapped around a sycamore tree, with Pongo himself wrapped around the steering wheel inside. He'd clogged the road for everyone else, but from the looks on their faces, they wouldn't have got far anyway.

Thirty yards away in the treeline the shadows were stalking us, matching us step for step, happy just to watch as we made our discoveries.

"Rebmemer! Rebmemer! Rebmemer!" they chattered from all sides, and I suddenly realised what they were saying. *"Remember,"* so I wracked my brains tried to remember what it was I had forgotten – the crash? The old stone marker? The dirt track into the village? The Black Fox? – but it wasn't until we got to the fertiliser plant that I realised they weren't speaking to me at all. They were speaking to Brian.

Another body lay in the grass. Another corpse. He lay by a hole in the perimeter fence, clutching wire cutters and a pick-axe and even though he was face down away from us, we both recognised him immediately.

It was Brian.

"What be going on?"

He looked at his own lifeless body and then at the

plant where a column of yellow steam was rising into the morning's air and then he looked at the phantoms taunting him from the shadows.

"Rebmemer! Rebmemer! Rebmemer!" they chuckled. *"Rebmemer!"*

"I remember," Brian finally said. "Yes. I remember now."

Brian turned to me and told me to go, to get back to my car and go. This was not the place for me.

"What is it? Brian, what happened here?"

"I did this," was all he would say, almost concussed with shock. "I did all of this."

Way off down the road Alex stood in the sunshine and stared at us. He'd come to see Brian remember, and now that he had, he turned and walked back to Long Fenton, satisfied that he wouldn't be the only one to burn there forever after past misdeeds.

"You have to go," Brian now insisted. "I can't come with you. You have to go. Go on, go now!"

I still didn't understand any of this, or why Brian couldn't come with me. Perhaps he was stuck here by some kind of black magic or perhaps he just wanted to stay to decorate his own hair with daisies, either way I was now on my own and I didn't like it.

"Where? Where do I go? How do I get out of here?" I asked.

"Back to Long Fenton. Back the way you came in. When the time comes, you too will remember," Brian told me before taking a step towards the trees.

"Wait, wait, what the hell are you doing?" I said, grabbing him by the elbows to drag him back.

"I have to go with them. It be my fate," he replied, before holding out a hand for me one last time. "God be with you for yours, John."

I knew his mind was set and that there was no

dissuading him. Never before had I met such a headstrong young butterball so I let him go. He crossed the road, jumped the ditch and walked up the short embankment to the line of trees. He turned, just briefly, one last time to wave goodbye and then stepped into the trees.

The shadows surrounded him instantly and welcomed him back to their fold, moving around him in ever decreasing circles but in no rush to snatch him away. Brian didn't look scared, he just looked sad, and as they caressed his face with their willowy fingers, he shut his eyes and resigned himself to his fate.

"I be ready," he said and they dived into him, swamping him with their darkness and snatching him through the very fabric of existence to a place of eternal night.

Which left just me.

xi

I did as Brian said and took the road back into the village. All was now quiet. The shadows were still with me but their vicious babbling had stopped. They merely bided their time, watching me from the thick undergrowth as the sun inched its way across the warm summer's sky.

I tried to remember what Brian and Alex had said, that when the time came I would know how to leave and it would be by the same way I'd come in, but this seemed impossible. The dirt track back to the main road was lined by trees and overhung by a thick canopy of foliage, allowing the spectres to move freely about these shadows. To set one foot on that path would've been to hand myself up to these fiends and I didn't trust Brian or Alex's vague assurances enough for that.

Yet this was the way I'd come into Long Fenton and

both of them had told me it was my way out. But I just couldn't see how.

I lingered in the village centre next to the stone cross outside the church and tried to formulate a plan in case inspiration didn't strike before nightfall. The Black Fox was burnt out, the church was already bubbling with evil and every cottage and barn looked like certain death. There was simply no shelter to be had.

There was also no food. If I'd been able to get into one of the houses I might've found some bread or ham or something but as it was I had nothing. An apple tree stood nearby in the ruins of The Black Fox, but the apples were withered and rotten on the branch. The same went for the plums on the plum tree behind the church. Nothing lived in this village. Only me.

Every now and then I saw Alex skipping amongst the graves. I tried to approach him but he would just run away, only to reappear half an hour later in the trees or amongst the wreckage of The Black Fox, dancing, skipping and singing to himself as if I wasn't there. In the end I let him be and just watched him play, but each time he appeared, he would remind me that the day was passing so that by the time the church's shadow stretched clean across the street, I knew my course was almost run.

The spectres once again began taunting me as their hour approached. It was the same old backwards gobbledegook and although I didn't fully understand exactly what they were saying, I got the general gist.

"Ruoy luos si srou Nhoj Laoc. Ew lliw evah uoy!" and so on.

"Go fuck yourselves!" I responded, figuring I couldn't do myself any more harm than they had in store for me. At least I'd figured that until they started replying:

"Og kcuf flesruoy!"
"Og kcuf flesruoy!"

"Og kcuf flesruoy! Og kcuf flesruoy! Og kcuf flesruoy!"

They shouted this at me, over and over again, from all sides, non-stop, laughing and cackling their derision until I had to cover my ears.

This had to be hell. It was the only explanation. My wrong doings had finally caught up with me. All that was missing was my father stepping out of the ground to tell me how proud he was of me.

Oh God, what had I done with my life?

Little by little my persecutors began to leave the trees, stepping out into the open, off the grass and into the road as the lengthening shadows stretched out towards me. Only now did I see them in their full glory. As I said, they were human in form, with arms, legs and a head, but nothing else, no other obvious signs of humanity, save for the odd indentation where a normal soul might have kept their eyes or mouth. They were smooth all over and as black as tar, only they didn't reflect the light as tarred surfaces might, they sucked it in so that they were less solid beings, more holes in the shadows where the souls of long departed sinners had once existed.

They reached and swarmed over the church's stone marker and were soon within smiting distance of me as dusk settled across the village. The sun was behind the trees to the west and only a few shrinking pockets of light remained between me and eternal damnation. I tried to meet my destiny head on as Brian had done with dignity and strength, but my cowardly default setting kicked in every time to spoil the moment.

This was it. This was the end of my road.

But then I'd thought that before and I'd found my way out of tighter scrapes than this and so it was to be again. For this was my moment. This was my time to leave. Just beyond the shadows of the church Alex was playing hopscotch with a pebble. He hopped and skipped across a charcoal grid and then back again, only to suddenly stop and look over at me. It was the first time he'd acknowledged me all day and I recognized the significance. I looked to the dirt track I'd been watching and at last saw my way out.

It was as clear as day.

I suddenly remembered.

It was my way back to the world.

The sun, having sunk beyond the trees in the west, now shone directly through the arcade of overhanging branches, like a light at the end of a tunnel. This was how it had been when I'd first blundered into Long Fenton twenty-four hours earlier and it momentarily vanquished all the shadows from the dirt track. I sprinted towards the sun, praying for all my wretched soul was worth that I'd not end up back outside The Black Fox again, and the demons swiped and spat their fury at me as I stumbled and bumbled my way back to the main road.

"Uoy tonnac epacse! Ew lliw dnif Uoy!" they snarled as I passed, but try as they might they could not reach me and I reached the end of the track to find the road I'd lost the day before.

I could've wept with joy as I stood there basking in the last few rays of twilight but my celebrations were cut short when I noticed the car I'd left in the ditch. As I drew closer I saw the car wasn't empty as it should've been. There was someone in the driver's seat.

It was me.

I looked down at myself through the shattered windscreen and wondered how this was going to affect my no claims bonus, only to be startled by the banshee screams of a thousand hurtling demons as the sun now vanished beneath the horizon.

Alex shouted at me from beyond the track to: "Go back! Go back the way you came!" and I just about dodged the first of a forest of claws by tumbling in on myself, through the windscreen, through the car...

... and through myself.

xii

"Come back to us mate! Come back!"

"Okay, that's it, we've got him. 1cc of Atropine and increase the oxygen."

"Can you hear me, mate? Can you hear me?" a voice kept asking somewhere beyond a blinding white light. "Can you respond? What's your name?"

The light finally moved away from my eyes and a man in a blue shirt clicked off a little torch and slipped it into his top pocket before asking me again; "Can you say something?"

"Like what?" I spluttered, choking on the words as if my throat were full of sandpaper, which wasn't necessarily beyond the realms of possibilities.

"Good enough," the man smiled and beyond him several others voiced their approval.

"What's your name, mate?" the man now asked.

"John... John Coal..." I coughed, suddenly aware that every inch of my body was in agony.

"Well John, I'm Phil, okay. Now listen to me, you've been in an accident, but you're okay. You're in an ambulance and we're going to get you to hospital so stay with us and don't go back to sleep, okay?"

Phil's mate said something about me having a weird blood type, which wasn't the half of it, and he hooked me up a bag of plasma to keep me going. Phil now locked down the stretcher to stop me rolling about in the back of the ambulance and thanked the assembled yokels who'd dragged me from the wreckage of my Cortina and phoned

999, then he pulled the backdoors closed as his pal got us underway.

They even sounded the siren just for good measure and I realised with a heavy heart that try as I might I would be spending the night in Lincoln in spite of my best efforts. But then again I guess that's just what happened when you came to Lincolnshire.

"You should be careful on these roads, mate," Phil advised, some might argue a smidgeon too late. "Treacherous they are. Deadly."

"Get away," I tried to reply but it was lost to the oxygen mask.

"That stretch where you crashed, that's particularly bad that is – a right black spot. Claimed dozens of lives over the last twenty years, it has," my cheery ambulanceman said, and it was a wonder he didn't take out his torch and hold it under his chin for his next snippet of trivia. "It almost had you an' all, it did. You know, you were officially dead for almost a minute back there. Oh yes, if we hadn't got to you when we had, you would've been just another statistic, you would've , mate. You're a lucky boy, you know that?

"A lucky, lucky boy."

CHAPTER 6:
AND THEN THERE WAS ONE

"I spent the next couple of nights in Lincoln County General just to get my strength back, but as soon as the nurses weren't looking I did a bunk, wheelchair and all."

"Why?" asked Colin, unable to take his eyes off the shadows that hung all around us.

"I had to, full moon was on its way so I had to get out of there and back home to my basement before I hurt anyone," I explained, taking a puff on my pipe and noticing it had turned stone cold again. I tapped it on my oil drum to knock the ash out and looked for my baccy pouch, refilling it, lighting it and savouring its flavours. "Ahh, nothing like a good shag," I sighed, prompting the kids to burst out laughing for some unknown reason. "What? What's so funny about an old man enjoying a good shag?" I asked, but none of them could breathe any more, let alone speak. "Bloody kids!"

When they were over the worst of it, Barry wiped the tears from his eyes and asked me what had happened to everyone at Long Fenton. "Were they real or were they ghosts like?"

"Bit of both," I replied, standing up to shake the cramp from my legs before picking a faded newspaper cutting off a pinboard over my workbench. "There, read that."

Tommy snatched it from me, though there weren't many details to the cutting

"SITE TO BE REDEVELOPED" it read and went on to describe how a holiday complex was to be built in the remote Lincolnshire countryside. At the end of the piece it said: "... the areas to be developed include the derelict village of Long Fenton, which was evacuated following a chemical spill in 1951 by the then newly built Connaught Watson Processing Plant. The plant closed in 1984 and this site will also be redeveloped."

"That don't say nothing about no monsters killing no one," Tommy objected, waving my cutting in my face. "See, he's full of shit, he is, *facking* shadow monsters and all that."

"People did die," I insisted, "about twenty families, but they died because a brash young man broke into a plant and smashed a load of pipes not knowing that this plant also made pesticides, not just fertilisers, and he poisoned the whole village with his folly."

"So what were the shadow monsters?" Farny asked, unable to join the dots for himself.

"I dunno, but I reckon they were from hell," I said, giving them my best scary guess as I stamped my feet and rubbed my buttocks to kill the pins and needles that were now eating away at my legs. The kids stayed where they were, four-square on my old knackered sofa and showed not a flicker of discomfort. Oh to be young and supple again. "No see, I woke them up I did, by stumbling into town like that when I had my crash. Well, not me, but my spirit like. And them old demons, well they came up from hell and dragged them all back down again."

"But why?" Farny persisted.

"I don't know. I ain't no expert. Perhaps the place gets reawoken every time a new soul wanders into it. Perhaps it even acts as a magnet for new souls. Judging from all the accidents on the roads around it, I wouldn't be surprised, but either way I reckon that weren't the first time Brian and his mates slugged it out with the shadow monsters, and I reckon it won't be the last either. The poor lost souls."

"But this happened in 1951," Tommy said, snatching

up the cutting and unscrewing it to nail my bullshit to the wall. "And you said it happened to you in 1975. You're a liar."

"No, don't you see," Colin interjected on my behalf, "they were ghosts. It was still in the past, but it happened then too, like when all them Roman soldiers walked through that building site in my brother's ghost book. Remember?"

But Tommy didn't remember and he didn't want to. He wanted me to be a "dirty old liar" and so that's what I was. At least, that's what I was to him. To the others however I was a man who'd had a near-death experience and who'd returned with tales of ghosts and demons to show for it.

Of the kids before me, I wondered who was the more satisfied?

"But that don't say nothing about no one dying from no chemical leak either, it says they was all evacuated," Tommy continued to nit-pick, despite losing the popular vote some time ago.

"Of course, it were covered up at the time. Too much money involved. Can't sell carrots to the public when they've been sprayed with the same stuff that's wiped out a whole village. Oh no," I said, trying to take my cutting back from Tommy, but unable to without it ripping because Tommy was purposely pulling on the other end. "If you don't mind," I asked politely, but a smile spread across Tommy's face and he would've torn my cutting had I not picked up the Browning off the floor to remind him who ran this basement.

"If you don't mind," I reiterated, this time a little more insistently.

Tommy relinquished both the cutting and the smile and slumped back in the sofa to sulk. Barry, Colin and Farny all looked at their brethren disapprovingly, as if to say, "what was all that about?"

"No, so the Government covered it up, records were lost and the village was boarded up and forgotten about for half a century, that was until Mickey Mouse bought the land," I said.

"Mickey Mouse?"

"Well, whoever them holiday people were, log cabins, nature trails and waterslides and all that. Ain't no place for that sort of malarkey," I lamented, although the real reason I disapproved was because they'd moved all the graves from the churchyard, including Alex's. I'd gone back there once every few years since my accident to plant fresh flowers around his headstone, only to find it had become a bike shed at some point in 2003. Nobody seemed to mind except me and I was pointed in the direction of Lincoln's municipal cemetery where they'd all been reinterred, but I never went up there to see Alex because Alex weren't there, just his old bones. And bones don't make a person.

It's a soul that does that.

I looked at my watch. It was coming up to midnight and I figured I'd kept the boys here long enough to learn their lesson. Farny, Colin and young Barry I could tell were good kids at heart and seemed to have enjoyed my old stories so I didn't think I'd have any more bother with them, but Tommy was another matter. He was the rotten apple in their barrel and the ugly fly in my ointment. No amount of ghoulish horror stories would ever reach him because he was a horrible kid. Some people say there's no such thing as a horrible kid, that it's all down to the parents, and this does have some merit, but only to a point. Some kids have it harder than most and become the best amongst us. And some have it easiest and become the dregs. I think we should give our caterpillars a little more credit for the butterflies they become and not defer entirely to God, Darwin and video games.

My own little girl was a case in point. She'd had a terrible start in life and the worst of all mothers, yet she'd overcome the most formidable of obstacles to turn into an angel. How I admired her for that. How she had saved herself with her choices. And no one had dictated these to her. She'd done it by herself.

The boys were finally starting to shift in their seats and I told them it was all right, they could go home if they liked.

"About bloody time! Sitting here all *facking* night!" Tommy predictably snorted, but the others were more gracious and thanked me for my stories, and in Colin's, case even apologised for breaking into my home in the first place.

"That's okay, Colin. We all make mistakes. I just didn't want you boys putting yourselves in the way of harm, that's all," I explained, opening a drawer in my work desk and dropping my Browning inside. I saw Tommy's eyes lingering on these actions so I figured I'd better head off the inevitable break-in by getting it out again and pulling the trigger. A little flame appeared at the end of the barrel and Tommy's face turned to thunder.

"It ain't even real?"

"Of course it ain't. You think I'd point a real gun at kids? What sort of a man do you think I am?" I asked, causing Tommy to swear all the colours of the rainbow while the others giggled with delight, partly at their own relief and partly at Tommy's ignominy. "Go home, go to bed, it's gone midnight already," I told them.

Tommy duly stormed off, only to return a minute later when he saw that none of his mates had gone with him. They'd become waylaid by some of the more obscure objets d'art I kept around the basement, such as my mouse crossbow, which I used for killing (not arming) mice, and my Seeing Eye mirror, which could tell the future of all those who looked into it, yet had failed to forewarn me I was about to waste £25 when I picked it up at a clairvoyant's closing down sale.

"Here, have some old bullets," I said, making the lads a present of a handful of old .22 shell casings I'd collected up off the heath after the pest controller had done his yearly rabbit cull a week earlier.

"Were they from the war?" Farny gasped, his imagination whizzing over enemy bunkers and into chests of advancing stormtroopers, so I decided not to disappoint him.

"They were from the Battle of Conning Heath; sixty brave souls met their maker in just one day's fighting, defending a series of command tunnels from a single enemy sniper (and each had big teeth and floppy ears). Remember their sacrifice, boys."

Farny clutched the casings lovingly to his chest and promised me he'd eBay them as soon as he got home, whatever that meant, and so I wished them a goodnight once more but still they wouldn't bugger off. Unfortunately I'd already shown them that my Browning was only lethal if used over about forty years and in conjunction with fags so I could scarcely go chasing them off with it, so in the end I asked if there was anything else on their minds.

"Yeah, come on you twats, I wanna go home!" Tommy snapped, unintentionally siding with me in a moment of non-thinking. It was Barry who finally spoke up and asked the question they'd all been reluctant to leave without asking.

"The coffin upstairs. Is it a real coffin?"

Oh yes my bait; the coffin I'd placed in the front room to lure them into my trap. It had obviously done the trick because even now, given the chance to leave, they still had to know what was inside it.

Or rather who.

"It looked like a girl," Barry said.

"It was," I told them. "That's Rachel."

"Who's Rachel?" Colin pressed.

"She… well, she came to me for help, so I took her under my wing... so to speak."

"Is she dead?" asked Farny.

"Alas yes, quite dead," I admitted.

"More bullshit!" Tommy butted in. "For a start I saw her moving, so she ain't dead, she's just of his mates mucking around. And for another thing he wouldn't just have her in his house if she was dead, would he? He'd have to bury her, wouldn't he, so there."

"Well, for a start, I haven't got any mates, I think we've already established that," I responded, answering each of Tommy's points in turn. "And for another, she *is* dead, but I can't bury her because like I told you, she came to me for help and so that's what I'm doing, I'm helping her."

"Helping her? Helping her do what, stink out the place?" Tommy hawed, still unable to see he was alone with his cynicism. The others were only too keen to hear and believe what I had to say, so I took them upstairs and invited them to gather around for a look.

"This is Rachel. She doesn't like to be disturbed."

I barely touched the lid before there was a sudden violent knocking from inside, making them all leap back in fright – including Tommy, who leapt the furthest I noticed.

"See! She moved, she ain't dead, he's a *fackin'* liar," Tommy rallied, but nobody flocked to his banner, particularly when I told them the reason Rachel was still able to move despite being dead.

"She's a vampire."

"Of course she is!" Tommy raspberried, but as far as

the others were concerned, I might as well have pulled out a red suit and black boots and told them I was Father Christmas.

"A vampire? A real vampire? You've got a vampire?"

"Please, tell us…" Barry implored, barely able to find the words, so I sat them all down (bar one, who refused to sit, yet also refused to leave) and looked upon my poor dear Rachel's casket.

She'd turned to me for help alright.

All the people in all the world and she'd turned to me.

And so for more than thirty years now, that's what I'd tried to do.

PART 4:

LIKE MOTHER LIKE DAUGHTER

A few years after I'd escaped Long Fenton and had returned to some semblance of a life, I came home after a less eventful business foray to discover a new smell in my home. As I may have mentioned I have a particularly good sense of smell, even when I'm not transformed, and I smelt something unusual in the basement straight away. It smelt like freshly turned earth, only freshly turned earth that seemed to be able to move about under its own volition, so I dug out my most powerful torch and peeped into the basement as carefully as I dared.

I couldn't see anyone at first, but a voice called up to tell me I was looking in the right place.

"Yes, I'm down here," she said. "Please come down. I can't come up."

"Who are you?" I demanded, ditching my torch in favour of a kitchen knife now that I knew it wasn't one of them shadow monsters who'd tracked me down.

"I'm Rachel. I've come to see you. I want your help."

"My help?" I asked, unwilling to accept this as any sort of guarantee for my safety. "How did you get in? Why didn't you knock on my door like normal people do?"

"Because I'm not like normal people. And neither are you, John Coal," she replied with a knowing hint.

As much as this was true, it still didn't answer who she was or what she knew about me, so I told her I was phoning the police if she didn't step out and show herself immediately. "This game's gone on long enough," I warned her. "This is private property and you are trespassing."

"I must say, for a werewolf you're something of a dick," Rachel observed, fairly stopping me mid-bluff.

"What did you just say?" I whispered, scarcely loud enough for myself to hear let alone Rachel down in the basement. But Rachel replied all the same, proving beyond doubt that she was indeed not like normal people.

"I said you're a werewolf. You are John Coal, heir to Tran Van Khan, and one-time Strangler of the Fens, nomad of the dusk and fugitive of the keepers of darkness. Oh yes, I know you John Coal. Now come down here at once because I want to see you for myself."

I wavered for a few more seconds, even more concerned and confused than ever before realising I had no choice. I could've done a runner, but Rachel didn't sound like the sort of girl I'd get very far from, so I slipped the kitchen knife into my pocket and started down the steps.

"Could you close the door as you come please?" Rachel asked, so I pulled it shut behind myself and inched my way into the basement, keeping my back firmly to the brickwork at all times.

Rachel didn't try to hide or surprise me; she was stood across the basement against the far wall smiling politely.

"Hello John. It's great to finally meet you in person," Rachel beamed, looking genuinely happy to be saying these things.

She appeared no more than about twelve-years-old, but her skin was pale and dirty, so it was difficult to tell. She had shoulder-length curly hair that might've once been auburn underneath all the dirt and grease but now it just looked black and lifeless. And she wore an old Victorian nightgown, which just about covered her grubby toes. The gown was white in theory but again like Rachel herself, it was clearly no fan of soap and water.

She was also stone cold to the core and smelt of freshly turned earth.

"Hello," I responded, unable to reply with a smile just

yet but sensing this was no time to lose my manners.

"I've come a long way to meet you," Rachel told me, as if this would jog a hug out of me.

"I can see that," I didn't doubt for a second.

"I'm not going to hurt you," she promised. "I just couldn't come upstairs, that's all. It's too light for me up there."

"Oh," I agreed, as if this was a perfectly acceptable explanation. A dozen questions bounced around my head, but none of them felt like stepping forward to be voiced, so in the end I asked her how it was going.

"Fine thank you," Rachel smiled. "We have a mutual friend in Alex Earlcott. He told me about you."

"Are you a ghost then?" I asked.

"No, a vampire," she replied.

"Ah, even better," I blinked.

"You can relax, I've given you my word," Rachel assured me once again. "Besides, take it from me, werewolf blood is *not* nice."

At this, I almost laughed – almost but not quite, because in order to know this, she must've surely tasted werewolf blood. And today didn't feel like the sort of day for upsetting little girls who could take down werewolves.

"Okay Rachel," I nodded. "How may I help you?"

It seemed Rachel had been a vampire for about seventy years now, which in vampire terms, isn't actually that old. The chap who'd originally turned her had been over five hundred years and counting at the time, so in both vampire years and physical years, Rachel was still a kid, despite being older than my long-dead dad in real terms.

Anyway Rachel was a pretty successful vampire, surviving happily on the streets of London and feeding regularly. I think her appearance helped her considerably because she was able to play the little-girl-lost card and lead all manner of good Samaritans off down dark alleyways, but after a while the psychological effects of looking like a gormless kid when she was actually an octogenarian started to get the better of her. Rachel found she was being more and more brutal, particularly towards young women and teenage girls – girls who had what she didn't, the ability to grow into women. It's funny, but if Ulay could bottle what Rachel had, I bet they'd sell a jar of it to every girl on the planet. But I'd predict just as confidently that they'd sell two of the antidote forty years later.

Rachel had descended into a spiral of unnecessary violence and this made her feel worse about herself, which would then lead to more violence. She knew she had to break the cycle but she couldn't do it on her own. She needed help.

Years of unhappiness passed into years of anger until one night she heard about a werewolf who would shut himself away every full moon and who had successfully managed not to kill anyone for more than ten years. Surely this was a beast after her own heart wasn't it? She had to meet him.

"But there's a difference," I told her, now sat a little more comfortably beside her on the steps. "I can take food as a man to sustain myself. And when the hunger pains get too much, I can buy myself an animal to eat if I need to make a kill – a goat, or maybe ten or twelve chickens if I really want to make a night of it. But surely you can – and must – only drink blood, if I've got this whole vampire deal right. Therefore you have to continue doing what you're doing to survive."

"No, I need to keep feeding. But in theory, I don't ever actually need to kill anyone. Not if I can get their blood voluntarily."

"Right," I pondered. "So how does that work?"

"Well it doesn't obviously," Rachel giggled. "But that's the theory."

"Okay," I said, scratching my head and wondering just how generous the neighbours around here were. None of the bastards had parted with a cup of sugar when I'd gone door to door the previous year. "Okay, let's talk measures."

Rachel needed just two pints a month in order to survive, but that was bare survival rations. In a perfect world where everyone walked around with cannulas in their necks, Rachel would've taken just a couple of pints a night, but people didn't give it up that easily and to take anything more than a pint or two from someone by biting them would be to infect the victim, so she killed when she attacked not just to feed, but to protect her territory. This meant in practice that she was making two or three kills a month and resting up in-between, which was an average rate for an experienced predator like Rachel, but every now and then she'd become consumed with rage after watching Pans People on the telly and her numbers would skyrocket.

"I shouldn't behave like that, and I'm always mortified afterwards, but I can't help myself. I just get so angry and lonely and scared some times, and before I know it I've done something I shouldn't," Rachel shrugged with genuine heartache. "I guess I'm just an emotional girl." Which was not only a contender for understatement of the year, it was also possibly the scariest thing I think I've ever heard anyone say – ever.

"Well I think you're great," I decided to tell her, again and again, as often as I could.

"Do you think you can help me?" Rachel asked.

I considered the problem long and hard and told her I'd give it my best shot. "But, if you want me to be honest, the only person who can really help you is you."

Rachel smiled once more and agreed. "Alex said you were a good man. I'm glad to know you John Coal," she said, leaning in to give me a little kiss. I didn't realise this was her intention, so I belted her in the face and dived off the steps, snatching up two bicycle pumps up as I rolled across the floor to form a cross with.

"Get back demon bitch!"

Rachel stared at me in mild amusement and shook her head.

"For a werewolf, you are *such* a dick!"

ii

First things were first. I hired a van and drove down to London to collect Rachel's things from a boarded up row of Victorian derelicts just off the Mile End Road. She had a couple of little keepsakes she wanted me to grab, like a silver locket on a chain that contained a few strands of auburn hair and a couple of dirty and scratched dollies I had assumed were treasured childhood toys until Rachel told me were just props for when she was out hunting. I had to remind myself that she wasn't a little girl anymore and that I had to stop thinking of her as such. The main thing I had to collect though was her casket. It was lined with earth from her original grave and it weighed a ton. After an hour of wrestling with it in vain, I stood on the street for ten minutes fanning myself with a handful of fivers and soon recruited a motley party of pallbearers.

Rachel told me to bring back some food too, so I sized up the misfits and asked the shakiest of the lot if he'd like to earn another hundred on top of the ten I'd already paid him, helping me out at the other end. The old boy fairly clambered over the coffin and into the back of my van, so I slammed the doors behind him and looked around to see if anyone had noticed.

No one had.

Over the coming weeks, Rachel and I got to know each other as much as we dared. We took midnight strolls around the surrounding countryside and talked about our families, our experiences and our regrets as we unburdened much of what we'd buried. This was a new experience for me because I had grown used to locking it all away, but Rachel had been around a lot longer than me and had talked with other supernatural beings on her travels.

"Like Alex?" I prompted, as we strolled down a grassy bank and towards the sound of running water below. It was a moonless night, with clouds piled thick overhead but neither of us had any difficulties seeing in the darkness. I guess there are some perks to eternal damnation.

"Yes, like Alex," Rachel confirmed. "If it wasn't for him, I wouldn't be here today."

"Where did you meet him? Did you go to Long Fenton or was he on a daytrip to London?"

Rachel giggled like this had been a joke, so I giggled too and pretended it had been.

"No, he came to me in my dreams," Rachel told me.

"You see ghosts in your dreams?"

"Of course, don't you?"

"No. I don't know. They're just dreams. I think," I said, to which Rachel predictably asked how I *knew* they were dreams. "Because my dad never wore a sari," I replied, and I could've added, "or rode a bike that could cycle up the side of skyscrapers" but Rachel was right, how could I know what the old bastard was doing these days?

"And of course I've known a few vampires in my time – arseholes most of them – and warlocks and hobgoblins, and even the occasional human," Rachel reminisced as she hopped and skipped across a series of stepping-stones that spanned the gentle brook she was leading me across. "But it never works out, not with humans. No matter how comfy you get with them, there's always a moment when they panic and get scared and I'm forced to deal with it, but that's because humans don't understand us. You're different though, John. You're a werewolf, so you know what it is like to be us. Which is why I think this could really work."

I agreed and I told her I thought she was great again before checking my watch when I caught up with her on the other side of the brook.

"Sun'll be up in a couple of hours. We should probably start heading back soon."

On our way home we passed a large farm that was set back from the road. Rachel asked if we could stop and get a chicken, or even a baby lamb, as it had been a week since her last feed. She wasn't a huge fan of feeding on livestock; it was not considered the "done thing" in vampire circles, but it would see her through for a couple more nights and it would save me driving down to London to snatch another bum off the streets, so we climbed over the gates and crept up to within thirty yards of the farmhouse.

"No baby goats," I said, sniffing the air. "But there are fresh calves in a barn behind the house."

Rachel tongued her fangs until they were fully engorged and told me she'd only be a minute. While she was away I wondered what would happen if she didn't kill the calf outright, would it become a vampire calf and stalk the land attacking other calves? Come to that, what would happen if I bit it? Would be become a werecalf? How did this work? I'd never really known. Not fully. Was it worth taking the calf home to experiment on, or would I run the risk of starting a Noah's Ark full of monsters and angering the resident's association who, and let's be honest here, had only just gotten over Mr and Mrs Singh moving into number 27?

I decided to let sleeping calves lie and wondered how I could get blood (human or otherwise) for Rachel on a regular basis without killing anyone. Alas I didn't have time to come up with any ideas because there was an almighty screech, and then a scream, and then a bang, like the sound of a gun being fired, followed by shouting from the direction of the barn.

I ran around to look for Rachel, to make sure she was okay and to drag her away from the danger, but there was no sign of her, just a lot of distressed mooing from the sprawling corrugated barn and several angry voices. I looped around to the rear of the barn, looking for a side entrance in, but again found nothing. I was just about to try the other way when a voice screamed at me that I was a dead man.

"You sick fuck!"

I spun around and found myself staring down both barrels of a loaded 12-bore and saw a young fella in pyjamas and overcoat on the other end pulling the trigger without waiting to hear my side of the story. The gun flashed and I was slammed into the side of the barn by the blast, but I opened my eyes to see Rachel wrapped around me. She'd appeared from out of nowhere and had borne the brunt of the blast, right between the shoulders. But Rachel didn't even seem winded. She just gave me a wink and flew off again, covering the distance between myself and the shooter in the blink of an eye. He fired another shot, but it had made not a jot of difference as Rachel thrashed her nails across his throat and wrapped herself around him as he fell to the ground. She feasted hungrily and quickly, gulping down his blood and jumping to her feet to reload his Purdey and blow off his head from the neck up. Then she slung the weapon and looked around with an alertness I'd last seen in Khan at his prime. Before I could stop her Rachel was off again, haring into the night to deal with the rest of the voices that had emerged to challenge her.

"No Rachel, come back!" I shouted, sprinting after her as screams and gunshots echoed all around the farmhouse. I arrived in every room just seconds too late, with blood dripping from the ceiling and the walls and another pyjama-clad gunman laid out for infinity. I guess they must've been the farmer and his three sons but they'd stood no chance once Rachel had got the bit between her teeth. She covered her tracks with each killing by gunning her bite marks to make them look like plain ordinary murders, but she dropped the ball with the farmer's [once] attractive wife, more or less decorating the bathroom with her to such an extent that I didn't see Rachel at first because she was the same colour as the walls. It was only when she moved that I realised she was there, perched on the toilet cistern like a gargoyle, breathless and exhilarated, if a little ashamed of herself.

"I've been bad," she admitted, staring down at the poor unfortunately farmer's wife, or at least what was left of her after one of her 'darker moments'. She twirled a filthy strand of hair around one of her bloody fingers and finally managed to look me in the eye. "Are you cross with me?"

Cross? I was out of my mind with horror, but Rachel needed reassurance at this point, not criticism, and we weren't going to get anywhere if I put her over my knee and spanked her every time she slaughtered a house full of people. So I told her it was fine, I wasn't cross, I was just disappointed, and this seemed to be enough of a ticking off for Rachel to bear with good grace.

"I'm sorry," she simpered, technically apologising to the wrong person, but it was a positive sign that she felt the need to apologise at all, so I took her by the hand and led her off into the darkness once more.

"Thank you for saving my life," I figured I should tell her.

"That's okay," she smiled. "Any time."

iii

At home Rachel got cleaned up, but only after a fight. She liked the feel of blood on her skin, particularly drying blood, and one of her normal rituals had been to wait until it flaked off by itself before going out hunting again. I told her this was not the sort of behaviour that was going to help her break her cycle, and she eventually agreed to a sponge bath. I ran a wet flannel over her hands and mouth, between her fingers and toes, and even made a little headway with her hair, but I stepped out of the basement when she stripped out of her nightgown and offered herself up to me. Rachel didn't like my reaction and accused me of looking upon her as if she was still a kid.

"I bet you'd be only too happy to wash me if I looked twenty-three and had big boobs and round hips," she sulked, but I assured her it wasn't like that.

"It's not that you're not... er, I mean don't look mature or nothing. If anything, I actually like girls who are... are young like you," I lied; pained at having to pretend I was some sort of kiddie fiddler when I was already the son of a serial killer and a werewolf. No wonder I couldn't get a girlfriend. But Rachel was right; I didn't feel comfortable washing down a prepubescent girl, particular a prepubescent girl who longed to be treated like a woman. Some men might've dreamed of the opportunity, and while I wasn't one of them, I would've been only too happy to introduce those that were to Rachel for themselves.

"Call me when you're finished," I told her, taking her nightgown upstairs to pop its washing machine cherry.

"Arsehole!" she sulked.

We didn't go out the following night because the moon had come full circle and I needed to transform. Rachel was interested to see this for herself and refused to leave the basement, no matter how much I pleaded with her. In the end I agreed it was her choice, but I was still concerned, not just for Rachel, but for myself. I really didn't want to wake up tomorrow morning having spent the night slugging it out with a vampire, but Rachel assured me it would be okay, she had a way with animals, so I locked the reinforced steel door and dropped the key into a drain in the corner of the basement.

"What's that for?" Rachel asked.

"For my own protection," I explained. "It's just big enough to get my hand into it as I am now, but too small for the beast so I can't get the key once transformed."

"What if I let you out tonight?" Rachel asked, a little mischievous glint in her eye.

"What if I wheel you upstairs for a suntan tomorrow?" I replied.

We sat playing cards for a couple of hours until Rachel noticed I'd stopped laying Jacks. The skin on the back of my neck was getting hotter and my muscles were tightening.

"It's started," I told her, shaking the knots out of my body as the fires took their hold. "God help us both!" I gasped and tumbled onto the floor.

I remember little else of the night. I remember Rachel clearing the chairs away and I remember her telling me that I looked amazing, but very little else from the perspective of John Coal. My memories once transformed are always sketchy, almost dreamlike. The thought process is gone, so too the ability to order the memories afterwards. They're all emotions and compulsions, sensations and instincts. I can remember certain events if they are vivid enough and I can remember being a part of them; I can even remember thinking they were a good idea at the time (like eating that chap from the Ordnance Survey department up in the Ben Armine Forest several years ago), but I can't remember why I ever thought they were acceptable. It was like my desires would have all their fuses replaced with six-inch iron nails so that no matter how overheated my impulses got, nothing would trip my conscience.

Until the next day.

My night with Rachel wasn't like that though. I couldn't remember any fighting and I couldn't remember any pain. In fact, I could hardly remember a thing, which meant it was probably an uneventful night. It was certainly one of the most relaxing nights I've ever had as the beast. Normally stuck in this basement as I am I give myself a few cuts and bruises trying to claw my way out, but the next morning when I awoke, I was tranquil and unscathed. Rachel sat nearby playing Patience and she looked unflustered too.

"What happened?" I asked, desperately racking my brains for some kind of an image.

"Nothing," she shrugged without looking up. "We just fucked all night."

Happily Rachel was only teasing, but she'd been right about one thing, she did indeed have a way with animals, particularly supernatural ones it seemed, because she'd held me in her sway all night long, talking me through my transition and even pampering me like a prize poodle when I was changed and I'd not gone for her once, not even when she'd started to groomed my thick mane.

Three pink ribbons remained tied in my hair and another ten lay on the floor to testify to this fact.

"Good doggy," she smiled.

I transformed again another three times over the coming nights and Rachel stayed with me each time. On the final night Rachel asked if she could take me out to the woods to transform. She said it would do me good to feel the bracken against my skin once more and she promised to keep me on a tight rein but I steadfastly refused. Rachel couldn't even keep herself on a tight rein; that was why she was here. I shuddered to think what might've happened if the pair of us had encountered a Girl Guide camping party.

She sulked that evening and the next morning I woke up with two black eyes and a swollen lip.

Rachel never cared to explain.

iv

The next day I set out to solve Rachel's feeding problems. I visited an abattoir and got the guy to sell me a couple of pints of blood, telling him I wanted to make my own blood pudding with it. And then I drove to Norwich and enquired as to where I went to give blood. They gave me the address of the local clinic, so I went along and checked it out, but stopped short of giving any of mine up for scrutiny.

Back home Rachel baulked at the cow's blood and tossed the lot back in my face – literally – though she seemed more receptive to the idea of the blood bank, so that night I drove her to Norwich and parked up outside, around the back of it. I didn't need to help Rachel break in. She was already an adept burglar in her own rights and successfully raided the fridge, bringing back with her a holdall full of blood bags to feed on over the coming nights. When we got home I noticed that most of blood she'd taken was of the rarer variety – AB positive and negatives.

"Does it taste better than the more common types then?" I asked.

Rachel shrugged. "Not really. But it'll fuck them up more losing this stuff than a load of boring O."

I was coming to learn that this was Rachel all over. Given a straight choice between benign and malignant, Rachel would go malignant every time. It wasn't even a conscious reaction to events; it was part of her character. She was at core a bad person. And the fact that she was a vampire too was just too bad on the rest of us. Rachel was the darkness that couldn't escape itself.

I wondered why she was even trying.

Rachel had come from a terrible childhood. Some might argue she hadn't come very far but not I – at least, not to her face. Her mother had been an East End harlot in the last days of the old Queen and Rachel had been just one of twelve occupational hazards to befall 'Happy Sue', as she was universally known back then. Rachel's eleven siblings had found the Workhouse or the cemetery within a day of arriving in this world, but when Happy Sue came knocking with number twelve, the Workhouse decided she'd spread quite enough happiness for one person and refused to take her new daughter. Under normal circumstances Rachel might've ended up in the river before the day was out, but the Workhouse Master was a vociferous champion of lost causes and warned Happy Sue to present herself and her daughter at the end of every month or else she'd find herself kicking air at the end of a rope. Obviously keeping a baby alive in those Victorian slums back then was no mean feat, but the Master insisted that even if little Rachel were to succumb to one of the many popular illnesses of the day, her body was to be brought to the surgeon for examination immediately.

Or else.

As you can imagine Rachel caught – and much to her mother's dismay recovered from – pretty much every illness known to medical science, but nothing could tear her from her mother's breast. And so for eight years Happy Sue played unhappy families to the most unwanted millstone in Bow and the pair only finally parted company in Christmas 1899 when Happy Sue was caught stealing a half a crown from her landlady's purse and broke her head on the stairs trying to flee.

Rachel saw this happen right in front of her.

And she barely cared.

I thought of the parallels with my own father. Compared to Rachel's upbringing, mine had been one long smoochy kiss after another, but both of our parents had played an important role in shaping our lives. For me, if I hadn't gone to sea to escape the consequences of my father's actions I wouldn't be the man (nor beast) I am today. But with Rachel it ran deeper. Her mother had moulded her very soul with contempt. I'm not sure Rachel even knew why she was so full of hatred, but it infested her like a cancer and it had nothing to do with her vampirism. If she'd been a normal kid I could've sent her for counselling but she was eighty years past that – although interestingly I didn't think she'd grown up at all. Her body was stuck in time and I finally got the sense that her mind was too. She may have been around since the last century but she had none of the emotional maturity or wisdom that should've come with age, just eighty years of bile. Her remorse was not for her victims – never for her victims – it was always for herself and for the way she felt afterwards during her post-kill comedowns. She dressed this self-pity up as regret because it was more attractive that way and wore it like a tragic curse, but really the anger was there long before the claws had been.

At her core, she was still a kid – eighty years plus and as dangerous as a tiger, but she was still a kid nevertheless. For Rachel it was all about tits and pubic hair and I eventually concluded she was right about the problem, she was just wrong about the region.

Naturally I played my cards pretty close to my chest as the weeks ticked by, because if there's one thing that upsets an emotionally retarded psychopath more than anything else it's telling them that they're an emotionally retarded psychopath, so instead I figured out a plan to help her.

First off were her material needs because we couldn't escape the fact that she drank blood to survive, no matter how many fluffy bunnies I lined her coffin with. So I researched all the hospitals within a one hundred mile radius and we agreed to systematically break into each over the coming months – not to ransack them, but just to take as much as we thought wouldn't be missed, because it was vital to Rachel's treatment that she no longer killed when she fed.

Rachel agreed and so once a week we would go on in the car, I would park up nearby, and she would scale the clinic walls to steal her supplies. She agreed to bring back only O and A+, and not to wreck the rest of the stock for her own private amusement and she even agreed not to kill anyone if she was disturbed, which marked something of a breakthrough for Rachel. However saying all these things and doing them are two different things, and I would bite my nails down to the quick waiting for Rachel to return, but to my relief she kept her word and really did just steal what she needed, giving us both half a chance to turn her life around for real.

And so to the second part of her treatment: Rachel had never known love nor warmth in eighty long years. Not the love of a parent nor the warmth of a friend. She'd

DANNY KING

only known resentment and fear and so as a result she only knew how to inspire resentment and fear in others. It probably ran deeper than that, of course, but this was my best amateur psychiatrist guess and so the answer was obvious. I had to be both a parent and a friend to Rachel. I had to show her all the love and the warmth she'd missed out on for almost a century and I had to reconnect her with humanity. She may have been a predator and preyed on humankind but that didn't mean she had to hate them too.

So we began at the beginning.

We began with *Peter Pan*.

I have to admit, it wasn't the subtlest of therapies – a boy who couldn't grow up flying about an enchanted island having magical adventures – but Rachel lapped it up and had me read each of J. M. Barrie's books to her over and over again until they were tattered and dog-eared. Rachel couldn't read herself and no matter how many times I tried to teach her, she couldn't even grasp the basics, so I remained her only window into Neverland and as a result I became that much more precious to her too. It was a little step forwards, not a massive one, just a little one, because these newly found emotions were still strictly speaking serving her own needs, but at least it proved there was something there to be worked with. All I needed was time.

All I got was two months.

v

For the third week running we returned to the same blood bank on Rachel's insistence. She told me it was the best stocked blood bank she'd raided over the last couple of months and it was also the easiest to get into, so it could sustain the losses better than the others and there was less of a chance of her running into anyone whilst robbing it. These seemed like all the right reasons for returning and so Monday after Monday I drove the fifty miles down to Colchester and parked up opposite the General Hospital while Tinkerbell went and got her dinner.

It wasn't until the third week that my suspicions finally kicked in after she didn't return for almost two hours. Not what you'd expect from "the best stocked and easiest blood bank to break into". And now I noticed specks of blood on her nightgown when she got back into the car despite the blood bags being completely sealed inside her holdall.

I didn't say anything at the time, but the next morning I returned to Colchester and looked around for myself. The hospital was exactly as she'd described it and no one reported seeing any intruders when I flashed them my bogus police badge. I took a further snoop around the grounds and traced the steps Rachel would've taken from the car to the blood bank window, scouring the ground for signs of violence, but there was nothing.

I widened my search and found a couple of acres of wooded parkland just behind the hospital, so I crossed the park to see what was on the other side. It turned out to be a large Victorian building set in its own grounds. It was three storeys high and about ten windows wide, and it had the air of an institution about it. A sign next to the front door read:

COLCHESTER CHILDREN'S HOME

Two police cars sat out front.

It seemed for three weeks Colchester Children's Home had been infected by a mysterious plague. The children on the top floor began to systematically self-harm, slashing themselves with razor blades or throwing themselves out of bed and down the stairs in the middle of the night, claiming not to know how they'd got there. A couple of the children reported having terrible nightmares about an evil spirit who'd attacked them in their beds, but most denied all knowledge of what happened or why, causing the staff to suspect it was some kind of bizarre pact dreamed up by the children to create a stir. They clamped down on it as much as they could, but no matter how tight a watch they kept on the children, each Monday night one of them would always go loopy and half-kill themselves at the first opportunity. At least that was until seventeen-year-old Rhiannon had gone the whole hog and thrown herself off the roof and onto the railings below. A terrible tragedy in itself but one that the staff simply could not fathom, because Rhiannon was a trusted helper and had volunteered to watch over the rest of the children on the top floor herself. It didn't make any sense.

At least, not to them it didn't.

To some of us, the events had an all too familiar ring to them.

vi

"I won't be long," Rachel promised, slipping out of the car and giving me a twirl of excitement as she slammed the door and hurried off into the night.

I started the car the moment she was out of sight and floored it, haring around the ring road that skirted the edge of the park until I came to the Children's Home on the other side.

I jumped on the brakes and leapt out of the car fifty yards short of the home, plucking my bag from the boot and running towards the front door with a sledgehammer hanging over my shoulder. I crashed through the door in one, shattering wood, glass and steel with a single swing and I let the hammer clatter where it fell as I charged for the stairs.

"Stop there! Stop this minute" came the cries from the Matron on duty, but I didn't falter a stride. I took the stairs three at a time, throwing myself around the banisters and ever upwards until I crashed through the top floor landing doors.

"Stop him! Stop him!" the Matron was screaming off somewhere behind me, and two burly orderlies jumped to their feet to tackle me before I could get anywhere near the children.

"Oi, come here you!"

"Stop right there!"

But I was in no mind to stop for them any more than I had been for the Matron and I rushed along the corridor kicking open every door I came to.

"I know you're in here. Out now! Out!" I shouted at the top of my lungs, pulling a large silver crucifix from my bag and scouring each dorm with it. The kids screamed as I burst into their rooms and the orderlies made a lunge for me, but I pulled my dad's old Webley from my bag and shot a couple of rounds into the ceiling to warn them back.

"Get back. I mean it!" I told them, gun in one hand, crucifix in the other and looking half-deranged like every orphanage's worst nightmare.

"Put the gun down and let's talk," the nearest orderly pleaded, changing tact slightly, but I told him the kids were in danger and if they didn't get out of my way another child would die before this night was out.

"No one needs to hurt anyone," the orderly urged, backing me into a corner until I had no choice. I lowered my gun and shot him in the foot, dropping him immediately and sending the other orderly sprinting for cover.

"Sorry mate," I told the orderly who was now squirming in a pool of his own making. "No time to explain but I'm here to help."

I had no doubt the telephone was glowing red hot downstairs, so I kicked my way through the remaining doors while the second orderly put himself between me and Matron as she evacuated the children I passed. Every room I came to I would hurl the screaming child I found within back to the orderly, who in turn would shepherd them back to the Matron. I could tell neither the orderly nor Matron understood any of this and both were frantic at the thought of what I might do, but as long as I was just handing them kids instead of exorcising them they were happy to let me continue my quest until the men with big butterfly nets arrived.

I reached the final couple of doors and put my foot through the second from last to find an eight-year-old girl standing in the linen cupboard next to an open window. There was no expression to her, she seemed to be in some kind of a trance but she was dripping blood from open wounds that ran up and down her arms, splattering the crisp clean sheets around her.

"Come with me sweetheart," I said, reaching out for her, only to become aware of something falling out of the ceiling at the last possible moment. I looked up just in time to feel the pinch of ten angry claws clamping around my face and I hit the floor before I could react.

"She's mine!" Rachel screamed, wrenching me into the shelves with enough force to bring them down on top of me. I scrambled out of the piles of linen and shot Rachel in the back with the revolver to get her attention, making the orderly and Matron outside turn and flee. Rachel snapped away from the window and scowled her nastiest scowl at me, which turned nastier still when I held out my crucifix for her appraisal.

"Get out of here!" I demanded, climbing to my feet and advancing towards her. "Leave this place at once and never return. You are forbidden from entering these walls for as long as you are sheltering with me. Do you hear me?"

I wasn't sure any of this was cutting any mustard with Rachel but she seemed suitably outraged and threatened to chew all sorts of shapes into my head if I dared to presume to talk to her that way again.

"I mean it," I reiterated, closing in on Rachel as she spat and hissed at my challenge. "Release the girl or your time with me is over."

The little girl in question was still none the wiser to any of this, but she was slowly being backed closer and closer towards the open window as Rachel retreated from my Sacrament. I knew I only had seconds before she was out and onto the railings below, so I got tough with Rachel and pulled out a well-thumbed copy of *Peter Pan in Scarlet* from my bag.

"This? You see this?"

I threw it onto the floor and shot it straight through the cover with a single round, scattering loose pages about the linen cupboard and putting a rather large hole in Barrie's plot.

"Nooo!" Rachel reacted, spinning the girl around and jamming her claws underneath her chin. She would've torn her head clean off in retaliation too had I not quickly dug *Peter Pan in Kensington Gardens* out of my bag to remind her there were three more beloved books up against the wall here.

"I'll destroy them all if you hurt that girl!" I promised. Rachel had clearly never been stood up to like this before in all her life and she didn't like it much. She roared her indignation into my face then hurled the girl aside in a fit of pique and scampered up the wall and out of the door.

I chased after her back down the corridor and in and out of the rooms as she raced around the ceiling bringing down lightstrips and ceiling panels onto my head. The Matron and orderly had evacuated the rest of the floor, hauling away their wounded colleague to leave Rachel no one else to take her frustrations out on – no one except me that is. And as I had a gun to Peter Pan's head she could only vent her frustrations at me for fear of losing all that she held dear. This was a new and unwelcome experience for Rachel, powerlessness, and she took it out on the fixtures and the fittings of the final bedroom, hurling beds and mattresses clean across the room in a childish show of might that left the place looking like a pillow fight in a poltergeist's bedroom.

"We're going home now!" I demanded. "Come on, back to the car this instant!"

Rachel curled up her lip in disgust. She seemed totally blinded by her own rage and her physical appearance changed to match her mood. Her eyes were milky with blood and her teeth engorged to stand clear of her mouth like a row of pincers, while black veins popped in her neck and face to distort her pale skin even further. She was no longer the little girl I knew and [sort of] cared for, she was an unspeakable spawn of Satan, a vile slug on the petal of mankind. I kept the crucifix between us at all times as she stalked me around the walls, suddenly unsure of my untouchability.

The sound of footsteps approaching on the stairs outside caught both of us off-guard and I looked out of the window to see a dozen blue flashing lights in the grounds below. The cavalry had finally arrived, although as far as they were concerned I was very much on the side of the Indians. Worse still, my momentary lapse in concentration let Rachel pounce. She flew across the room to swipe the crucifix from my hand and slammed me headfirst through several MFI wardrobes and onto the floor.

I ended up on my back with her fangs just inches from my neck, wondering how I'd been so naïve as to think I could rehabilitate a remorseless killing machine such as she, while at the same time marvelling at the strength she held within her tiny frame. She kept me pinned to the lino as if she were made of concrete and screamed her dissatisfaction into my face.

"You are nothing! You are a worm-riddled mongrel of no consequence whom I have honoured with my kinship. Do not for one moment assume you are my keeper. You are my pet, no more, and I have the power to snap your filthy neck as soon as look at you, you mangy half-breed!" she bellowed, peppering my face with spittle and spite.

Voices now sounded in the corridor outside demanding I showed myself and we had but seconds to spare before we were discovered. Rachel snarled at these further interruptions and snatched me up off the floor as if I weighed no more than a coat, running for the sash window at the end of the dorm and jumping us both through it and out into the night.

Glass, wood and screws showered the police cars below, but Rachel and I didn't land for another thirty yards, crashing to the ground in the woods beyond and disappearing into the shadows before anyone knew where to look for us. By the time the police caught up we were long gone. They scoured the woods with torches and with dogs but found no signs of any intruders, just a few broken branches twenty feet up and a page from the J. M. Barrie classic *Peter and Wendy*.

It was just the latest in a long line of unexplained and unexplainable events to befall Colchester Children's Home. Though it was not to be the last.

vii

It didn't escape my attention that Rachel's feelings had focussed on the books themselves, rather than the stories contained within their pages. It hadn't occurred to her that she could've easily tossed them all on the fire and sent me out for new copies the next day. The way she saw it, these books had brought her a great deal of comfort and happiness, therefore these books had become very dear to her. It was an affection that belied an innocence behind the malice. Likewise it didn't occur to her that she could've easily found someone else to read them to her if she'd tried. Like the books, I'd become [almost] as precious to her, though that didn't stop her from dragging me through every thicket in the park as we circled the cops to sneak back to the car. Rachel laid out the policeman we found snooping around it, but to my surprise she didn't kill him. I think she only abstained because she realised this would've turned up the heat on us unnecessarily, but it was still a welcome relief. Instead we drove home without breaking any more laws and without saying a word to each other for the entire journey. It was Rachel's first teenage tantrum and I would wear the scars from it for the rest of my life.

Having been a teenager once I knew what tricky, unpredictable and proud creatures they were so I made most of the running when we finally sat down to "talk about it".

I apologised for shouting at her and I apologised for making her feel stupid and I apologised for failing her and for not considering her feelings and for night turning into day and for just about everything else I could think of until Rachel eventually cracked.

"I shouldn't have called you a mangy mongrel," she conceded and I waited for the rest of it, but that was it. That was all I got. The attacks, the maiming, the killing and the terrors she'd inflicted on the orphanage, they didn't count for anything. She was only prepared to apologise for a name I couldn't even remember her calling me. Still, I accepted it as graciously as I could but refused to let the other stuff slide until she'd at least acknowledged some of it. Finally she did.

"I didn't ask you to drive me to a kids' home, did I? You drove me there and you pushed me out of the car knowing what I was like, telling me to collect food when there was young blood on the wind and then shouting at me when I had one of my episodes," she snapped. "You're meant to be looking after me. You put me in that situation and now you're having a go at me. Well fuck you!"

Believe it or not she was right in a bizarre sort of way. I had presumed too much of her and I had got complacent. I should've researched my locations better and not under-estimated her capacity for malevolence. She was a savage and out of control predator, after all, not a Girl Guide on bob-a-job week. I had let my guard down and been caught out as a result.

"I'm sorry Rachel, you're right. I didn't think. I should've been more considerate," I admitted, quelling the fires that burned behind her eyes a little until she was ready to bare the real pain in her soul.

"And you didn't have to ruin my books," she sniffed, catching me out by even shedding a tear or two. "They were mine. You had no right."

I completely agreed and said I had gone too far, shooting holes in a couple of old paperbacks just to stop a killing spree, and I promised not do it again. "I guess I just wanted to show you how precious that little girl was to me, just like your books are to you," I told her, which Rachel had trouble understanding.

"Precious to you? You didn't even know her. How could she be precious to you?" she asked.

"All life is precious to me," I replied. "Particularly those who cannot defend themselves. It's my human side I guess. And I know it's in you to feel it too, so I'm sorry if I upset you, I just wanted to show you how I felt."

Rachel's eyes narrowed. I sensed she thought my feelings were about as important as evacuating ants during a forest fire but she didn't elaborate on the point. Instead she drew the conversation back to her books and went on about how far she'd come with them and how much they'd been helping her understand who she was and all the rest of it until I stopped her in mid self-analysis by telling her I knew where I could get my hands on more copies.

"Where?" Rachel demanded to know.

"Better yet, why don't I go and get them for you?" I suggested, buggered if I was going to hand her my head on a plate as well as my library card.

viii

There was far less fallout from the children's home incident than I'd been anticipating – both from the authorities and from Rachel. I'd expected a nationwide manhunt, a media frenzy and pitchfork sales to rocket throughout the land, but there was barely one word about it in the papers, just a little story in *The Times* concerning the Social Services budget being questioned in the House following "a series of incidents at children homes in recent weeks".

A "series of incidents"? That was the term they'd used to describe the multiple injuries, the death of a child and the bizarre attack and escape by a [seemingly] religious maniac on one of the nation's care homes. No wonder Rachel had been getting away with murder for best part of the last century. It beggared belief.

That said, if that was weird Rachel's behaviour was weirder still. After a day of sullen sulking she became the very picture of contrition, apologising completely for her behaviour and assuring me that she finally understood the pain she'd been causing all these years. Admittedly she only came to this conclusion after I'd bought her a new set of Peter Pan books, so there was still a certain amount of self-interest there, but she was remorseful nevertheless. And she seemed genuine too. On our way across the fields one night we encountered temptation in the shape of a courting couple who were going at it like badgers under the light of a silvery moon. They were making such a performance of it that I almost felt like ripping them to pieces myself, but Rachel simply watched them from the shadows. Then, when they were finally – and theatrically – finished Rachel turned, took my hand and led me away.

"Have you ever done that before?" she asked as we climbed over a stile and into a hedge-lined country lane, fags lighting in the distance behind us

"A couple of times, when I was younger, but not for a long long time. That sort of thing never really worked out for me I'm afraid. And I just sort of lost the urge," I shrugged.

Rachel nodded like she understood, then said: "I've done it before."

It was a brave confession and I thought she meant since she'd been undead, but the truth was more unsettling than that.

"Sue made me do it," she said, meaning Happy Sue, her mother. "She made good coin from me, particularly those first few times, so good in fact that she never had to do it again herself, especially not with anyone she didn't want to." She looked away into the night and into her dim and distant past before passing judgement on the experience. "I never liked it, but she kept on making me do it. Said I had to support her how she'd supported me. That was on my sixth birthday."

In the absence of anything constructive to say, I simply said; "I'm sorry," but it barely registered with Rachel. It was like putting a sticking plaster over a guillotine wound.

"Do you really like young girls like me?" she asked after a little silent thought, dredging up the bullshit excuse I'd told her when I'd made her wash alone. I quickly turned this one over in my mind and tried to second-guess her reactions to a selection of different answers, but in the end I plumped for the truth, simply because I figured it was better to have my head ripped off for the truth than for a lie.

"No, not really," I admitted. "I just didn't want to upset you, that's all."

Rachel just nodded and smiled.

"You're a good man, John Coal," she said, then added; "for a mangy mongrel."

The following week we took a break because it was my time of the month. Rachel helped me get ready for my transformation and even moved her coffin to the corner of the basement to give me room to stretch my claws. I can be a little edgy and a little cranky on transformation days, particularly those last few hours before I change, so we sat down and played a board game to help me take my mind off the impending agonies. *The Game of Dracula* I had thought was an inspired choice, and something I'd picked up when I'd bought Rachel her new set of Peter Pan books, and thankfully Rachel thought so too. We played a couple of rounds of it and I let her win, then she asked me how long I had when she saw me cricking my neck.

"Maybe just over an hour, I guess," I told her, and that was the last thing I remembered. Pain flooded my senses and the world turned to darkness and then nothing.

When I awoke I didn't recognise where I was because the room was dark, but I knew I was no longer in my basement. What's more I could tell I hadn't changed yet, so I hadn't ended up here after a night on the claw. No, my changing was imminent, yet somehow I'd passed out and ended up here, outside of my sanctuary, in harm's way. I snapped awake, now alert and jumped to my feet.

What the hell was going on? Where was Rachel? I needed her to help me get home safely without hurting anyone.

I felt around in the darkness until I found a light switch and flipped it on. In that instant I knew where I was.

And how I'd got here.

ix

Linen.

Piles and piles of linen. It had been washed, ironed, folded and stacked away on the shelves since my previous visit. The young girl I'd encountered before was no longer here and her blood had been cleaned up, but I recognised the cupboard immediately.

The window at the far end had been forced, which must've been how Rachel had smuggled me in, and beyond the woefully flimsy door, I could hear footsteps both little and large as the residents got ready for bed.

They had no idea I was in here. They had no idea

what was to come.

And they had no time to flee.

The fires swept over me as my transformation ignited. I tried to scream a warning to those outside but my throat was crushed by a thousand agonies that ripped me apart. I kicked out at the door, but only succeeded in bringing a pile of freshly folded linen down on top of me.

"Run!" I gasped beneath the sheets. "Ruuunnn!!"

But nobody heard. Nobody responded. And nobody ran.

Razor-sharp talons sprouted from each of my black fingers and my feet made short work of my shoes. The rest of my clothes soon followed, falling from my body as I ripped through the seams until I stood in the cupboard naked as the day I was born, except for a coat of coarse black bristles.

I sniffed at the ceiling, now barely an inch from my snout and tasted the air around me. Beyond the musty smell of institution was the unmistakeable scent of young meat. It skipped and frolicked just beyond the feeble door and my mouth watered at the prospect of sinking into soft, pink flesh. I'd not had wet meat in such a long time. I'd been caged and denied for over a decade by my selfish keeper but I would be denied no longer. I had to feast. I had to gorge. I had to tear and crunch. My hunger knew no bounds.

With one swipe, I knocked the cupboard door clean off its hinges and bounded out into the corridor a single stride.

Four juicy pups and an alpha guardian jumped out of their skins when they saw me and I responded in kind, barking my ravenous intentions at their backs as they fled for the furthest room. I advanced on them slowly, howling at their screams and flooding their little hearts with terror for my own delectation. Terror is delicious; terror gets the juices pumping and makes the meat richer. Terror is exciting. It's all part of the hunt and it was the thing I missed the most on those long and bitterly frustrating nights when I found myself locked in that dingy little basement, even if my keeper had left me a goat to chew on. But the bleatings of tethered animals paled into insignificance next to the demented squeals of young flesh on the hoof and they drew me in with their songs until I was drowning with want.

I stood in the doorway of a large end bedroom, filling the entire frame to deny my quarry even a sporting chance of slipping by. I would have every morsel tonight. There wouldn't be so much as a toenail spurned, I owed that much to myself and I was delighted to see a few extra courses had fallen out of bed to join the platter. At least a dozen little faces looked up at me in abject horror, desperately trying to wake themselves from this most desolate of nightmares, but there would be no reassuring cuddle and fresh blankets for them tonight because I was only too real.

As their succulent little bones were about to find out.

"No you dog!" the alpha guardian shouted, charging headfirst at me with a broomstick in a futile attempt to prolong his mandate. He didn't get to within six feet of me though; I swung an open claw and swatted him into pieces, filling the air with an arterial mist that basted the pups to perfection. How could this get any better?

I snatched the first up by a flailing foot and dangled him by the ankle. He looked so tiny I could've almost swallowed him whole, but to do so would've been to miss the crunch of flavour, so I gave him a cursory lick, tonguing the hot blood and tears from his ruddy little face until my palate would be tantalised no more.

I stretched wide my jaws and placed the little pup inside, but at that moment of satisfaction a cry more resonant and more reaching than I'd ever known before commanded me to put down the pup and back away. Such was the power of this command that I had no choice but to obey – to do otherwise would've been to refuse to breathe.

The cry came again.

"Don't eat us! Please don't eat us!"

It was a plaintive cry from a fear-ravaged mind but the very forces that changed me from man to beast compelled me to do as the voice bid. I backed away to the door, confused and frightened, and barked my unequivocal acceptance at whoever had ordered me to refrain, scouring the sea of faces to see to whom I answered. In the centre was a familiar-looking eight-year-old girl with bandaged arms. She was sprawled just in front of the others and shone like a solstice moon, her supremacy was simply overwhelming, yet her demeanour was cowering, as if she didn't realise the dominance she commanded over me.

"Please don't eat us!" she was crying so once again I barked my assent and awaited her pleasure, only to tumble forwards when an axe was planted into my back.

I spun around to see a second alpha guardian swinging his weapon at me but this time I caught it just below the blade and yanked the guardian's head into my jaws before he could let go of the handle. One bite and my mouth filled with bone and brains as his head came apart at the seams. The meaty slop was almost orgasmic in its deliciousness, but I spat it all out when the girl with the bandaged arms once again commanded me to desist.

"No, God no! Leave him!" she shrieked, so I let the carcass fall from my mouth where it dropped and stepped away in deference.

Around her the other children were still screaming random pips and squeaks but the girl was all I could hear. She pleaded with me to spare their lives and cried for her mummy over and over again, and it was almost an entire minute before she realised I'd done all she'd asked – except fetch her mummy, and I would've probably done that had she given me an address. The girl stared at me in bewilderment for the longest possible moment and I stared right back, basking in the heat of her attentions. After a time I had to look away, it got too much, but I was soon looking again, her draw was too much to resist.

The girl was confused, that was plain to see, but she was thinking fast. She looked around at the other children going ballistic about her and saw I only had eyes for her. She did a little more adding and subtracting before eventually she spoke again, very very quietly, barely a nervous squeak in fact, but I have seriously excellent hearing.

"Bark," she uttered, so I barked.

The girl choked on a breath and put her hand to her mouth. After a moment she removed it and told me to do something else.

"Stand on one leg," she said, so again I did.

Where she'd been irresistible before, she now erupted authority when she realised the extent of her powers and I could scarcely remember ever being able to think for myself before she'd come into my life.

The girl now urged the other pups to be quiet but unbelievably they refused to obey. She repeated her instruction, telling them over and over to "stop crying, please listen to me," but still they ignored her so I barked my loudest howl at them all, blasting out the window panes behind them and toppling several of the lighter tots over as I blew every other noise from the room.

When the blinds finally stopped rattling the room fell in silence. No one dared interrupt the girl with bandages after that and I snorted my disdain at their proximity to her beauty, but I let them be. If this was what she wanted, this was what she got. Let any man or beast try to dictate otherwise and they would have my unbridled fury to answer to.

"Do not kill us," the girl now repeated. This time she spoke so clearly and so precisely that I was left in no doubt as to her will. "Do not hurt us or anyone else here; the Matron, the orderlies or no one. You are not to hurt anyone you see around here. Anyone. Do you understand?"

I understood the remit if not the logic, but that was neither here nor there. The girl with the bandages had decreed it and so that was good enough for me; I would not hurt anyone else while inside this building so I barked again to demonstrate my submission.

I might've stayed there standing on one leg and woofing deferentially all night had another voice, just as loud as the girl in the bandages', not demanded to know what I was doing.

"Don't just stand there you mangy mutt; kill them! Kill them all!"

x

Rachel's directive was every bit as compelling as the girl in the bandages' but it was diametrically opposed to what I'd already been commanded to do, causing me confusion. Rachel bawled at me louder still, appearing in the hallway behind me and shoving me in the back towards the pups.

"Do it! Tear them to pieces! Do it I say!"

I wasn't strong enough to defy such an authority so I lurch forward to do as she said, but the girl in the bandages threw up her hands and ordered me to halt.

"No, don't do it! Stop! Stop there!" she pleaded, blocking my path and wrong-footing me with uncertainty.

Rachel refused to let it lie though.

"Go on, you're supposed to be a killer you mangy mutt, so prove it, kill them all!"

I barked at my mistresses to make up their minds and the girl in the bandages pressed home my indecision. "Don't do as she says. She's being horrible to you. Do only as I say and do not hurt anyone."

Remarkably, up until this moment, Rachel hadn't even noticed the girl in the bandages, probably because my immense frame was sandwiched in the doorway between them but she noticed her now all right and was thunderstruck at her audacity.

"You bitch! You thieving little bitch! You took that from me and now you think you can take him too? I'll kill you myself, you bitch!" Rachel screamed, launching herself past me and bang-smack into the little girl. They smashed into a chest of drawers that quickly splintered to matchwood and rolled around the room scattering pups and beds in their wake. The girl in the bandages did brilliantly well to hold Rachel off for as long as she did, but Rachel's experience soon began to tell and blood and hair started flying in all directions.

"Help! Please help me!" the girl called to me, now in pain as well as fear.

Rachel shouted at me to keep out of it and told me to "kill the others" if I wanted to do something useful, but I could stay on the sidelines no longer. The girl in the bandages' authority may have been less sure of itself, but her pleas shone far truer than Rachel's lie-infested commands, so much so that even in my savage state I could tell when I was being used. And if there's one thing an unstoppable force of supernature like me likes less than being called a mangy mutt, it's being duped into doing someone else's bidding for them.

I spun away from the pups and roared at the girls

fighting on the ground to get their attention. Rachel and the girl in bandages looked up at me in surprise but my fury knew no bounds.

"I command you…" Rachel got as far as saying before I swiped her into the wall with a swing of the paw.

Rachel crashed right through the wall and into the next dorm and I was already after her, roaring and hurling myself through the ragged hole as she leapt to her feet to greet me. I charged right through her, bowling her over with bulk and claws, only to receive several large gouges across my shoulder for my troubles. Before I could turn to protect myself Rachel came after me, swiping and biting as she tried to find my throat, but I had speed as well as strength on my side and bolted through the next wall without so much as missing a stride. I tumbled onto my back to try to catch her with an outstretched talon, but Rachel skated across the ceiling to avoid my grasps and dropped on me from above, her fangs on a direct course for my Adam's apple. Luckily Rachel never made it that far south; before she got within three feet of me, I swung a lucky foot at her and drop-kicked her through the closed door and into the corridor beyond.

A trio of firearms officers who'd been called to subdue a rabid dog now looked through the hole in the door in disbelief and began blasting away at me without even asking if I had rabies or not. I charged through their hail of lead and jumped into the oily vampirene in their midst, scattering the four cops to four corners as me and my ward went on slugging it out around the orphanage.

The police continued to pepper me with their Smith & Wessons and I lost count of the number of bullets that found their way into my back, but Rachel wasn't pestered by a single shot suggesting looks counted for everything with these bozos, so I flung a chest of drawers at the nearest copper and knocked him clean out of the window and into the rose bushes below.

"We need back-up! Everyone you can get! Bring all the guns in the world!" I heard a policeman crying into his radio as he and his remaining colleague emptied and reloaded their handguns into me until they were all out of luck. Unfortunately for them, they made not the slightest bit of headway with me. Rachel was my entire focus and I chased her from room to room, swiping down ceiling panels, strip lights, cables and pipes as we took our fight on a whirlwind tour of the care home until smoke and dust filled every room.

At last the police gave up trying to kill me and concerned themselves instead with evacuating the kids. They ran them in a line down the stairs as if this was a fire drill and Rachel was apoplectic to see the children slipping from her grasp once again.

"Nooo, they have to die!" she screamed, breaking off from the fight to race towards one of the stragglers. She was too quick for me, but the girl in the bandages appeared from out of nowhere, grabbed Rachel by the ankle and swung her full circle and back into my loving arms.

"Take her. Take her and go!" she told me, so I grasped her as tightly as I could, clenching my hand around her tiny throat and charging through the mayhem, out of a recently boarded up window and into the night below. I ran as fast and as far as I could, dragging the wriggly Rachel with me through the park and then the woods, but it was taxing keeping a hold of her as she was free to rake me at will with her savage nails. All I could do to distract her was to slam her headfirst through every tree and fence post I came to until after three miles of destruction Rachel agreed to a truce.

"All right, all right, you've made your point!" she protested as I ran her north through farmland and woods and back to the sanctuary of our basement. "I'll not harm the brats again. I'll leave them be, just let me go, you mutt."

But I didn't let her go, not for another forty miles. Not until the approaching dawn had barred her from returning to Colchester. I'd been charged by the girl in the bandages to do this much and I had no choice but to obey.

I managed to steer a path back through Essex, Suffolk and back into Norfolk without running into too many humans along the way, just the odd startled motorist who'd never be believed by anyone and who'd spend the rest of his life trying to rationalise what he'd seen, before I finally released my stranglehold on Rachel once we were on the outskirts of Thetford.

It had taken most of the night but we were almost home.

Rachel brushed the splinters and twigs from her hair as I looked on and huffed. Neither of us had the time nor the inclination to continue this squabble as the sun was rising in the east and we had maybe only an hour at best before we were transformed once more, me into a man, Rachel into a pile of dust, so we put our differences to one side and made plans to return to the basement.

Beyond this last stretch of heathland lay a couple of smallholdings and the occasional cattery before the varicose veins of suburbia reached out towards the sticks. Mine was one of the most outer-lying houses on the estate (deliberately so) but it was still going to represent something of a minor miracle sneaking home in my present state. See, my hungers had returned with the discharge of my duties, but fortunately for my neighbours, so had Rachel's sway over me and she couldn't allow me to run amok this close to her resting place, so she brought me to heel with a few choice words.

"You fucking dick! Why did you take that bitch's side

and not mine? You ruined everything, you did! You ruined the whole night! You should've ripped them all to pieces like I told you to. I'm your friend, remember? Not some milk-sucking little brat barely out of her mother's cunny, who wouldn't even be walking around if it wasn't for me! That was your fault, that was, making me leave her last week. You're a coward, John Coal. A dirty stinking lily-livered coward!"

I shrugged these observations off with a ripple of my coat. Names could never harm me; neither could sticks, stones, knives or bullets come to that and as if to prove the point some of the slugs I'd collected over the previous evening fell from my back as I waggled my mane.

"Arsehole!" Rachel fumed, biting her lips and chewing her anger as she brooded over what might have been. She looked to the stars above and then at the pink clouds drifting along the horizon and just shook her head. The best laid plans of mice, men and murderesses. Some things just weren't meant to be.

"Ohhh, come on, let's go home," she eventually sighed, taking me by the claw and leading me back through the grasses and back to our unfinished *Game of Dracula*.

xi

Obviously my memories of the previous evening were sketchy at best, but they came back to me in dribs and drabs, like flashes of a horrible dream, so that by the early evening I could more or less account for most of the five dozen gouges I found across my arms and neck after I came to with my head in the toilet the next day.

"What the hell?"

Rachel tried to deny all knowledge of the incident at first, but confronted with the numerous radio reports of a wild dog loose in Colchester and my own explicit recollections from within the care home she finally admitted her part.

"I didn't want to do it, you made me do it," she insisted. "I was just *showing you how I felt*."

Hmm, my own words used against me. I had to hand it to Rachel, she really knew how to stew.

"See, I can't control myself any more than you can in those circumstances," she continued. "That's why I came to you for help, if you remember. Now are you going to help me or what? Or are you going to be like all those other selfish pricks I've ever known and run out on me?"

Poor old Rachel, she was such a long way from shore – even for a messed-up psycho vampire bitch – that she didn't even know which way to swim. I know it sounds bizarre after all she'd put me through but I still felt genuinely sorry for her. And I knew I was the only person who could help her overcome her 'episodes'. After all, I at least was another supernatural being. What man could ever reach out or understand her as I could? And vice versa for that matter. I knew I had to continue with her therapy, even if it killed me. I was all she had. And by that same token, I was all the orphanage had too – much as I'm sure they'd be delighted to hear.

"You're right Rachel. You're right. I finally understand how hard this must have been for you," I told her, looking at the clock on the basement wall by the stairs. "But listen, I'm going to change again tonight, in a little under six hours, so let me do it here, okay? Let's give the kids a night off tonight shall we?"

Rachel's hackles retracted when she saw that was the extent of her telling off and she agreed to play the game tonight. I didn't doubt it for a second, as fun and games were her little distraction, so when she returned to her coffin to rest up for the evening I jumped on the lid and screwed it down with six silver screws I'd forged from a solid silver crucifix Lincoln Cathedral had generously, if unwittingly, donated towards Rachel's rehabilitation.

"What are you doing? Let me out of here you mutt! How have you done this? Let me out! Let me out now!" she demanded, lashing out and kicking against the lid of her casket from the inside, but as formidable as she was, even Rachel lacked the power to escape her own grave, particularly when held there by the strength of the Almighty. "Undo me! Undo me this instant!"

"I'll undo you, alright," I promised her. "But I can't do it in an instant. It's going to take rather longer than that. Have patience. But I will undo you. Eventually. You – and all you've become."

I opened the book I'd brought with me, pulled up a chair and began to read.

"All children, except for one, grow up. They soon know that they will grow up, and the way Wendy knew this was this..."

xii

There was only one thing left to do.

I transformed three more times over the coming nights, all thankfully in the confines of my reinforced basement, but these transformations delayed and frustrated me in what I had to do.

Come the fourth night the moon left me alone so I grabbed my bag and headed out into the darkness, hoping and praying I wasn't too late.

I no longer had a car thanks to Rachel, who'd used it to take me to Colchester earlier in the week and who wouldn't tell me where she'd left it. And I couldn't report it stolen either in case she'd left it near the scene of our crimes so I was forced to borrow my neighbour's car. I

275

hoped to have it back by the morning before I had to ask his permission.

I headed down to Colchester once more and parked in the hospital car park across the woods from the care home. I picked my way through the bushes and was surprised to see, despite all it had been through in recent weeks, the home was still open for business, albeit with a police car decorating its drive. Getting into the home was going to be hard. Getting out again was going to be almost impossible.

I weighed up my options, went back to the car and wondered what to do. That was when the obvious finally caught up with me and I climbed out of the car and wandered around to Accident & Emergency. The usual array of broken legs and biros up noses sat waiting to be seen so I held my arm as if it were hurt and limped through casualty until I found myself in a corridor beyond A&E. I followed the signs down to the laundry room, picked myself out a slightly blemished white coat and set off again.

I grabbed the first nurse who wandered by and tried to look as Doctorly as I could with seven days worth of stubble and bloodshot eyes – which is probably pretty Doctorly for the NHS as luck would have it.

"The patient from the care home, which ward is she in?" I asked, taking a shot in the dark.

"You mean the mystery case?" she replied. "She's up in Isolation, on the third floor. Who are you?"

"I'm a Specialist, up from Great Ormond Street. They've asked me to come up and take a look at her," I said. The nurse looked me up and down in confusion and just nodded in a way that told me she had no idea what I was talking about. Not that it mattered. Us Specialists weren't duty-bound to keep every bed-pan-handler informed as to our movements so I thanked her for her assistance and hastened off for the stairs.

The Isolation ward was made up of a couple of long corridors and a series of rooms on either side. Only authorised medical staff were allowed to see the patients, which I imagined didn't include me, the "religious madman" and "rabid dog" of recent weeks, but it's incredible what a white coat can do for a man's authority.

The room I was looking for was right at the end of the second hallway. I could tell it was the room I was looking for because it was the only one with a policeman sat outside it. I approached as confidently as I could, coughed a couple of times to get him to look up from *Jaws*, and asked if this was the room with the girl from the care home.

"Who's asking?" the policeman replied, putting his book aside and looking me up and down just as the nurse had downstairs.

"Doctor Coal, child specialist," I informed him with a click of the heels.

"Doctor Coal huh? Well what are you wearing kitchen overalls for if you're a doctor then?" the policeman asked. This was a good question and one that deserved a good answer, but instead it just provoked a smack in the mouth and a whack over the head.

I looked around to see if anyone had seen me, but the corridor was empty, so I dragged the policeman through the door and into the darkened room.

A nurse looked up, as did a real-life Doctor who didn't have gravy stains all over his tunic, and they watched me drop the policeman on the cold hard tiles and dig a revolver out of my bag.

"Not a word either of you!" I insisted, training the gun on them and holding a finger to my lips.

"I don't know who you are but you've got to get out of here this instant. This girl's desperately ill, the slightest infection could kill her," the Doctor insisted right back, ignoring the gun and my threats for the sake of his patient. It was a commendable attitude, but one which was likely to win him a look at his workplace from the other side if he persisted.

"I don't want to shoot you but I will if you try to stop me," I promised him.

"Stop you from what? Who are you? What do you want?" he demanded.

"Just a friend," I replied. "And I'm here to help."

I approached the bed and looked down at the pathetic sight that greeted me; the girl no longer had bandages down her arms, she had them all over, as well as pipes, tubes, wires and straps. She looked as pale as a ghost, even in the half-light of her room, and as thin as a pipe cleaner. She looked at me, alert, yet frightened, and a tear appeared in the corner of her eye.

"Please, don't be afraid, I'm not going to hurt you," I reassured her, lowering the gun from her line of sight. "My name's John, what's yours?"

The girl swallowed a couple of times to find her voice and eventually coughed out her name. "Wendy," she told me, panting for breath after such an effort.

Wendy. Perfect.

"Wendy, listen to me, I can help you, but you must come with me," I said but the Doctor stepped up to the bed and told me not to be such a fool.

"You're mad man, she can't leave here and you're no Doctor," he said, trying to reason with me. "Look, I don't doubt your intentions are good but if you take her from this place she'll die, it's as simple as that. You have no idea what you're dealing with here."

"That's where you're wrong Doctor," I told him. "You are the ones who have no idea what you're dealing with and you are the ones who are killing her. I know what's wrong with Wendy and I can save her, but she must come with me."

To illustrate the point, I pulled a penknife from my pocket, sliced open the palm of my hand and slipped it under Wendy's oxygen mask. The Doctor flipped when I did this and tried to tear my hand away, so I laid him out with the butt of my gun and warned the nurse she'd get the same if she tried anything similar. The nurse backed into the far corner of the room so I returned my hand to Wendy's mouth, making her baulk and gag at the violation until some of my blood made it between her lips. When it did, she stopped struggling and let out a shudder that ran up and down the length of her body. This shudder seemed to transform her in an instant and Wendy now pulled my hand towards her where before she'd been pushing it away. She lapped against my palm, then sucked and finally guzzled until I could feel myself growing dizzy from the loss. The nurse watched all of this with abject horror and began to cry. I told her to sit down and close her eyes and she did as I said, desperate to block out this nightmare and only too willing to give me free reign. I let Wendy feed for a little longer, just to get her strength back, then pulled my hand from hers.

"How do you feel now?" I asked, wrapping a bandage around my palm to stem the bleeding.

"Still hungry," she gasped, straining against straps that up until a minute ago had kept her in her bed with their sheer weight alone.

"Wendy, come with me and I can take care of you," I told her, but Wendy's bottom lip began to wobble and the tears returned to her eyes. In spite of the food I'd just given her, I had to remind myself that Wendy was still a frightened, confused and desperately unwell little girl. And like her poor tormented benefactor, she would stay this way for centuries. Of course Wendy didn't know any of this and I couldn't tell her. Not yet. But I would in time. I'd find a way but for now what I needed was her trust.

"Wendy, do you know who I am?" I asked, stepping around bed and into the light of the single lamp in the corner so that she could see me more clearly.

Wendy shook her head and looked away so I told her to look again.

"You do know me," I assured her, retracting my left leg so that I was standing on just my right. Wendy didn't get it at first but when the penny dropped she put a hand to her mouth just as she had done before.

"Oh my God! I... yes. Yes, I know who you are," she finally said.

"Then you know I'm not going to hurt you, don't you?" I asked.

Wendy thought about this then agreed, she did. "Yes. I don't know how, but yes, I know you won't hurt me."

"Will you come with me then?"

Wendy took a deep breath, nodded and broke out into a frightened smile.

"Good," I said, returning her smile with a mightily relieved one of my own. "Let's go then."

The nurse was good enough to let me tie her up with all the tubes and wires I ripped from Wendy and the Doctor and policeman continued to sleep peacefully so there was no need to trouble them further. I bundled a blanket around Wendy, lifted her in my arms and carried her from the hospital without a question being asked of me.

"Can you really help me?" Wendy asked when we got to the car.

"Yes," I sincerely promised her. "We can help each other."

CHAPTER 7:
GOOD NIGHT AND GOD BLESS

"And Rachel's been in there ever since?" Barry asked, stepping away to give the coffin a little more room.

"That she has. I never let her out after I rescued Wendy from the hospital because she was just too dangerous. So I read to her in the evenings, play her music and sometimes stick on the radio, but mostly she likes books, fantasy and adventure stuff, little bit of sci-fi and occasionally Peter Pan, even after thirty years."

There was an audible bristle of excitement as the boys (or at least three of them anyway) stroked the cedar lid with their eyes and tried to imagine the girl beneath. Unfortunately, thanks to a childhood wasted playing XStations and BoyGames they couldn't see her, so Farny asked if I could unscrew the lid so that they could get a proper look.

"Sure, no problem" I told him, "just as long as you're happy for her to be the last thing you ever see."

"What d'you mean like?"

"He means she'll kill us," Barry transcribed.

"Oh," Farny nodded, then asked again; "Not even a quick look, like?"

I smiled, so Colin asked the obvious; "How long are you going to keep her in there? I mean you're an old man. You can't keep her in there forever," he pointed out before blushing. "Sorry, I didn't mean to be rude calling you an old man or nothing."

I gave Colin a wink. "I am an old man, and there ain't nothing I can do about that. No, I'll keep her in there as long as I can, until she learns her lesson, maybe another ten or twenty years say. She's a lot better than she used to be but she's still a handful," I said, patting her lid lovingly. Barry went to do the same, but I told him not to get too close. Not at this time of night. She could still be a bit touchy with strangers. Barry backed away accordingly and looked at the others. Farny smirked.

"And what about Wendy?" Colin asked. "Where is she? Is she in there too?" He scoured the piles of junk stacked up all around for signs of another coffin, but I had only the one. Some people might think that would be enough for most two-bedroom end-terraced bungalows but I guess I'd raised the bar this evening.

"No, Wendy's not in here anywhere. She doesn't live with me no more. She left home a long time ago but she occasionally pops by from time to time."

"And is she still a vampire too?" Barry asked.

"Oh yes, that's one thing you can't shake off. You can get it under control and do just enough to survive, but you can't ever be human again." Which is how it had been with Wendy, I told them. For the first few weeks I had nursed her back to health with cows' blood and a bed of freshly turned soil, but the hardest task had been preparing her for the life to come. There'd been tears, there'd been despair and there'd even been the desire to end it all but eventually I'd brought her around; at least my alter ego had. I'd transformed a little over four weeks later and Wendy had stayed with me throughout the night, settling me, comforting me and taking great solace from eight hours of werewolf whispering. The next morning when I changed back into a man I found Wendy had transformed too.

"Thank you, John," she said, giving me an embrace that lasted most of the morning.

"Where is she now?" Colin asked.

"London," I said. "She's pretty settled now, gets most of her food from blood banks and voluntary contributions. There are a few folks who know the score and are only too happy to help if it saves lives. Wendy's doing okay, making friends and getting by. I don't see her as often as I'd like, but what parent ever does?" even a surrogate parent like myself, I could've added but they'd joined the dots themselves. "At the end of the day, she don't come back much because she don't like being around her mother," I said, indicating towards Rachel's coffin.

"Was she her mum then was she?" Farny said, scratching his head in confusion.

"Only her vampire mother, if you know what I mean. She made her, but they don't get along. Rachel likes to kill. Wendy doesn't," I explained. What families don't have such problems?

"So like, she don't kill no one or nothing never?" Farny complained, clearly annoyed that there were pacifist vampires in the world that he'd not heard about.

"No, Wendy will kill occasionally if she thinks it's called for. She'll hang around a playground late at night after all the other kids have gone home and accept rides from whatever dodgy fellas come along and offer. She has no problems nibbling at the edges of society."

"Righteous," Colin said, making a gesture with his left hand similar to the one I sometimes made when my arthritis flared up.

I looked over at Tommy who'd stayed uncharacteristically quiet throughout my latest story and its subsequent inquest and I wondered if I'd finally got through to him too. Tommy noticed me looking but just went back to leaning against the doorframe with his arms folded, staring into space and chewing on his tongue. Finally he snorted, looked at his watch and told the rest of them they should all go.

"It's gone midnight. We're in for a wallop if dad finds out we snuck out again," he told Barry. But Barry was beyond walloping. He was stood in front of a coffin that contained an actual vampire that was being looked after by a werewolf serial killer who could talk to ghosts. Who cared about wallops when life was this good?

"Oh don't you get it? It's all bullshit!" Tommy suddenly snapped. "All of it, bullshit! And you dickheads believe him. *Facking* unbelievable."

"But we saw her, remember, she moved when we looked in," Colin pointed out.

"He's got some dolly in there or something and rigged it up to a bit of string. Don't you watch *Scooby-Doo* for *fack's* sake?" he dismissed, storming towards the coffin and kicking it off its trestles and onto the floor. The cedar panels cracked and for one horrible moment I thought it was going to break open but I guess they knew how to build them in them days.

Colin, Farny and Barry all jumped out of their skins and got ready to leg it but Tommy just laughed.

"Pussies, the lot of you! Grow the *fack* up."

He now pointed a finger directly at me. "As for you; werewolves and vampires and demons. You can stick 'em up your arse, mate. Oh don't worry, I ain't coming back here again, but not because you is some sort of monster or something. It's because you is a boring old bastard and I've had enough of it. *Facking* Victoria Crosses and Peter Pan. You wanna get your *facking* head checked out you old scarecrow because you're mad, you are!"

And with that Tommy finally left, stomping through the hall and slamming my front door back on its hinges.

He thought I was mad. He thought I was a bullshitter. He thought I was boring. And he wasn't coming back.

That would do for me.

Farny and Colin now saw themselves out too, rallying to Tommy's pied pipe and dismissing my salty yarns as a "load of old tosh", presumably for their glorious leader's benefit. Only Barry lingered. He watched me roll Rachel onto her back and ignored his brother's impatient calls to stay and say his piece.

"Mr Coal?"

"Yes Barry?"

He looked to the door to make sure no one had returned to hear what he had to say then leaned in and whispered; "I believe you."

Barry took one last look at Rachel's coffin and headed towards the door. I called to him before he disappeared and thanked him for his faith.

"And please, my friends call me John."

EPILOGUE:
MONSTERS IN OUR MIDST

Remarkably I got no trouble from the boys after that. My milk stayed in its bottles, my bins left themselves alone and my neighbours' dog shit stayed on the pavements outside the chip shop where my neighbours thought it ought to go. All had returned to normal.

But what was most remarkable was the reaction I got whenever I encountered them on one of their street corners. Gone were the catcalls and abuse I'd suffered for most of the year, in its place was courtesy and even humour.

"Watchya John, eaten anyone today?" Colin would shout, as I'd saunter by with a length of guttering or half a dozen bricks I'd rescued from a nearby scrap pile.

"Only a couple of Jehovah's Witnesses, bleeding do-gooders, hardly a snack," I'd reply much to their amusement, making even the lads who'd not been with us that night laugh and howl in deference. I guess word had gotten out as to my "secret identity" but I didn't mind. After years of shutting myself in it felt good to have a modicum of accord for a change, even if it was just from the local reprobates.

"Hiya John," Barry would wave from his bedroom window as I passed.

"Alright mate," Farny would call as he bombed past me on his bike.

And word clearly spread around town because one afternoon two young boys I'd never even met helped me carry my shopping home for me, while some spotty Herbert with a runny nose knocked on my door and offered to sell me a car stereo he didn't want no more.

My turnaround was complete.

Obviously I still wasn't the best of buddies with Tommy but he didn't give me a hard time about it. He would just ignore me whenever I wished him a "good morning" or smirk sarcastically when I went by, but that would be it. I guess I'd made him feel foolish the evening I'd locked him up, and he'd not liked how his friends had sided with me, albeit only for an hour or two, but these were big hurdles for such young legs and it was hard for Tommy to get over them. But then I guess that was what being a kid was all about. At least, I think it was. It had been such a long time that I couldn't really remember, but there'd been plenty of humility and humiliation in my dim and distant past, of that I was sure. That said, Tommy was true to his word and left me alone from that night forth, which I guessed qualified as respect – especially from someone like Tommy.

And it could've gone on like that as far as I was concerned. I'd not been this content for longer than I could remember but an unexpected knock on the door changed everything, as unexpected knocks on doors have a want to do.

Standing on my front door step was a shaven-headed man I didn't recognise, in a football shirt and tracksuit bottoms. I thought he'd come to ask for his ball back, but instead he grabbed me by the throat and barged me into my house.

"You dirty paedo scum!" he shouted, throwing me to the floor and stamping on my face before I had a chance to ask what the problem was. "*Facking* touch my kids will you! I'll *facking* kill you, you sick bastard!"

I raised my arms to defend myself but he was too big and too heavy to ward off. He booted me in the face, kicked me in the stomach, stamped on my chest and rained blows across the rest of me with his tattooed fists.

He was well-schooled in the art of beating up old aged pensioners and I stood little chance against him.

"Pervert! *Facking* animal!"

I think that would've been my lot had Tommy not charged in and grabbed the shaven headed man, pulling him away and pleading with him to leave me be.

"Dad, don't, he didn't do nothing to us, honest, please, just leave him!"

But the shaven headed man turned his fists on Tommy instead, shouting at him that he weren't his son no more and that he was a "*facking* queer" who'd let his little brother get "knobbed by a scarecrow". Tommy denied it all, even when he was on the floor himself, and insisted I hadn't touched anyone, least of all Barry, and that all I'd done was tell them ghost stories.

"Fink I'm daft or somefink? Fink I just come off the banana boat from *facking* banana land? I know what sickos like him are like. Want shooting the *facking* lot of 'em, grooming my *facking* kids like that!"

"He weren't grooming us, dad, honest!"

"You're a *facking* disgrace!" his dad decreed, and had he been the calibre of gent who could negotiate a belt and buckle, I don't doubt we would've both tasted its lick. But Tommy's dad was straight-up elasticated waistband man and made do with fists and feet, slapping Tommy and kicking me all over until it hurt no more.

The irony of the moment was not lost on me and I even managed a broken smirk in response. I'd shared tales of werewolves, ghosts, ghoulies and vampires with the boys but when all was said and done who were the real monsters in this neighbourhood? My stories must've seemed tame by comparison. Poor young Tommy, he didn't stand a chance. I finally got it.

But that was it. One final punch in the epicentre of my thoughts and then there was nothing.

*

Alex was standing in front of me. I got the sense he'd been there for some time because he was at his wits' end, tearing his hair out and shouting at me to get up.

"Come on John, please, get up! Move it. I know you can hear me. Just get up. Get up now!"

"Alex?" I said, trying to push myself up to see him better but unable to do so as my arms felt like lead. "What's happening?"

"You're out of your basement. Quick, you've got to get back into your basement. Come on, John, move!"

I didn't know where I was or what was going on, and when I tried to lift my head, I felt sick to my stomach, but Alex was determined to see me up.

"John, please listen to me, you've got to get into your basement now, you need to wake up. Come on John, you can do it. Open your eyes. Just open your eyes!"

I knew it must be serious because one dodgy referral asides Alex had never steered me wrong in over thirty years of friendship so I focussed every ounce of my strength into a single point and finally –

– I opened my eyes.

Everything was quiet.

Alex was gone. So were Tommy and his dad. I was all alone on the floor of my hallway and it was dark. I could hear my carriage clock in the next room chiming out for midnight and I could see the basement door open just a few feet away.

Oh Jesus, Alex was right, I was out of my basement and it was almost time.

I tried to crawl towards my sanctuary but every movement was agony. Some of my ribs felt broken and my face was stuck to the carpet with blood. I didn't manage an inch but I had to keep trying. I had to reach that door.

But it was already too late, my body began to burn

and my clothes fell away in rags. Oh God please, this couldn't happen. Not like this. Not here. Not now. But God had forsaken me for the best part of seventy years and he saw no reason to answer my calls now.

Two rows of savage teeth cut through my gums to fill my enormous black mouth. And jagged claws sprouted from each of my thick and powerful fingers as my hands grew to the size of dustbin lids. The pain suddenly slid away too; my bruises became but memories and my invalidities were put on hold as I clambered to my full height, smashing the overhead light bulb on my snout and not even feeling it.

My mind was a fog of thoughts and emotions but my senses were needle sharp. I could smell the dead chicken that had been placed in the basement by my keeper, but beyond the flimsy door in front of me there was fresh meat – lots of it, and it was grazing unawares. There wasn't even a decision to be made but in case I was in any doubt after all of these years on the leash, Rachel called to me from the next room, from behind her dusty cedar lid, to tell me what I had to do.

"Go on John, what are you waiting for? You know what you've got to do so just go and do it!

"Kill the bastards! Kill them all!"

The End

Danny King was born in Slough (UK) in 1969 and later grew up in Hampshire. He has worked as a hod carrier, a supermarket shelf stacker, a painter & decorator, a postman and a magazine editor and today uses this rich smörgåsbord of experiences to dodge all of the above. He lives in Chichester with wife, Jeannie and four children and divides his time between writing and wondering what to write about. dannykingbooks.com.

Printed in Great Britain
by Amazon